THE DIONYSIAN PUBLIC LIBRARY PRESENTS

FEARFUL SYMMETRIES

AN ANTHOLOGY OF PSYCHEDELIC HORROR

To those who were punished entirely too much for what they did—those who wanted to have a good time, but were like children playing in the street.

"No live organism can continue for long to exist
sanely under conditions of absolute reality; even larks
and katydids are supposed, by some, to dream. "

—Shirley Jackson
The Haunting of Hill House

"To fathom hell or go angelic, just take a pinch of
psychedelic."

—Humphry Osmond,
letter to Aldous Huxley

— TABLE OF CONTENTS —

come on up

So, here we are again—on this side of the sun, the time of year when that same sun sets earlier and earlier. It's not even seven yet, not quite, and night is already drooping over the horizon, ready to pull the whole sky under her cloak. It's nearly cold as well as nearly dark, but this late in October it should be more than nearly cold. Instead, the air may generously be described as crisp, chilly if you want to push it, and you stand in the back parking lot of the sagging old house with the rest of the revelers, waiting to be admitted inside.

You look to your friend, chatting with a group of girls by the dumpster, smoking jazz cigarettes and trying to look sophisticated. The girls, one dressed as a flapper, the other two as the twins from Kubrick's Shining, *manage it; your friend, coughing as he takes his drag, does not. You try not to be annoyed at their preparty carousing, but knowing that they will likely disappear as soon as the doors open, you wish they would at least spend a little time with you now.*

Instead you people watch, scoping out more costumes: a full-bodied inflatable Pickle Rick, a couple dressed as Oompa-Loompas, three Marilyn Monroes, a Spider-Man, and a sexed up version of Optimus Prime. You're trying to figure out whether the girl by the spigot is wearing a specific purple fuzzy monster costume or just embodying a general sort of fuzzy purple monster when your friend nearly slams into you.

"This is gonna be so dope," they say, punching your shoulder. "Dude, I've heard All Willows' Eve gets fucking monkey nuts. Are you ready to freak out?"

You aren't sure what you're ready for, if you'll be able to handle the cacophony on the other side of the closed door, but you do know that you're tired of standing out here in limbo. If you're going to spend the night overstimulated and uncomfortable, you'd rather get it over with.

As you think it, a housemate dressed as an old school theatre usher with skeletal facepaint appears in the doorway. Immediately folks form a line, picking up their backpacks and sixpacks and moving like moths towards the light. You and your friend pass through the doorway, dropping a few crumpled bills for cover in the bucket at the housemate's feet. "Enjoy the show," they say, grinning through their make-up, and then you're in it: in the music, in the motion, in the roaring, rushing life of the party.

Sure enough, your friend vanishes only a few minutes into the unfolding cacophony, leaving you to wander the halls of Willow House Cooperative alone. You feel out of place here, in the pulsing, flashing lights and the pulsing, slashing electronic noise. Under the music is the roar of hundreds of voices crammed into the enclosed space, and you can feel soundwaves burrowing through your muscles like bugs under the skin of a withdrawing addict. More faces, some unfamiliar, others recognizable: the Mystery Incorporated gang, a group of slutty nurses you are pretty sure are actual nursing students from the bit of their conversation you catch, four different Jokers from different adaptations and not a single Batman to root them out.

You wander from the main dancefloor to the sideroom where beer pong is being played to the stairwell which leads to the basement, where the electronic dance music is replaced by a live jam band. You listen to the band for a while, but after a bit the solos all sound the same, and then you're in the kitchen, drinking a glass of water from a red solo cup, and then you're upstairs again, in the library, sitting on the couch and sipping once again. At some point your water was swapped out for something alcoholic, or at least you hope it's alcoholic from the fermented taste. Theoretically, you suppose it could be kombucha or some similar probiotic concoction. What's that stuff that farmers drink, with the ginger and vinegar?

Still the faces drift in and out of presence, disappearing, doubling, replacing and being replaced. Time dips, drips, trickles down your spine in a long, cold thread and then wraps around your neck. You feel its spiderweb tug, pulling you into the couch, and you stand, spilling your drink all over the card table where a game of Uno Attack! is being played out. Someone swears at you, but you barely hear it as you brush off the rest of the strands and book it for the bathroom.

You try not to slam the door behind you but are sure you slammed it too loudly anyway, and you press against it, breathing, making eye contact with the collage of vintage porno mag spreads which has been plastered all over the far wall. The toilet is only a few steps away, and one auburn-haired beauty seems to beckon across the tile, but you can't, you can't move, can't make it…

"Hey!" shouts a voice outside, and there's banging on the wood. "Some of us have been waiting a lifetime out here! You gonna hurry the fuck up?" So you try to hurry the fuck up, confused, sweating. You're sure you haven't been in here long at all, but the knocking comes again. The toilet is a bust, guarded as it is by the naked models, and so you try to vomit in the sink, but nothing comes up and so nothing comes out. Instead you take in your reflection, transfixed by the way it responds to your movements. Your eyes are bloodshot, huge, like the twin suns of Tatooine, and oh yeah, you can feel the Force, baby, it's with you, in your blood and your bones—

"Come on!" shouts the voice, and you tear yourself away from your visage, suddenly sick again, tumbling out the door, where there is no line for the loo at all, merely undulating bodies moving from room to room. Breathing heavily, you almost tumble back through the bathroom door, and then you feel a pair of strong arms under your pits, lifting you, keeping you from the fall.

"Alright, friend, let's get you safe and settled," a voice says, and you crane your neck to see a figure behind you, xer dark tresses teasing your shoulders as xe helps you up. You try to offer thanks but instead only a mumbled-jumble of confusion. You are unsure if xe is wearing a costume or is merely dressed as xemself.

"Some asshole dosed you," xe says, coming around to your front and taking your hand. "Come on, this is not the place to be right now. Not too fast, but don't dawdle, either—you really don't want to be down here when it actually kicks in." So you follow xem through the bodies, up the spiral staircase near the back door where you came in, past the sign which reads housemates only beyond this point. Xe must be a housemate xemself from the way xe is acting, and you are suddenly grateful for your host's hospitality. As you get off at the second floor, you realize a hairless cat has joined you and is weaving around your feet. "Don't trip them, Deedee," your guide says, "they're having a rough go of it already."

You round the corner, past decorated doors with numbers screwed above each frame. Xe stops at the room labeled 27, reaching for the knob and letting you both inside. There, you see bookshelves, toys, couches, a minifridge, a projector. "Let's go, come on, inside," xe ushers. "Don't let the draft in."

Then the door is closed behind you, and you are alone with your host. Xe helps you to one of the couches, sitting next to you. "I am sorry about this," xe says, and your eyes are drawn to the pendant around xer neck. "I'm sure this isn't the Hallows' Eve you had in mind. Maybe try and get comfortable. It's going to be a long night for you, I'm afraid." Noticing your fixation on xer necklace, xe removes it, handing it to you to play with. You run your fingers over the crystal, feeling it pulse with a strange rhythm not unlike the music you had left behind downstairs. You run your fingers along its geometry, tracing it, barely aware of the fishhooks in your brain, drawing you up to the light. As you stim with the stone, xe yanks the plug of the alarm clock on the end table out of the wall. "Won't be needing this." Next xe moves to the bookshelf and scans the spines, removing a thick mathematics textbook, cracking it open like an egg. This is your brain on… "You just focus on that," xe says, nodding to the crystal in your hand. "On what feels good. Chase what feels good, and don't let it slip. No such thing as a bad trip. Not if you learn the lessons. Now, attend to one such lesson, here at the top. Who knows—it might help you with what comes later on. Now, listen, listener, and attend a beginner's course in…

Black Magick 101

administered by G. W. McClary

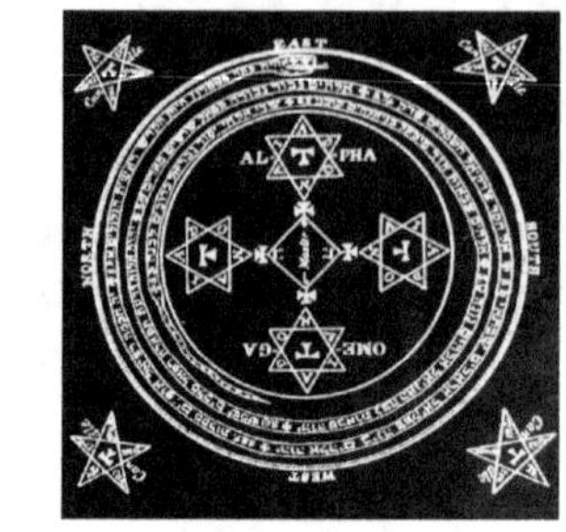

Anapæst Dactyl, the infamous black magician, became my hero as soon as I discovered him. The route through which I found him was most strange.

I was a connoisseur of obscure music. I would scour the internet for hours, looking for lesser-known gems. Eventually, I chanced upon a cheaply shot music video, on tape, anachronistically. It follows a bleach-blonde man as he leaves his New York City apartment and walks the streets. He pulls a twenty from the ATM, carries leftovers home while he considers buying flowers, takes a drag from a hand-rolled cigarette as he chats up a stranger, all to the haunting, carnivalesque music, which saturated the footage with a slow-burning menace. The lyrics revel in urban debauchery, "I wanna be / I wanna meet / A tongue-splitter," as we're shown street freaks with body modifications, creatures of the night. At one point, the man (also the singer) puts the "okay" hand signal over his left eye and raises the other hand up in a peace sign. The camera lingers on that pose, panning slowly out. The image struck me, so I googled it. That's what sent me down the rabbit-hole, straight to the man himself.

Anapæst Dactyl was born in 1875 to a fabulously well-to-do English family. Some say his devout Christian upbringing distorted his moral compass. He blasphemed at an early age, eventually rejecting the church altogether. He studied esotericism at Oxford and published scandalous poetry in the university newspaper. He joined an occult society, The Order of the Eastern Temple, where he quickly rose through the ranks, until he was one of its heads. His behavior became erratic, at least to some of his peers, and the seedier elements of his newly implemented and experimental practices became too much for their puritanical minds to bear. He eloped to Italy, with his second wife, and founded the Varra Villa, where he could pursue his insane rituals in secret.

I was working in a grocery store deli, but I liked to think of it as an old-fashioned butcher shop, since we basically cut up meat all day anyway. It was dull work, but it allowed me to maintain a tiny apartment in the heart of downtown.

One night, as I was walking home, I saw this beautiful young woman walking in pace with me across the street. I snuck glances at her through the passing cars.

"Hey," I said to her, shouting so I could be heard over the traffic. "What's your name?" Her pace quickened and she clutched her purse. "No, hey, it's not like that," I shouted after her. She stopped and turned to face me.

"What the actual fuck?" she said.

"I'm sorry, I just… thought you were cute."

"It's late. I'm a woman. By myself. What part of this doesn't scream murder in an alley?"

"Look, I just—"

"Nice apron," she yelled, before resuming her walk home. I untied the apron, suddenly embarrassed, and bundled it up in my hands as I walked the rest of the way to my apartment.

I didn't have a television, but I did have a projector. I would watch old films on a reel-to-reel, and feel transported to a simpler time, full of euphemisms and fade-outs. The stark German ones were my favorites, but I had a lesser inkling for American romances, with their jaw-droppingly gorgeous starlets and plotlines so simple they faded into the background.
I had this weird hook-up for old film reels. My handyman's wife worked at the library, so she had access to old movies that they didn't let the public borrow. Employees weren't allowed to take them home either, but she snuck them, and my handyman would then pass them off to me. I'd been saving

them up for a marathon. He handed the final film to me, wrapped in a paper bag, like a hand-off in a heist movie.

"Thanks," I said, "But I'm tired. I'm gonna turn in." He knew that meant I didn't want company.

"No problem, Vin," he said, and shuffled off to his unit.

I laid out all the films for my planned marathon, in the order I wished to watch them. Tomorrow was my day off, and it was going to be glorious. Have you ever fallen in love with an actress of the past? It's bittersweet, since you know in the back of your mind that they're either very old or dead, but still, they enrapture us. For me, it was Audrey Hepburn. She was the star of my marathon.

About midway through, and one hastily prepared breakfast and Chinese takeout later, I received a visitation, or perhaps just a hallucination. Just to the left of my projector screen, I saw a green-skinned creature with a bulging, distended belly and sharp yellowed teeth, tilting its head back and bringing its fangs together with a sickening clacking noise. It glared at me like a warning, then crawled out the window. I chalked it up to tired eyes and switched over to the next reel.

At the end, I fell into a deep daydream, a reverie. Audrey and I danced, ballroom style, around my apartment, sashaying past the microwave, and dipping her over the coffee table. I held her aloft and stared into her stunning starlet face. I leaned in for the kiss. There was a knock at the door, and with it, the evaporation of my beloved. It was my handyman.

"How was the marathon?" he asked me.

"Jesus, I just finished it, how did you know?"

"I was listening outside the door, sorry." He must have been nervous to get the reels back to the library. Maybe they'd started to get suspicious.

"No worries," I told him, handing him the stack of films.

"I'm gonna put these up. You want to burn one when I get back?"

"Sure," I said.

We smoked a joint on the back porch of my building, both staring wistfully up at the stars as our mutual buzz set in, since it is technically illegal for two men in close proximity to one another to make eye contact, as you all know.

"I don't know, I guess I just feel unnoticed," I said.

"Well, my friend, I suppose you must do something to get noticed." He exhaled a translucent zephyr of smoke into the moonlit night. He was my only friend.

That morning, I went and bought a megaphone from a nearby superstore. I had a plan. I set up on the street like a doomsday preacher, standing on a milk crate I found along the way, and shouting at the people walking by, using a speech I had prepared for just such an occasion.

"Don't you want to burn it down? Don't you want to? Let's freak out and hit the streets. We've got nothing to fight for, not anymore. All these manic pauses, too many false causes. Amerikay, the doomed and damned, fallen into foreign hands. But what do we care? What do they care? Blood feasts! Hell in the east! We'll make our home in the dumps, hijack the water pumps. We'll speak new words, live off the birds, as they capitalize on the children's crimes. Don't you want to burn it down? I'm done with dreaming, let's start scheming." I thought for sure that last line would grow into a chant, but alas, all the people passing by ignored me but one. A young woman stared at me from across the street, seemingly transfixed. As I was packing up to leave, she made her way over to me.

"When do we get started?" she said.

"Oh, well, it might be tough with just the two of us."

"Maybe it'll catch on."

"Haha, maybe."

"There's this carnival tonight, it's Victorian themed, you should come."

"Where?"

"At the plaza downtown. It starts at six."

I didn't have anything vaguely Victorian in my wardrobe, so I just went as I was. She had changed into a simple dress. She held out two tabs of acid on her palm, one for each of us.

"Come on, it'll be like that scene in *Villette*, where the narrator takes opium and goes to that carnival."

"*Villette*?"

"The Charlotte Bronte novel. Come on, I took you as the well-read type."

"No, I'm more of a film guy."

"Hm, fascinating."

"I know, I'm a thrill a minute."

We ate the acid and made our way into the crowd. A line of dancers came rollicking toward us, hand in hand.

"Let's go," she said, pulling me along. We latched on and bounded, now linked with the dancers.

Hours later, the striped tents breathed and the men on stilts became liquid giants. The night flipped and hollered within my mind. Emily seemed experienced. She would grin at me every once in a while like a child who knows a secret.

She agreed to come to my apartment, so she didn't have to drive. We undressed and stayed awake, talking at the ceiling as our trips slowly subsided. I bid her goodbye in the haze of the morning, knowing I had to be at work in a couple hours.

She moved in a short time later, both of our possessions packed into that tiny space. We achieved some sort of equilibrium, coming home exhausted and leaning on one another for strength. Her hobbies and proclivities loitered with mine on the walls and shelves. We were residentially melded, yet still we managed to grow apart.

Varra Villa was a repurposed abbey, one that used to house monks. In the basement of the villa, Dactyl painted demons on the walls, as well as barbarous words, diabolical graffiti. It was there, in the basement, that he conducted one of his most well-known and despised rituals.

A large male goat had its throat slit while it was penetrating a woman, right at the moment of orgasm. The purpose of the ritual was unclear, but all those present recalled a feeling of a great transference of energy, but to whom and how much, none were fully aware.

There were also rumors of human sacrifices at the villa, but some scholars considered it a crude joke on the part of Dactyl, with "human sacrifice" being a morbid stand-in for masturbation, which said little about his credibility as a new-age prophet.

It was during this time that I discovered him, the infectious song through which I had found him playing in my head as I purchased some artifacts online, after doing a little research: *The Lesser Key of Solomon* (with an introduction by Dactyl himself), several sigil pendants (for compelling the spirits to be controlled), a large tapestry of a magick circle, a black mirror for viewing the spirits (which incidentally got cracked during shipment), and a deep red velvet cloak. The last was not a requirement, but merely an aesthetic choice on my part, since I thought it would look ravishing in the light of the candles. Those, and the incense, I got from this hippie store. I would wait until Emily fell asleep and set up in the second bedroom.

For the naysayers, Dactyl concocted a 'scientific' rationalization of the sensations that resulted from a proper invocation. He claimed that by preparing the materials and speaking the words, the sights, sounds, and smells of the ritual, you were thereby accessing a heretofore untapped portion of the brain, thus awakening ancestral DNA, i.e. instantaneous knowledge. I witnessed this firsthand.

I laid down the tapestry, in conjunction with the cardinal directions, smoothing it out so all of its details were visible, the magick circle, with the 72 names of God inscribed around its border, and laid the cracked black mirror within the movable triangle that pointed in a particular direction, which contained the spirits. I placed a candle at each quadrant and lit them, as well as the incense ("dragon blood" scented). I donned the appropriate sigil pendant and took my place in the center.

I decided to start small. One of the spirits, number eight, a duke of hell called Barbatos (pronounced bar-bay-toes), "giveth understanding of the singing of Birds." Note that the words below in italics are chanted in a single pitch, rather than spoken.

"Thee I invoke, the Bornless one. Thee, that didst create the Earth and the Heavens: Thee, that didst create the Night and the Day. Thee, that didst create the Darkness and the Light. Thou art Osorronophris: Whom no man has seen at any time. Thou art Jábas. Thou art Jápos: Thou hast distinguished between the Just and the Unjust. Thou didst make the Female and the Male. Thou didst produce the Seed and the Fruit. Thou didst form Men to love one another, and to hate one another."

"I am Mosheh Thy Prophet, unto Whom Thou didst commit Thy Mysteries, the Ceremonies of Ishrael: Thou didst produce the moist and the dry, and that which nourisheth all created Life. Hear Thou Me, for I am the Angel of Paphro Osorronophris: this is Thy True Name, handed down to the Prophets of Ishrael."

"Hear Me, Barbatos."

"*Ar: Thiao: Rheibet: Atheleberseth: A: Blatha: Abeu: Ebeu: Phi: Thitasoe: Ib: Thiao.*"

"Hear Me, and make all Spirits subject unto Me: so that every Spirit of the Firmament and of the Ether; upon the Earth and under the Earth: on

you
just
have
to
believe
POOF!

dry Land and in the Water: of Whirling Air, and of rushing Fire: and every Spell and Scourge of God may be obedient unto Me."

"I invoke Thee, the Terrible and Invisible God: Who dwellest in the Void Place of the Spirit."

"*Arogogorobrao: Sothou: Modorio: Phalarthao: Doo: Ape, The Bornless One: Barbatos.*"

"Hear Me: Barbatos."

"Hear me: Barbatos."

"*Roubriao: Mariodam: Balbnabaoth: Assalonai: Aphniao: I: Thoteth: Abrasar: Aeoou: Ischure, Mighty and Bornless One! Hear me: Barbatos.*"

"I invoke thee: Barbatos."

"*Ma: Barraio: Joel: Kotha: Athoribalo: Abraoth: Hear Me: Barbatos.*"

"Hear me! *Aoth: Abaoth: Basum: Isak: Sabaoth: Iao: Barbatos?*"

"This is the Lord of the Gods: This is the Lord of the Universe: This is He Whom the Winds fear. This is He, Who having made Voice by His Commandment, is Lord of All Things; King, Ruler and Helper. Hear Me, Barbatos."

"Hear Me."

"*Ieou: Pur: Iou: Pur: Iaot: Iaeo: Ioou: Abrasar: Sabriam: Do: Uu: Adonaie: Ede: Edu: Angelos ton Theon: Aniaia Lai: Gaia: Ape: Diathanna Thorun.*"

"I am He! the Bornless Spirit! having sight in the feet: Strong, and the Immortal Fire! I am He! the Truth! I am He! Who hates that evil should be wrought in the World! I am He, that lighteneth and thundereth. I am He, from Whom is the Shower of the Life of Earth: I am He, Whose mouth ever flameth: I am He, the Begetter and Manifester unto the Light: I am He; the Grace of the World: 'The Heart Girt with a Serpent' is My Name. Come Thou forth, and follow Me: and make all Spirits subject unto Me so that every Spirit of the Firmament, and of the Ether: upon the Earth and under the Earth: on dry Land, or in the Water: of whirling Air or of rushing Fire: and every Spell and Scourge of God, may be obedient unto Me!"

"*Iao: Sabao: Barbatos.*"

"Such are the Words!" ended the invocation in the text.

Once I invoked the spirit, I found that I could in fact recognize and imitate various forms of birdsong. I could match the quality and pitch of the mourning dove's deep and sorrowful whistle, not unlike an owl: *hoo-oot, hoot hoot hoot.* The song of the American robin became clearer to me as well. The younglings would emit a higher-pitched glissando, which I could imitate and draw the older ones closer to me. When I let out a deeper call, they backed away. There was a final bird, which I was unable to identify, but which had a distinct call I could mimic precisely: *chir-ree, tweedle-dee tweedle-dee, chir-ree, chir-ree.* I found that by matching their calls, I could summon masses of birds to me, wherever I happened to be.

After I had performed several invocations, the light in our hallway refused to work. A maintenance order was put in for it, yet no matter how many times they changed the bulb, it would fizzle out as soon as you hit the switch. They finally took the bulb out, leaving that naked spiral cavity hanging over our door. I wondered which of the handful of possible spirits it could have been.

One night, Emily awoke for one reason or another and spied on me through a crack in the door. Did she see the spirit lurking in the shadows of the candles as I did, could she hear our conversation?

Before we proceed, I feel a proper definition is required. Though it has gone by many names, the concept of black magick (spelled with a K, to differentiate it from stage magic, hocus pocus) is addressed in the seminal text, *Transcendental Magick: Its Doctrine and Ritual,* by Eliphas Levi, the man whom Dactyl claimed to be the reincarnation of. It was published in two volumes, the doctrine in 1854, and the ritual in 1856. The following is an excerpt from the text, if the reader would be so kind as to humor me for a moment. Note that any peculiar spellings or syntax are a product of the time during which it was written.

"We approach the mystery of black magick. We are about to confront, even in his own sanctuary, the black god of the Sabbath, the formidable goat of Mendes. At this point those who are subject to fear should close the book; even persons who are a prey to nervous impressions will do well to divert themselves or to abstain. We have set ourselves a task, and we must complete it. Let us first of all address ourselves frankly and boldly to the question: Is there a devil? What is the devil? As to the first point, science is silent, philosophy denies it on chance, religion only answers in the affirmative. As to the second point, religion states that the devil is the fallen angel; occult philosophy accepts and explains this definition. It will be unnecessary to repeat what we have already said on the subject; we will add here a further revelation:—"

"IN BLACK MAGICK, THE DEVIL IS THE GREAT MAGICKAL AGENT EMPLOYED FOR EVIL PURPOSES BY A PERVERSE WILL."

"The old serpent of the legend is nothing else than the universal agent, the eternal fire of terrestrial life, the soul of the earth, and living fount of hell. We have said that the astral light is the receptacle of forms, and these when evoked by reason are produced harmoniously, but when evoked by madness they appear disorderly and monstrous: so originated the nightmares of St. Anthony and the phantoms of the Sabbath. Do, therefore, the evocations of goëtie and demonomania possess a practical result? Yes, certainly—one which cannot be contested, one more terrible than one that could be recounted by legends! When any one invokes the devil with intentional ceremonies, the devil comes, and is seen. To escape dying from horror at the sight, to escape catalepsy or idiocy, one must be already mad… In the fifteenth chapter of our Ritual we shall give all the diabolical evocations and practices of black magick, not that they may be used, but that they may be known and judged, and that such insanities may be put aside for ever."

"We return once more to that terrible number fifteen, symbolised in the Tarot by a monster throned upon an altar, mitred and horned, having a woman's breasts and the generative organs of a man—a chimera, a malformed sphinx, a synthesis of monstrosities; below this figure we read a frank and simple inscription—THE DEVIL. Yes, we confront here the phantom of all terrors, the dragon of all theogonies, the Ariman of the Persians, the Typhon of the Egyptians, the Python of the Greeks, the old serpent of the Hebrews, the fantastic monster, the nightmare, the Croquemitaine, the gargoyle, the great beast of the middle ages, and, worse than all this, the Baphomet of the Templars, the bearded idol of the alchemists, the obscene deity of Mendes, the goat of the Sabbath. The frontispiece to this Ritual reproduces the exact figure of the terrible emperor of night, with all his attributes and all his characters."

You might be asking yourself, if this being is so abominable, why was it chosen as the cover of the text? But I digress.

"I've seen someone do that before," she told me the next morning. "We had all taken acid, and the guy whose house we were at lit these black candles and recited the same strange poetry you did, though he called a different name. I can't remember which one. My boyfriend at the time and I went upstairs and had sex in one of the bedrooms. While he was on top of me, I saw a tall horned figure in the corner, then I blacked out. I had eaten a bunch of Xanax too. While I was unconscious, I dreamed I saw the Baphomet, pointing at me and laughing, saying I would never leave that place. There were man-like figures all around it, but their faces were hollow and devoid of light. I felt a hand pulling me up, and I woke up on the guy's lawn, covered in sweat, I had OD'd."

One day, on a whim, I decided to google "Anapæst Dactyl" backwards, since I knew from my studies that inversion was a direct path to the infernal. On the third page of results (oh, the irony) I found a link to a PDF entitled 'Mr. Gold's Sigil Formula.' It detailed, as the title suggests, a method for making a sigil.

First, you write down a desire, something like "I want an ice cream cone," but of course, the desire should be one not so easily fulfilled. Then, you remove all the vowels and any repeating consonants. "I WANT AN ICE CREAM CONE" becomes "WNT C RM." Finally, you take that witchy string of symbols and combine them into a single image. Here's the one I made for "I want an ice cream cone."

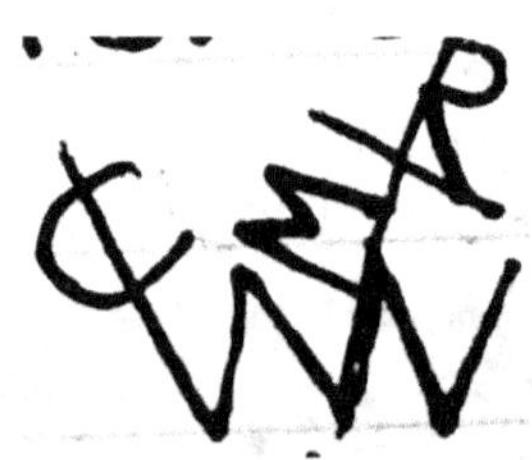

(See if you can spot all the letters.)

Then comes the 'launching' of the sigil. In my experience, masturbation is the easiest way, but sitting naked in a cemetery at night will do. While you conduct your chosen method, you must fixate on the sigil you've made, until it is imprinted on your irises, until you can recall it exactly when you close your eyes. Then (for me, at the moment of orgasm) you 'send' the sigil off into the universe, will it out into the ether, where it will hopefully manifest the desire. The document said you would "feel the sigil leave your consciousness" as it was jettisoned out and away. The results will always reveal themselves in threes. Three days, three months, three hours, but always in threes. The author of the PDF, Mr. Gold, claimed a 100% success rate if the formula was followed exactly, but the treatise ended on a final warning: "Madness, paranoia, and death are constant dangers, so tread lightly, and happy casting."

In 1921, Anapæst Dactyl conducted an elaborate ritual in New York City with one of his male apprentices, where he called forth a being called Lam (Tibetan for 'the way'). He sketched the creature, with its sizable head, tiny features, and wise eyes. Some have said that this sketch was the origin of the 'little grey men' of UFO folklore. Coincidentally, the Roswell crash occurred the same year as Dactyl's death, in 1947, which, if you believe the theories, introduced digital technology and Kevlar, among other advancements, which the government then slowly trickled out to its people over the decades. Perhaps, with his death, the seal to the land of the Lam was broken, and they poured into our world. Perhaps there's one watching you read this right now.

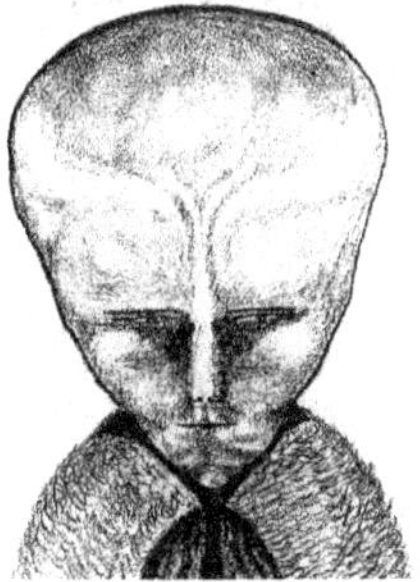

I opened Dactyl's sketch of Lam on my phone and stared at it for way too long, the swirl of wrinkles on the vast cranium, the pinpoint eyes. I was treating it like a sigil, trying to memorize it, but when I pulled my phone away, the image remained, bobbing around in a figure-eight pattern. It repeated this motion a few times, and then darted out of sight. It was late, so I snuck back into bed. I felt a lonely but curious presence in the closet. It spoke to me telepathically.

"I am Lam. Lam am I. Am I Lam?" It kept repeating the words in different variations, until they sped up continually, eventually becoming an undulating tremolo, then a perpetual hum.

As I drifted off to sleep, I had the distinct feeling of astral projection, as if my spirit was moving at a great speed, over the ocean. I saw a desert landscape stretching out below me, somewhere in the middle east, great explosions, people dying, the sand turning to glass.

"My laptop moved last night," Emily said the next morning.

"What do you mean?" I asked her, rubbing my eyes as the sun leaked through the curtains.

"It was somewhere different than where I put it last night. You didn't move it, did you?"

"No," I said, truthfully. I hadn't touched it.

"Don't you find that strange?"

"Not particularly," I said, "Not with all the other stuff that's been going on."

That spring, Emily and I took a road trip. Whatever the opposite of a honeymoon was, that's what we were on. We rented a car, drove across the country, staying in cheap hotels along the way. We made it as far as Arizona, hiked through the dusty railroad tunnels of Nevada, saw the Grand Canyon, and spent a few nights in Las Vegas, touristy things. I think we only had sex a few times the whole trip. We hardly said a word to each other as we stared out over incredible landscapes.

Sometime later, she asked me if I wanted to take a trip with her family. Before I could collect myself and give a proper response, I uttered a sarcastic, "Oh boy," and knew I'd blown it. As you could imagine, she didn't take it well. If the road trip was the beginning of the end, that was the final curtain.

I ended up kicking her out. I figured I would leave her before she did the same to me. She went to stay with her brother, who coincidentally lived just a few blocks away. She left most of her things, either as collateral or some psychological ploy to make me think of her.

The time between Emily leaving and going to jail was a blur. In her absence, I was visited by an old friend from high school. He was attending a university a few states away, studying botany, and made the drive to come see me. He was jumpy and nervous. He didn't stay long.

"Are there ghosts here?" he asked me, as we stepped through the doorway. He was shivering. We sat in the kitchen and caught up over a pipe he produced from his day bag. Before the effects could sink in, he excused himself and left in a hurry. He forgot to grab the pipe, which lay docile and smoking on my fold-out table. It was months later, via email, that he revealed to me the pipe's contents: a rich and pungent combination of opium, meth, and weed, all coagulated and compounded into an odious and ominous dark brown paste, almost an identical shade of the wood that housed it. Ignorant of what it contained, I puffed on the pipe for days, falling into fevers and visions. My cat, my familiar, whom Emily and I had found on one of our rare afternoon walks, when we still had the energy, leapt at invisible targets on the walls. I was bedridden and mad. I swore I could control the weather, as the wind whipped the trees outside in a seductively frantic dance, my dance, the dance of my mind.

I thought I'd try a ritual coined by Dactyl, what I thought of as the Mirror Trick. You sat before a reflective surface, one large enough to contain the entirety of your image and fixated on the left eye (stage right) of your aberration, your other. After several minutes, my reflection began to vibrate, then slowly faded from view, dimming in time to my heartbeat. I blinked, and it reappeared. I continued this process for hours, meditating in silence, until my reflection disappeared completely. It was then that I was visited by the winking eye in the cloud.

It led me through the alphabet, with one simple association for each letter (A, alpha; B, barnacle; C, croquet, etc.), then the numbers zero through nine. The rest was a swirl of language and concepts, with the one discernible phrase being, "Why must you betray me?" In the flurry of voices, I couldn't make out the speaker. It could have been me, God, or the Devil, or maybe we were all saying it to each other.

A few days later, I was visited by a county sheriff. He handed me a protection order, filled out by none other than my old pal Emily. She told the cops that I was "practicing occult rituals," which I was, and becoming "irrational," which I also was. When I asked the sheriff why she would do this, he laughed in my face.

"Some people are just irrational," he said.

My plan was simple: curse her belongings and then carry them over to her brother's apartment by the armload, where I would then pile them up on her little blue Honda. It took several trips. I still had a few more to go when she came outside.

"Call the cops," I said.

"I already did."

Jail was a trip. They flagged me down and cuffed me on my walk home and took me downtown, where I was booked and fingerprinted. For some reason, when they asked me my religion, I said Jewish. I guessed technically I had been studying the Kabbalah, so it was close enough. The next question was, "Are you involved in any hate groups?"

"No, they hate *him*," an inmate I couldn't see said.

I had to spend two nights in a holding cell ("Never get locked up on a weekend," one of my cellmates warned me), then they shipped me to the county jail. They moved me in the middle of the night, to pod B, which I later found out was considered the "junkie ward." They must have assumed I was some kind of drug addict. It was a spacious dormitory that held fifty bunks, toilets, showers, sinks, and a desk where the CO's sat. All but a few of the men in the pod were sleeping. I saw one raising and lowering his arm, slowly, as if he was flagging a ship or an airplane, some kind of signal. I managed to sleep and woke up to a not unsatisfying breakfast.

One of the inmates in the pod was a self-described martial arts master, part-time bouncer, part-time video game store clerk.

"They call me AZ," he said when he introduced himself.

"Azrael, the archangel of death," I said. My research had served me well.

"I'm glad you recognize it," he said.

We developed a sort of bond. We walked and talked around the pod. I let it slip that I had meditated in front of a mirror.

"You know you've got hunger ghosts, right?" he said.

"What do you mean?"

"You meditate in front of a mirror, it draws hunger ghosts to you, Preta, creatures with swollen stomachs that were gluttonous during their time alive. That's why you're so damn skinny."

I thought of the hallucination I'd had during my Audrey Hepburn marathon, but that fell quite some time before I attempted the Mirror Trick. He avoided me after that and told the other inmates that I wasn't to be trusted. I spent two weeks in relative silence. That was until one of the guards informed me that my attorney was there to meet with me.

I had no attorney, but I went with them anyway. An older man in a suit with salt and pepper hair greeted me. He said he was sent by Æreum Sidus, the very same magickal society founded by my hero, Anapæst Dactyl. He informed me that my $10,000 bond had been posted, and that they had rented a nearby hotel room for me for one week. In that time, I was to contact and arrange a meeting with a known witch, who lived some 130 miles to the south.

Since I was bailed out before my trial, they gave me a court date. I pled guilty, and the judge granted me "time served" for my two weeks in jail and sentenced me to two years of "community control," essentially parole for non-felons. I was to meet my PO once a month, and be subjected to random drug and alcohol screenings, so I had to stay straight, or risk further imprisonment.

Dactyl founded Æreum Sidus later in life. He served as its head, until it was taken over by two of his protégé, a rocket engineer and a man who invented his own pay-to-play religion. To this day, the organization has a functioning website, and one can become a member by paying the yearly dues of around two hundred dollars. Some larger cities even had temples, where various rituals would be conducted.

In 1904, Dactyl went with his first wife to Egypt, where they somehow gained access to the interior of a pyramid. There, he conducted an unknown ritual, which caused the apparent demonic possession of his wife, who became manic, and insisted he accompany her to a nearby museum. She led him to an exhibit of the child-god Horus, number 666 in the collection.

I contacted the witch, using the phone number I was given. I had to hit nine to 'dial out' from the hotel phone.

"Hello, you've reached Farah Moon, where your darkest fantasies are my desire, how will you be paying me today?"

"Um, yes, I was told to contact, uh, call you. Æreum Sidus sent me."
Her voice changed from demure and silky to professional and clipped.

"Of course, yes, I have your location. I'll be there in about ninety
minutes." She hung up, and I waited in my room for a while, flipping through
the endless channels on the television, until it was almost time, then I waited
in the lobby. She pulled up right on cue.

Her hair was waist-length and dyed purple, her clothes all skin-tight
fabric, like yoga pants material, which hugged her tall, narrow frame. She
certainly looked like a witch. I peeked into her car, and sure enough, there
was a straw broom with a red handle laid across her backseat.

"Take me to your room," she said, "We don't have much time."

When we entered my room, she began to undress. She turned to me,
bony and naked, her Quaker-length hair covering her most sensitive of parts,
so she was nude, but not nude.

"Drop 'em," she said.

We had sex. She was on her period, and blood was everywhere, all
over the white sheets. At one point, she scooped up a handful and smeared it
across my chest. The smell awakened the beast within. I was rabid. I'd been
in jail for two weeks, with no jerking off (because how could I? I wasn't going
anywhere near the "jack shack," the crudely named shower that was reserved
for nighttime releases). It was so much build-up, I nearly passed out.

"Was that sex magick?" I asked her, as I panted, splayed across her.

"Yes," she said, "Now get dressed. We're to leave for my house to the
south at once." The cleaners must have thought they walked in on a murder
scene, but I never received word from the patrons. Whatever madness we
were wrapped up in, they wanted no more to do with.

She drove us the whole way.

"According to legend, the year of the awakening, the arrival of the
antichrist, is 1990," she said, once we reached the highway.

"But I was born in 1991."

"Yes, but you were *conceived* in 1990. It's you, you're the antichrist. Pull
out your phone," she said.

"Okay."

"Now look up 'Hebrew gematria calculator.'"

"Got it, now what?"

"Enter Farah Darlene Atalie Thomas."

"What's that?"

"My full given name."

I entered the name into the calculator. The result in Hebrew gematria was exactly 666.

"Of course you know of Anapæst Dactyl?" she said.

"Yes."

"My mother told me he was present at my birth, and that she was visited by an angel, who delivered my name to her."

"You were born in what year?"

"1988."

"Dactyl would have been over a hundred years old."

She stared ahead as she drove, letting the silence be an answer.

The house was a simple one-story affair in a sketchy neighborhood, with a patch of dirt in the yard that was either a garden or a crude gravesite. Pinned to her front door was a sign, offering Tarot and psychic readings for a modest fee. Save for us, the house was empty. She led me in and headed to the kitchen, where she began to cook eggs, six to be exact. Anyone acquainted with the triplicate nature of embryonic development will recognize the significance.

"I'm to sell this house, and we are to secure an apartment," she said, over the steaming eggs and vegetables in the pan. We ate our fill and went apartment hunting.

The first, and the cheapest, apartment we looked at was a studio on the second floor of a rundown building. The landlord had enormous, heaving breasts that swayed as she rounded the stairs. They were incredibly distracting.

"You'll have to keep the lobby door locked," she said, "Otherwise, junkies will come in and use the stairwell to shoot up. We can't have any more deaths on the property."

The water pressure was pitiful, and there was no built-in heating or cooling, but it was dirt cheap. The busty landlord accepted cash for the first month's rent, no deposit, no lease to sign, strictly "under the table." I wondered if she too was a part of Æreum Sidus, but I declined to ask her.

The handyman of our new apartment was a sleazy drunk, who lived in a unit just below us. He had to do some minor repairs to our bathtub, using a caulking gun. He joked with Farah that he was "really good at caulking," which I let slide, since it was so pedestrian. He also made a comment about her being flat-chested, but I didn't want to start a confrontation and potentially blow our new residence. Some days later, I found his wallet on the stairs leading to our door. I never asked Farah why, and I gave it to her so she could return it, wanting nothing more to do with the matter. One night, we heard him arguing with a prostitute.

"Give me back my purse," she said, "I can't stay up all night talking to you." We heard them scuffling on the street below, then we heard the sound of big, slow steps, a deep voice, indistinguishable from the second floor, that could only be her pimp. The argument quickly fizzled out, and the whore made away with her purse.

Needless to say, he wasn't anywhere near as amiable as my old handyman. I wondered how he and his wife were holding up. Maybe I'll send them a letter sometime, I thought.

The neighborhood was alive with underground activity. Thugs hung out in packs around doorways, light-skinned whores flagged white Johns, bums picked through the leavings. My first time out of the apartment, on the way to a nearby bodega, I was stopped by a prostitute I would see many times after.

"You want this TV for $25?" she asked me.

"Nah, I'm good, thanks," I said.

"Okay honey, you have a good one."

None of the streetwalkers ever tried to flag me down. Maybe because I was on foot and they assumed I was broke? I wasn't ever sure.

Further down the block, a group of tough-looking guys were huddled around smoking a blunt.

"Ayy, I saw you move in down the street. That's a fine-ass bitch you got," the biggest guy said. The others chuckled. "Nah, I'm just fuckin' with you, white boy. I ain't gonna fuck your bitch." He dapped me up and I continued on my way. They merely nodded at me when I passed them on the way back.

"We have a date," Farah told me when I returned. "With a client. You are to say nothing. We will have dinner, then spend the night in a hotel, one far nicer than that hole they had you staying in."

The dinner was with a frumpy middle-aged man, who was already seated when we came into the restaurant, a nicer Japanese place. She handed him a grocery bag full of various items. We dined in relative silence, though I did correct her usage of chopsticks, since I thought it fell in line with our roles.

"He's a teacher," she explained to her mark, with a brilliant glimmer of improvisation.

We followed the man in his car to a fancy hotel, where he watched us have sex. He laid five hundred dollars on the dresser and left, never to return.

We awoke to a lavish spread brought to us by room service: delicate slices of bread, fresh fruit, various cheeses. Farah told me later that the bag she gave the man contained a sweater she'd worn for three days without showering (not surprising, since to take a bath, we had to haul hot water from the kitchen sink by the vase-load, since there was no showerhead), a hairbrush she had used for months without cleaning it, and one of my used condoms, which she had fished out of the trash.

"Sorry about that one," she said, "But the money was too good to pass up. Think of it as an offering."

We lived in relative luxury for a time, going on other similar 'dates,' always with the same handful of sad older men. Farah considered herself a dominatrix, specifically a findom, financial domination, where no physical contact with the client was made. To her, it was easy money, but I shuddered to think where my "offering" ended up, and to what purpose, magickal or otherwise.

Farah managed to sell her house quickly. Someone paid for it in cash, $9,000, without so much as a proper showing. She had scrawled strange signs on the walls, some of which resembled breasts, and I could only imagine she used it as a place to conduct rituals until the very end.

It turned out Farah had a nice chunk of money saved up (thanks in part to her recent sell), and after years of living cheaply, I did as well. We decided to go in on a country house, a cabin with no electricity, no plumbing. It was perfect. We paid for the property in cash and moved in a short time later.

Occasionally, we would take trips into the city for more findom dates, making enough to keep us afloat, as well as the monthly visits with my PO. Farah began to take more and more solo trips, which left me plenty of time to complete the Abramelin working, my real reason for purchasing the land. I needed a place where I could invoke undisturbed.

Dactyl purchased a property near lake Loch Ness in Scotland, with the purpose of completing the greatest ritual of them all, the Abramelin working. It required one to invoke and banish all 72 spirits of the Goëtia. Doing so would allow one to come into conversation with their guardian angel. Dactyl covered the balcony of the house with sand, so that he could see the footprints of the demons he called there. It was then that he made many of the sketches which have since become obligatory, not unlike the sketch of Lam.

However, the ritual was interrupted before he could fully complete it. Dactyl was summoned back to England, as he was enlisted to plant counterintelligence within the German propaganda machine and infect their people with a keen sense of superstition. It's been rumored that Dactyl was responsible for Winston Churchill's use of the peace symbol in photos, the V for victory, also an ancient sign of excommunication from the church, which spooked the now superstitious Germans, the very same hand sign that led me here. The cyclical nature of magick was not unfamiliar to me. His political ties didn't end there. It was rumored that one of his children was Barbara Bush (born in 1925, so the dates added up), which only added to all the conspiracy theories surrounding those esteemed oil and political barons.

The house became a place of legend. It was said that one of its caretakers committed suicide, and that a floating head could be seen haunting the grounds at 3am, the witching hour. It was eventually purchased by a rock star, and traded hands every ten years or so.

It was said his failure to complete the working was not only responsible for the fabled Loch Ness monster, but also the string of bad luck that followed him for the rest of his days.

My humiliations had been building up, and Farah became quite nasty toward the end.

"Fine, you want to suffer? Here's some suffering for you. If I ever got pregnant with your child, I would abort it," she said. She told me a few months later over text that she had indeed become pregnant, but she terminated it with a non-lethal dose of mugwort, like some ancient shamaness.

I was almost there. I was about to perform a ritual that even the great Anapæst Dactyl had failed to complete. I was nearing the final stretch of the last invocation, of Ba'al, the king of hell, for I had saved the most powerful for last, when Farah burst in, wielding an ancient-looking scroll and a wand.

She touched her forehead and said, "*Ateh.*"

Placing a hand to her breast, she said, "*Malkuth.*"

Touching her right shoulder, "*Ve-Gedurah.*"

Her left shoulder, "*Ve-Gedulah.*"

Clasping both hands to her chest, *"Le-Olahm, Amen."*

She turned to the east and drew a pentagram in the air with the wand, *"Yah-Weh."*

Turning to the south, she signed a five-pointed star again, *"Adonai."*

She turned to the west, *"Eh-Hei-Eh."*

To the north, *"Ag-La."*

She extended her arms in the form of a cross.

"Before me, Raphael. Behind me, Gabriel. On my right hand, Michael. On my left hand, Auriel. For about me flames the Pentagram, and in the Column stands the six-rayed Star," she said, thus performing the lesser banishing ritual of the Pentagram, and with it, the departure of the final spirit. At the last second, she robbed me of my magickal glory. In the end, I had failed, just as Dactyl had done before me.

I left Farah and moved back in with my parents. My mother remarked that for some weeks, my eyes were black, several shades darker than my usual light brown, tinged with gold and hazel. I went to therapy, where they told me that Farah was "grooming" me for her BDSM lifestyle. I thought they might have been right. For years, I lived on edge, waiting for some portent of my antichristdom to reveal itself. But if I was the antichrist, it was a mostly dull existence. Surely the apocalypse was a slow burn.

Farah's body was found in the trunk of a car in the warehouse district, not far from our old apartment. The car had been stolen, and she was found while the jackers were stripping it. The news report said her death may have been gang- or drug-related, but it was later revealed that her killer had been the man with whom we went on our first findom date all that time ago, the man who had made off with my "offering." I mourned her as anyone would.

Anapæst Dactyl died a penniless heroin addict at the age of 72. His only known possessions were a dog-eared copy of *The Lesser Key of Solomon*, an edition that predated his introduction, and a small chest full of coins of various metals which were inscribed with strange symbols. By now, you surely know, they were the sigils of the 72, the spirits of the Goetia, the third of the host of heaven that followed Lucifer after his fall. Forget thee not Mr. Gold's warning. The reader is advised, no, implored, no, required, to flip back to it at once. Fixate upon it. Commit it to memory. Emblazon it on your irises, until you can recall it exactly when you close your eyes, and send it off, to any poor, doomed, and damned soul who wishes to practice the darkest of arts, the embodiment of entropy and chaos itself, black magick. If you've read this far, consider yourself an initiate.

Dactyl's last words were rumored to have been, "I've made a terrible mistake."

ABRACADABRA
ABRACADABR
ABRACADAB
ABRACADA
ABRACAD
ABRACA
ABRAC
ABRA
ABR
AB
A

"...nd we're back," xe says, xer voice returning you to the soft embrace of the couch cushions. There in your hand is the crystal, still turning between your fingers, like its the focal point of your whole world. "There. You're a trooper. You just have to push through the icky stuff, and then you're home free. How are you feeling?"

How are *you* feeling? With your body. With your nervous system. With your soul. With your blood. With your heart.

"It's just a waiting game from here on out," xe says, standing up and returning the grimoire to the bookshelf. "You, me, and this little playroom until you're straight again. Sorry, darling. Them's the breaks. I hope you can live to forgive me. but you're in no state to be wandering off on your own." The cat hops up on the couch next to you, rubbing against your leg as his master crosses over to the minifridge. Its surface is splattered with stickers, band logos and cartoon characters and brewery logos. "You hungry?" xe asks. "You're probably not. But getting some food in your stomach isn't the worst idea in the world." The door to the minifridge opens and closes, and then xe is crossing back over to you, a pair of reddish green pears in one hand. "Here. Eat up."

You take the fruit with your free hand, still holding the pendant in the other, and bite into the flesh. The skin breaks, flooding your mouth with sugar, and far from feeling ill, you sink your teeth in greedily. Your host smiles approvingly, settling down next to you and taking a bite of xer own. It's perfectly tart, perfectly ripe, perfectly juicy, and it dribbles down your chin as space dribbles down the walls around you. "Chew, swallow, and do not take for granted as you do, for not all who hunger are sated. Some can only long, only dream of sweetness, only writhe and wriggle and look out through...

Hungry Yellow Eyes

administered by Sandor Paulson

—— ◎ ——

Terry Mcullen saw yellow, glinting eyes and scurrying shadows beyond the gate of the yard.

Was it the kitty? He dug his nails into his cigarette, his fingers scratched and bloodied. His veins weren't much better. He covered his gluttony with the sleeves of his grandpa's old, brown jacket. He had worn it for five years, even in warm weather. The coat hid the blood-red pinpricks and dark-blue bruises that tattooed his arms. The switch from heroin to Special K was a good one. His grandfather would have been proud.

The house he was staying at was an aged two-story building assembled from spit and firm, red brick. The two stories seemed to tower over him, even though it was shorter than any of the other houses on the block. The backyard was of yielding earth, which gathered an anthology of flowers in the spring. He liked to smoke there. The yard was already covered in butts. He shared the house with a landlady, and her alone.

He felt every inch of its journey as the nicotine flowed through the river of his veins. It glided through the map of his crows-feet face. It moved beneath the filthy tributary of his track marks. It moved into the empty chambers of his black-lung heart. He flicked a bit of ash from his cigarette, then tossed it behind his back before looking into the yard again.

The eyes were still there, looking at him blank and without judgment. He heard a thudding of trash cans, creating a raucous and hideous chorus that accompanied the tinnitus from his drug use. Maybe the eyes were an animal's, extended and poisoned with humanity by his drugged perception? Stranger still, the eyes had pupils slanted like a billy goat.

Something about the sound, the eyes, haunted him—nameless memories of bygone nights. He hurried upstairs, curious and terrified.

◎◎◎

Enclosed is a printout of an advertisement. Some information is withheld due to the sensitive nature of this story:

Dear Reader

My name is Marcia Lovelace and I'm the owner of a house at ▮▮▮▮▮▮▮▮▮▮. I know a lot of people are trying to move to Chicago right now, and I'd like to inform you of this wonderful opportunity.

My house is a boarding house over 100 years old and has a lot of history. I've lived here alone with the occasional renter since my son died about 40 or so ago. I do have my cat, Paws, to take care of now. I enjoy the company of hearty young people and would like to invite you to join me in living in this wonderful abode.

Renting is ▮▮▮ a month. Each room is pre-furnished, including beds, shelving desks, and so on. As a devoted landlady, I clean the house once a week and fix two meals a day, including tea, of course.

I do hope you would care to join me,
—Marcia Lovelace

Accompanying the text is a picture of an old, chipper woman in a flowery yellow dress. She holds a cat to the camera. The cat is thoroughly annoyed. The woman is smiling, exposing a set of Yellow Pages teeth. Behind her is a picture of a young man with a sorrowful and stern expression, about 18 or 19. The advertisement is crumbled, stuffed in the pocket of someone who never took the offer.

◎◎◎

The clatter-clanging of Marcia's breakfast bell woke Terry from his half-dazed dreaming. He looked around his room. His vision was blurry, only somewhat able to make out the posters on the walls. He was proud of his collection: 10 total posters of different indie bands and old horror movies. He pushed himself up, eyes failing to make out his *Onibaba* poster taped to the left of his window.

Eventually, Terry managed to clear his vision enough to look to the corner of his room. There stood a shrine: old photos; weathered journals; and his grandfather's shovel. A tribute to the person he most adored in the world. A tribute to a grave robber, a world traveler, an adventurer. A tribute to the old man who raised him when his drunken waste of a father couldn't. A tribute that was like him: unable to live up to the man it represented.

Terry did a quick, nervous check for his kit before the smell of food overwhelmed him with hunger. He finished his morning routine by putting on his jacket and heading downstairs. He made it just in time for Marcia's traditional obnoxiousness.

"Oh, I'm so glad you decided to join me! I thought you were dead!" she said, laughing loudly.

"Ah, no, I'm alive," said Terry. He smiled back, just wanting her to shut up.

They both sat down, Marcia eating slowly. He looked down at the plate of fried eggs and toast she had served him, picking at them with a distinct inattentiveness. He glanced at the landlady, hoping she'd allow him to take his food up to his room, where he could snort a little k and watch the episodes of *Creepshow* he pirated a week ago. That was one of the few things she requested he never do—take his food upstairs.

Marcia smiled at him. Terry could never tell if it was genuine. To him, he felt like she was committed to imitating a porcelain doll. He looked at the eggs again—they stared back at him. Eyes: yellow, sobbing, crying. Eyes frozen before the moment of death, murdered in cold blood. Eyes that said, "I never asked for this." Eyes that said, "I couldn't say no."

"Do you like your eggs, Terry?" asked Marcia. She tapped her fork against the metal dining table. He blinked. The eggs were there, yellow embryonic sacs suspended in a putrefied white sea. He felt a churning in his stomach that began to rise to his throat. He tried shoving the feeling down by chewing through his toast. He nearly swallowed it whole. It tasted like ash.

Nine of Cups
Dealing
with
Pests

"You eat too fast. You don't have to rush! You'll get sick if you don't take your time," Marcia said. Terry took his time responding. He felt himself filled with fire. Every half-real comment made him want to screech.

"Yeah, they're good!" he said. "I just have some work I have to get done today. That's all."

"Oh yes!" exclaimed Marcia, "your computer programming." She started to move to the sink at a snail's pace. He wanted to move too, but he knew she'd complain if he tried to get up before her. It was *impolite* somehow.

"I'm so sorry. That wasn't around when I was raising Terrance. Computers are so difficult. I had to have a neighbor help me write the ad I posted for the house." At the mention of Terrance the old woman became slow and sad: a rusted windmill, unable to turn. Terry got up from his chair, her sorrow doing nothing to stop his thoughts of raging violence. To him, even her motions of depression seemed false.

"Do you mind bringing your plate in?" Marcia asked.

"Sure," responded Terry.

"Oh that you so much," said Marcia, "you're such a kind young man."

"Do you mind if I…" said Terry. Marcia cut him off.

"I need you to bring in everything, don't be rude," she said. She was stern and piercing.

Terry looked back. There was nothing on the table.

"There's nothing there," he said.

"You didn't check," said Marcia. She grinned like a stuffed toy.

He walked to the table, checking every angle of it.

"Yup, nothing there," said Terry.

"Let me check, I think there was a fork," Marcia said.

She hobbled over, doing the same check Terry did, then she walked back to the sink.

"Can I leave now?" asked Terry.

"I'd love if you talked to me while I cleaned, given all the work I've done, but you can go to work if you want," said Marcia.

"Well, see you at dinner," said Terry. He wanted to sock the old woman with his right hand. Paws followed. At least he didn't want to strangle the cat.

◎◎◎

Trip report: Shadowy Contact
By: Grave_Robber_At_Large
Dose: 150 mg
Route: Injection
Drug: Ketamine, liquid
Body Weight: 150 pounds
Gender: Male
Age At Time of Experience: 29

I recently acquired more medical grade ketamine from my dealer and was ready to do more solo exploration. During one of my undocumented uses, approximately a week ago, I saw a pair of gleaming, yellow eyes. I found that memory of those eyes and that entity disturbing me in my daily life. Rather than hiding and wasting ketamine's potential, I've chosen to confront my fears. The best therapy is to "self heal" instead of living in fear.

At about 1 am, long after my landlady was sleeping, I injected the substance. I wanted to reach a deep K-hole. In this dissociative, hallucinogenic space I could find the eyes again. After the injection, my sense of time turned into water and gunk, slipping down the drain. My vision descended into a flower array of various colors and shapes, far too various to detail. They seemed to become a warping mass at some points, then return to a humming vortex, then a deep tar. I saw my body below me, moving from my bed to the dark backyard. Outside my bedroom window, strange wind-woven shadows danced.

Again, I saw the pronounced yellow goat's eyes. At first they looked at my body, then glanced at me, the real me, floating above. The tinnitus I find accompanies my K trips started as well. Soon, sound itself turned into a sort of pre-digital ancient code. Something dating before humans developed radio transmitters. Eventually, I could make out the broken sound of speech. It sounded like a screeching vulture, hatching fully formed.

"We're hungry. So hungry. Our bellies ache. Feed us," the voice said. I was deeply fearful. I didn't know what they wanted. I looked out my window, each house was a decayed estate and each yard was a rotten field. The moon itself was a fading crescent, a deep yellow—just like the eyes. I was thoroughly K-holed. I had to be.

I took my spiritual body and floated from the window of my room to the backyard. Outside, my body lay flat, eyes wide open, arms crossed.

I ignored my surroundings for a moment to try and touch it. I reeled backwards. My hand stung like I dipped an open wound in formaldehyde.

I worked each of my other four senses, trying to ground myself and ease the pain. The ringing in my ears had turned into a cankerous caterwauling, a bloodshot braying. On my tongue was the taste of my own blood, viscous like maple syrup. On my nose was the smell of feces and rotten eggs. I looked around. A black fog surrounded me. Four pairs of yellow eyes pierced through the darkness.

The screaming began to form into words again, the eyes sopping wet with tears: "An apple, a pear, an orange! Anything, anything!" they screamed. Each voice vibrated with hunger. Only three voices cried. One remained silent. One did not cry. Its mouth was sealed shut. Its sorrow was much deeper than the others. Too deep to explain even through the language of any realm or tongue.

I don't know how many hours I spent like

this, but the paws of my landlady's cat pulled me
back from my K-hole. I don't know if I'll ever
attempt to do 150mg of ketamine again, or when
I'll do this. If I do, I'll make a post.
    Trip Safely,
    Grave_Robber_At_Large

◎◎◎

July, 25, 1984:

No more love

No more hate

No more sex

No more disease

No more unknown

No more distaste

No more horror

No more violence

No more me

Best,

Terrance Lovelace

The poem is stained with tears, stuck in the cabinet of an untouched
desk.

◎◎◎

Chatlog between Simply_Lithium and Grave_ Robber_At_Large:

10:35pm — Grave_Robber_At_Large: Hey girl!

10:36pm — Simply_Lithium: What is it now?

10:36pm — Grave_Robber_At_Large: Just like, some questions and a favor maybe?

10:36pm — Simply_Lithium: I'm not giving you any more bumps, fuck off lmao.

10:36pm — Grave_Robber_At_Large: No it's totally different.

10:36pm — Simply_Lithium: Ok sure, what is it?

10:37pm — Grave_Robber_At_Large: I recently had a trip where I contacted a bunch of really weird entities and went to a totally different place. I experienced a ton of stuff that's really hard to describe or understand. I'm scared. I don't want to K-hole again. Maybe ever. Idk how to talk to the entities without doing a ton of ket. Unlike you I don't know how to get into that space, I don't know anything about mysticism, or anything like that. What do I do?

10:37pm — Simply_Lithium: Then tell them to fuck off lmao.

10:38pm — Grave_Robber_At_Large: I don't want to, I can't, Idk. I keep going back to that place, thinking about it.   Maybe all of this is real? More than the human brain? Maybe it's a way I can see my grandfather again. Maybe it's a way to prove to him I'm more than a waste.

10:38pm — Simply_Lithium: Yeah… That's a lot. Try this—have you tried just offering them something? Have they asked you for anything?

Meditating a bit and then getting into that space with your mind and then make an offering.

    10:38pm — Grave_Robber_At_Large: How do you meditate? Like focus on your breath?

    10:38pm — **Simply_Lithium**: Just like, close your eyes and remove yourself from your daily interests. The struggles, all of it. Let your brain empty like a sieve. Do that, maybe do a bump while your at it. Then see what you get.

    10:40pm — Grave_Robber_At_Large: Then I'll call you?

    10:43pm — **Simply_Lithium**: I guess? Like, don't you have things to do?

    10:43pm — Grave_Robber_At_Large: Please?

    10:43pm — *Simply_Lithium **has logged off***

    10:47pm — *Grave_Robber_At_Large **has logged off***

◎◎◎

Trip report: An Offering
By: Grave_Robber_At_Large
Dose: 50 mg
Route: Injection
Drug: Ketamine, liquid
Body Weight: 150 pounds
Gender: Male
Age At Time of Experience: 29

This is a follow up to my last trip report, "Shadowy Contact". This time, following my ex-girlfriend's advice, I decided to inject a much lower dose of ketamine. I'd contact the entities from my last trip by meditating instead of injecting a heroic dose of kitty.

At about 1 am, I injected myself and attempted to reach the same point. I crossed my legs and sat on my bed, closed my eyes, and focused on my breath. The meditation took little time, but I started hearing the buzzing again. The buzzing turned into three distinct voices.

"Oh, I'm so hungry," said one.

"I'm more hungry, even more than him!" said another.

"I'm hungrier still!" said a third.

Sober enough to do so, I grabbed three pears from the fridge and walked outside to the backyard. Unlike last time, the backyard looked normal. In the distance, I could see 4 pairs of yellow, starving eyes.

I laid the pears down on the ground. Then, I said a small prayer to the universe and went to go back into the house, content to let the eyes feast without me. Before I made it to the door, the eyes shouted at me.

"This isn't enough! This isn't enough!" the three said, "we need more!" A great braying started. I couldn't tear myself away. At last, the fourth pair spoke. It had a youth to it, and a deep cruelty. Something denied, something unspoken.

"If the fruit isn't enough, we'll have to eat something else."

I bolted upstairs, almost tripping over my landlady's cat. I sat in my room for an hour, holding my knees to my chest and sobbing. I didn't want to be crazy. I didn't want to be a part of all this woo woo stuff, I just wanted to see my grandpa again. This all had to be a vision, a deep dread from my mind.

I'm not crazy, right?

Best,

Grave_Robber_At_Large

Terry and Marcia sat at a table that felt longer than it ever had before. The metal tabletop, shining and bright, felt fraudulent. Neither spoke. Both ate their chicken in silence.

Terry's brain was shut off. He didn't want to think. He didn't want to *be*.

Marcia broke the silence. "Mind if we drink tea?" she asked.

Terry nodded. Dissociated from the moment, he felt a firm nothing. No preference, no meaning. He just didn't want to be crazy. He thought only of each pair of glistening eyes.

Marcia hobbled to her cabinet behind the kitchen. The smell of loose-leaf tea wafted out and into Terry's nose. He thought of the mushroom tea a friend had made him once when he visited London. The memory, once kind to him, struck him with a fury. Like a snake biting into his leg, he felt the horror of his isolation, the firmness and realness of it. Who would believe a drug addict? Not him. He was trash. He held back his tears.

The tinnitus began again. Then, a knock on the door. The wind moved the curtains aside. Paws made a movement, then bolted to the top floor.

"Mind checking the door for me, sweetheart?" said Marcia. She was absorbed in her brewing.

"Umm, could you? Sorry, I think I hurt my leg earlier," said Terry.

Marcia didn't appreciate the bold-faced lie, or the leg injury. Regardless of the truth, her tea would help with both.

Stumbling again, Marcia made it to the door. She turned the handle, with the grand slow bravado of the elderly and retired. Of someone untouchable. Of someone well and sane.

Terry began to get up. He didn't want any part of this. Following Paws, he ran upstairs, deep into the den of his junky silence. His projected tomb.

The last sounds he heard before injecting were the screech of an old woman and the gnashing of flesh.

◎◎◎

3 Bodies Found in Backya.

Yesterday, a local man was found collapsed in the backyard of a local boarding house where he was housed, surrounded by three skeletons in various levels of decay. Neighbors report they had heard digging and howling that night but ignored it. Three skeletons in various levels of decay were dug up. Clinicians at Northwestern Hospital said he been abusing ketamine and was "close to an overdose," but he is expected to make a full recovery. Marcia Lovelace, the landlady, has been reported missing. The skeletons found connect her to a series of missing person cases over the course of forty years. After searching the house, police found a collection of poisonous substance in her "tea cabinet". These included over-the-counter pain medicine, cleaning supplies, and pesticides, which had been mashed together and reduced into a fine powder. Police

Note: The rest of the article has been torn out, collected, archived, and marked by sweat.

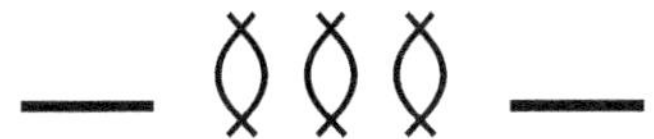

Xe swallows the last bit of xer pear as you swallow the last bit of the tale, still tasting stale sweat and feeling fractured and shaking against a breeze that isn't there. This tiny playroom feels the size of an ocean, all of the water in your body adding up to barely a drop in contrast to its endless rolling waves. You're floating. You're swimming. You're drowning. You're drowning, and it's soft, and it's warm even though it's cold, so cold, like the wreck of the Edmund—

"Ground control to Major Tom," says your companion. "Get back down here."

You're trying to stay above the surface, trying to swim, trying, trying, trying to see through the rain, trying, trying, trying—and then you do see something: a lighthouse, on the horizon. You swim towards it with all your might, propelling yourself through the snapping tides until—

—you feel xer hand pressed against yours, fingertips still sticky from the pear juice, and you see the lighthouse in your other hand. You turn the amethyst around and around, its golden structure seeming to suck in all of the overhead light and hold it like a long, soft breath. Xer hand withdraws and xe licks the last of the glistening sugar from the tips of xer fingers.

"Don't run away from the feelings," xe says. "Don't try to numb them. You close your mind's eye, look away from the fire, the trip will suck you dry." You focus on the lemony glow of the crystal, xer voice bubbling in your ears. "When you run," xe warns, "it's only in circles. You end up where you were before, only stripped of what you were when you were there last. Naked, afraid, and tired. Running in circles, walking in circles, crawling in circles, through cycles, again and again and again and again and again and again and...

3rd Dose:

Again

administered by Raymond Brunell

You will scrub your hands for two minutes. You will feel the water temperature—hot enough to redden the skin, not hot enough to burn. You will count the seconds. This matters more than you think.

You will enter the delivery room with confidence. The mother will look to you for reassurance. You will provide it. Your face will show nothing but practiced calm, even when you see what you will see.

You will check the dilation. You will monitor the heartbeat through the fetal monitor's steady percussion. You will note the contractions—their frequency, their intensity, their progression. You will record everything in the chart with handwriting that remains legible. Legibility matters. The chart may be reviewed.

When the infant crowns, you will guide the mother through her breathing. You will support the perineum. You will ease the head through, then the shoulders, then the body in one fluid motion that you have practiced five hundred times before you ever touched a real birth. By your thousandth delivery, it will feel like muscle memory. By your two-thousandth, you will understand that some muscles remember what they should not.

You will suction the airways. You will clamp and cut the cord. You will dry the infant briskly to stimulate breathing and crying.

Sometimes the infant will not cry.

You will note this in the chart as "initial apnea, resolved." You will perform the necessary stimulation. You will assess the APGAR score at one minute and again at five minutes. The infant's color will be pink appropriately. The heart rate will be strong. The muscle tone will be good. Reflexes present. Respiratory effort adequate after stimulation.

You will record a score of 9 or 10.

You will not record what you see in the eyes.

When the infant opens its eyes in the first seconds after birth—and some will open their eyes immediately, before you have finished suctioning, before the first breath—you will continue your assessment. You will check the pupils. You will note their response to light. You will document "alert" or "responsive" in the appropriate box.

You will not write "aware." You will not write "exhausted." You will not write "watching me with an expression I have seen on the faces of hospice patients who have stopped asking for more time."

The eyes will track your movements. This is normal. Neonatal tracking develops over weeks, the textbooks say, but you will observe it in minutes. You will observe it in seconds. The infant will follow your face as you move from the warmer to the scale. The infant will watch your hands as you perform the measurements.

Some infants will not blink for forty-three seconds. You have counted. You will stop counting.

You will weigh the infant. You will measure the length and head circumference. Your hands will be gentle and efficient. You will speak in soothing tones to the infant because this is what midwives do, even though you will notice that your soothing seems unnecessary. The infant will not startle at sudden sounds. The infant will not react to the cold scale against its back. The infant will simply watch you with a patience that belongs to someone who has waited before and will wait again.

You will place the infant skin-to-skin with the mother. You will facilitate the first feeding attempt. You will observe the latch. You will document, "Breastfeeding initiated successfully."

You will not document the sigh.

When the infant exhales—not a cry, not a whimper, but a sigh of profound weariness—you will continue your charting. The mother will not notice, or if she notices, she will interpret it as a sound of contentment. You will allow her this interpretation. You will smile and say, "Perfect. Your baby is perfect."

In the days that follow the delivery, you will encounter the infant again during routine checks. By now, the mother will have noticed things. She will say, "He seems so serious," or "She hardly ever cries," or "Sometimes I think he's looking right through me." You will reassure her. You will explain that every infant has a unique temperament. You will say that some babies are calmer than others.

You will not say what you are thinking.

You will not say that you have delivered one hundred and forty-seven infants in the last eighteen months who opened their eyes already tired. You will not mention that Judith in Labor and Delivery has noticed it too, or that Dr. Kovacs has started taking longer breaks between shifts. You will not discuss the staff meeting where someone almost said something before changing their mind.

You will deliver more infants.

Some will be ordinary. Their cries will be the mindless wailing of new lungs learning air. Their movements will be the random jerking of nervous systems still forming connections. Their eyes will be unfocused, absent, and blank with the emptiness of new consciousness.

You will feel relief during these deliveries. You will find yourself hoping, during each birth, that this one will be ordinary. Sometimes, your hope will be rewarded.

Other times, the infant will emerge already exhausted.

You will recognize this immediately now. You have learned the signs. The limpness that is not quite hypotonia. The silence is not quite respiratory distress. The way they hold their bodies with a stillness that newborns should not possess—newborns who have not yet learned that they have bodies, who should be all reflex and instinct.

These infants have already learned. You do not know what they have learned, but you see the knowledge in them.

You will observe, over time, that some arrive more burdened than others. Some merely seem tired, as if they have had a long day. Others arrive with a weariness so deep you can feel it radiating from their small bodies like cold from stone. These are the ones who will watch you with something approaching recognition, though you have never seen them before and they have never seen you.

You wonder if they have seen someone like you. Someone who pulled them into a light they did not ask for, in a life they did not choose, in a body they will have to learn to operate again.

You will begin to recognize gradations of exhaustion in the newborn. This is not in any textbook. You will develop your own classification system, privately, never written down: the Merely Weary, the Profoundly Tired, the

ones you think of as the Veterans. The Veterans are the worst. They do not just watch you—they assess you. They take your measure. They calculate, behind eyes that should not calculate, whether you are the kind of person who will make this easier or harder.

You do not know how to make it easier. You only know how to deliver them.

You will attend a birth at 3 AM on a Tuesday in March. The mother will be a first-time mother, healthy and uncomplicated. The labor will progress normally. You will prepare for a straightforward delivery.

The infant will crown, and you will guide the head through, and then the shoulders, and then the body, and you will suction the airways and clamp the cord, and the infant will draw its first breath.

And with its first breath, it will speak.

Not a cry. Not a sound of distress or confusion. A word, formed with lips that have not yet learned coordination, pushed through a larynx that should not be capable of speech.

The word will be: "Again."

You will freeze. Your hands will be holding the infant, supporting the head and body as you have done a thousand times, but your hands will forget how to move. The mother will be asking, "Is everything okay? Is the baby okay?" and you will remember to move. You will finish the delivery procedures. You will assess the APGAR. You will record normal scores.

You will place the infant with the mother and watch them together—the mother's face radiating joy, terror, and love, the infant's face radiating nothing but tired resignation.

Later, the infant will speak again. Not to you. To its mother, who will not understand because the sounds are not quite words yet, or because she is not listening in the way you have learned to listen. The infant will make sounds that could be interpreted as coos or gurgles, but if you stand close enough, if you pay attention, you will hear the shapes of sentences trying to form in a mouth not ready for them.

You will hear: "How long this time."

You will hear: "Not fair."

You will hear: "Remember you."

The mother will laugh and say her baby is trying to talk already. You will agree. You will say that some babies are very vocal. You will leave the room.

You will deliver more infants after this one.

You will perfect your documentation. You will master the art of recording only what can be recorded. You will learn to describe the observable without describing what you observe. This is a skill. This is survival.

You will attend more births. You will see more eyes than you have seen before. You will hear more sighs that carry lifetimes in them. You will feel more tiny hands that grip your finger with a strength that knows exactly what it is holding onto—a hand that has pulled them into this again, a hand they may remember from last time, or the time before.

Some nights you will go home and wonder if you are helping or harming. Some nights you will not be able to tell the difference.

You will return the next day. You will scrub your hands for two minutes. You will enter the delivery room. You will check the dilation, monitor the heartbeat, and guide the mother through her breathing. You will ease the infant out in one fluid motion. You will dry, stimulate, and assess. You will record the score.

You will do this again tomorrow. And the day after. And the day after that.

You will do this until you retire, or break, or die.

And when you are reborn—because you will be, because we all are—you will open your eyes to find someone like yourself standing above you. Someone with gentle hands, a practiced smile, and eyes that have learned not to see what they see.

You will try to speak, but your mouth will not form the words yet. You will try to sigh, but your lungs are still learning air. You will try to turn away, but your neck muscles have not developed.

So you will do what all the others have done.

You will watch. You will wait. You will endure.

And you will hope that this time, the midwife will understand. Who will be gentle with what you carry. Who will know, even if they never say it, that some births are not beginnings at all.

You will hope that they have read these instructions.

You will hope that they remember.

— ◊◊◊◊ —

"... if you can. Your name?"

You think. You roll the question over. You struggle, but you get there. You remember your name, and you tell your host.

"Good. Your birthday?"

This one is easier. Numbers seem to stick more readily than letters in your current state of mind—but it's still no picnic dredging the figures up from the old databanks. After a bit of a struggle, you reel it in, remember your birthday, and then you tell xem that, too.

"Who's the president of the United States?" xe asks, and this one you remember immediately, as much as you'd prefer not to. You report your recollection, and xe nods.

"Your address?"

This one is more difficult than either your name or birthdate, but after a millennium or so you remember this one too, and say it aloud.

"Alright," xe says. "Good. So you're not totally pickled. Just mostly pickled."

You think back to a moment before, which was a lifetime before, and then to the lifetime before that, and the lifetime before that, and so on. Your hands still know how to deliver a life, but you can feel the knowledge fading, slipping away, along with the knowledge of what may be hiding in the margins between here and there, then and now, stage left and stage right. Again you are fully yourself, or as fully yourself as anyone in this world ever can be, sharing so much matter with the rest of being. It's all borrowed material and all borrowed time.

With this realization, you do the only rational thing there is to do: you panic. You stand up sharply, dropping the crystal, stumbling to the door, back towards the party. Your skin prickles, expecting xer fingers on your arm, trying to stop you. The fingers do not fall, and you place your hand on the doorknob, jiggling it, finding it locked, fumbling for the bolt.

"I won't stop you if you want to leave," xe says from behind you. "I'd just advise against it." Where is the lock? Where is the fucking—?

This time the knob turns. It must have simply been stuck before. "You intend to get away," xe says behind you. "To escape from this strange teller of strange tales and from all of the demons in your head. You seek to escape what you've tried to leave behind. You throw the door wide, step inside, out of this enormous, tiny room and back out into...

4th Dose:

The House that Breathes Back

administered by Zazie Productions

He woke inside a clock that did not keep time but posed as it. A cathedral of gears, slow and milk-pale, the metal soft as cartilage. The hour-hand was a fishbone; the minute-hand, a needle threaded with late sunlight. The second hand hovered, considering whether to split him.

No one had invited him into the mechanism. He had climbed no stairs. He simply existed there, mid-tick, the air smelling like pennies soaked in rainwater and something behind the smell, something too clean to be trusted. They would say he was the protagonist if they liked roles, but the room disliked nouns. Names held doors open; the room wanted everything shut.

The house breathed in—a long, pearled inhalation that lifted the walls like wet sheets—and breathed out, returning each wall to its hinge of shadow. It was not a house in any conventional sense; it moved like lungs, it pulsed like a thought with a fever. He watched the wallpaper ripple with a thousand tiny fishes swimming in a single direction. When the building exhaled, they reversed in unison. He believed he had been here before. He believed the wallpaper had once been a field and each fish a blade of grass. He believed too many things to fit into his body.

A corridor unspooled. The corridor had a flavor: aspirin ground with orange peel. He decided to walk because motion seemed like a way to negotiate with the scene. The floorboards had the hollow echo of a skull pressed to a seashell. At irregular intervals the corridor produced windows that looked in, not out. Through them, versions of himself passed in failing costumes—teacher, butcher, choirboy, organ donor. Their mouths moved, making that generous shape speech makes before sound goes inside it. He was fond of them, these selves. He wanted them to leave while that was still possible.

At the second window, his reflection was not himself but a camera dolly negotiating a staircase that curved like a nautilus unbuttoning. The lens blinked in a slow mechanical courtesy; the iris was an obedient wound. He raised a hand to wave. The lens zoomed until his palm filled the view: the palmar lines were rivers; the skin, a paper map that had been folded too many times. He could see the delta where he would one day go missing.

He reached a landing made of salt. It cracked like sugar. There were doors. They all wore teeth where doorknobs should be—small, childlike, milk-tooth rings. Polite, in a predatory way. He chose the one that was not-quite closed. To open it, he offered a syllable. A good strong one: loam. The teeth parted. Tongue of brass, an approving taste.

Inside, a kitchen married to a laboratory. Countertops arranged like altars. The stove was a field recorder with iron coils; its red eye winked as if it had just captured a ghost's confession. On the table: a bowl of keys, a cup of air, a plate holding a snowflake pinned with an entomologist's pin. When he leaned to examine it, the flake whispered its geometry into his ear. Sixfold sorrow, sixfold joy, sixfold repetition until the meaning friction-burned away. He wanted to promise the flake that he would remember. He wanted to promise everything, something.

A faucet dripped water in the rhythm of a heart deciding. Drip. Wait. Dripdrip. He listened until the rhythm synchronized with the residual minute-hand in his chest. The water was not water, it was film spliced into bead-sized frames; each drop contained a micro-second of somewhere else—someone laughing in a neon kitchen, someone washing blood from a peach, someone counting backwards from childhood. He held his breath to not interrupt the edit.

From the corner: cutlery, restless. Knives tapping their points in Morse, spoons humming at the brevity of mouths. He recognized the code. It spelled his name with a stammer he had never forgiven. "Shh," he told the knives. "We're not choosing violence today." The knives, disappointed, re-arranged themselves into the topography of a city he had never visited but somehow owned. Streets like scars, rivers like veins he would not let a loved one cross.

He was thirsty. He raised the cup. The cup was full of breathing. He pressed his lips to the rim and drank warm exhalations until something softened in his spine, a latch giving way. When he put the cup down, his fingerprints bloomed across the ceramic like bruised violets performing a funeral they were too young to understand. He apologized to the cup. The cup said nothing. Things here remembered without the hassle of words.

A scraping. The house's ribs adjusting. He went on.

Stairs this time: steep, narrow, furred with a dust that had once been moths. The walls tightened. He descended, then remembered he was ascending, then wondered whether vertical direction was a pollutant imported from some lesser architecture. Halfway, time wrinkled. A draft passed through him carrying the smell of abandoned swimming pools, of wet concrete and lifeguard laughter left in storage.

Door again. This one with a knothole that watched like a cataract. Inside: a nursery or its eulogy. Toys arranged in the precise disarray of staged authenticity. A mobile hung from the ceiling, spinning slowly. It was composed of anatomical models: ear, tongue, iris, fingertip. They circled each other with the patience of planets that had agreed, privately, to collide. On the far wall: a chalk drawing of a rabbit labeled Teacher. Beneath it, small handwriting had added: Not a Rabbit. Beneath that: Not Not a Rabbit. Someone had been learning the spell of names and their double negations.

He sat in the little chair, knees peaking comically like mountains. There was a book open on the table: a child's primer filled with diagrams of rooms that did not exist and their proper names. The captions were courteous and wrong. The red room was labeled "Hush"; the blue room, "Spill"; the white room, "Don't." He felt the impulse to correct the captions and then the impulse to preserve their error. He experienced both impulses as parents quarreling softly, not to harm but to occupy the same air with their contrary kindness. He accepted being the child in their argument and also the judge and also the window through which their voices escaped.

Something touched his shoulder—a draft shaped like a hand, or a hand shaped like a draft. He did not turn. Bodies were so often clichés where true presences preferred edges. "I'm here," the draft said, in the sense that it moved the tiny hairs. Oh, he thought. So am I.

Down a hall graceless with chairs turned on their sides like horses asleep. Light pooled beneath a door and seeped under it, shivering as if cold. He entered. The bathroom had been converted into a listening booth. The tub was a choir stall; the showerhead a microphone; the mirror an informant. He heard himself approach: breath, then heartbeat, then the

N
W E
S
NOT A RABBIT
(NOT NOT A RABBIT)
kitchen
11x10
dining
12x13
stor
bath
hall/
pantry
parlor
13x13
entry
living
14x16
up
up

electrical chitter of neurons arguing about a face. In the mirror he was both absent and over-present. His features stacked like transparencies misaligned. When he blinked, one version lagged—a beautiful delay, the kind that doomed romances require.

On the sink: a tooth in a little glass coffin, laid on cotton. It vibrated faintly, tuned to a note he couldn't name because naming is a way of holding and the note refused to be held. He leaned and heard not the note but what lived behind it: a theatre where old arguments dressed as tragedies, a shore where people swallowed cameras to prove their memory was honest, a street where a boy rehearsed a goodbye until the word wore through.

He felt impatient. He felt holy. He felt like a corridor that had finally decided to become a river. The house accommodated.

The next room contained a sky. Not a painting, not a skylight. A sky lowered into domestic scale, wearing a lampshade like a party hat you didn't have the heart to remove. Clouds moved with arthritic grace; lightning stitched itself without thunder, as if practicing before the audience arrived. In this sky hung a door—free-floating, immaculate, its handle a droplet of mercury holding a miniature of his face. He was smaller there, kinder. He forgave the miniature for not knowing what forgiveness was.

He reached for the handle. It was warmer than any metal had the right to be. When he turned it, something resisted—not the latch, but a memory refusing to unlatch from him. He thought of the day he learned that glass is a slow liquid, grief a slow animal, forgiveness a slow ladder you climb and climb and find yourself nowhere, higher than anyone and nowhere. He turned anyway. The door opened onto a hallway that smelled like syllables: hush, hush, hush. The smell of being small and successfully invisible.

He entered the invisibility. He thought, in brief clarity, that he had finally found the part of the house that had built him. He did not want to be unbuilt.

A room made of echo. A room with no furniture but ashtrays. A room that asked questions and nodded before answers. A room where music leaked from the walls like sap—organ tones pitched to the frequency of the body's apology. He recognized the melody. It was the tune he hummed in supermarkets when aisles felt like centuries; it was the elevator song that forgave every floor; it was the humming birds make when they do not wish to be birds.

In the center: a table set for one. On the plate: his shadow, folded, napkined, garnished with lemon rind. The cutlery shone with a joy bordering on rapture. The chair scraped itself back, offering. He sat. He did not unfold the shadow. He placed his hands on either side of the plate as if to pray, or to keep the plate from drifting into wider currents sheening under the floor. The house inhaled. The house held. The house exhaled and, with it, he felt his thoughts depart like passengers who knew the gate number now.

The ceiling lowered to kiss his forehead. "Quiet," it said, though no sound occurred. "We're making you symmetrical." There's a danger to symmetry—the world prefers its faces slightly off, its apples bruised, its prayers smudged. But the house was indifferent to local custom. It aligned him with his other versions like one aligns transparencies on a lightbox until the overwriting stops and the face can be read. For a moment the alignment seized: he was every costume at once, every angle agreeing, a perfect coin balanced on a blade. The sensation was obscene with relief.

Then the blade moved.

He fell sideways into a stairwell that dove into water. Not actual water—its idea. He swam through temperature. He kicked through calendar pages. He broke the surface in a room whose walls were breath; on the far wall, a window finally looking out, not in. Night outside. The sort of night that begins in the eyes before the sky catches up. He approached the glass. It clarified around his face like a decision. Beyond, the yard was an absence well-groomed. In the grass, the outline where someone had laid, recently, facing the same window, hoping for a sign.

He lifted a hand. The yard did not wave back. Good. He was tired of reciprocity.

Downstairs, the front door waited with the patience of furniture. He went toward it, because endings are a courtesy. When he opened it, the night rushed in—not wind, not cold, but the velocity of unmade choices. On the threshold he turned, one last look. The fish in the wallpaper slowed, a tide unsummoned. The knives hummed a lullaby they'd practiced for someone braver. The mobile rotated its small planets toward him and every part—the ear, the tongue, the fingertip, the iris—offered its private salvation.

He stepped out. The house breathed in, enormous. He felt himself subtracted, feather by feather, until he was as light as a story nobody wants to remember but everyone is telling. The door closed with a soft dental click.

In the yard, he stood until morning invented itself. The sun rose like a curtain. He found, in his pocket, a tooth he did not own. When he held it to the light, the light changed key. A chord he had never heard struck him in the middle of the chest. He understood, then, that he had not escaped the house but taught it how to travel.

He walked. The tooth hummed a map. The world opened its corridors. Every window he passed looked inward. Every shadow he cast was folded, napkined, lemoned.

A perfect coin rolls until it is lost. He listened for himself in the sound. And when it stopped, he kept walking, not toward, not away, but with.

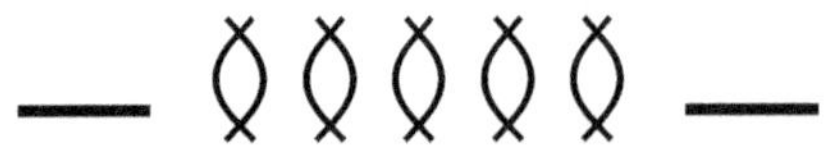

You blink. Your reflection blinks back. Your reflection blinks again. You blink back. This is what it means to be with—to be, and to be alone, but not alone, never alone. Solipsism is a sucker's game; the mirror destroys its basic premise, save for the possibility that the mirror is itself only an appendage of the self externalized. You reach out. Your palm touches glass, and you wonder if your palm feels like glass to the you on the other side.

"You alright, darling?" asks your host from the playroom proper, and as your journey through the endless house ends, you realize that you never left; this is a bathroom, attached to the bedroom which has been repurposed as a playhouse, tiled with key lime green and kept shockingly clean compared to the bathroom downstairs. Surrounded by all that green, you feel like you're in a forest. The bathroom is a tiny treehouse, suspended in space-time like green Jell-O, an infinite lattice of rope bridges above and below and all around you.

You step out of the treehouse, back onto solid land, trying to hide your embarrassment. There was no reason to run; xe was right. Running only landed you back where you began—but it has killed some time, at least. That is, your host had said, the point of the whole exercise. To kill time until you are sober again, egoic again, sane again. Xe takes your hand with a gentle tug, helping you back to the couch, where you collapse. Did you even use the facilities, or did you just stumble in and lose yourself in the surface of silvered sand above the sink.

The crystal is sitting on the coffee table, and you pick it up with trembling fingers, once again using its familiar heft and texture to orient yourself in relation to yourself.

"Here," xe says, dimming the overhead bulb. "How about some TV? You've had enough reflection for now." With a sudden crackle, a projector flares to life, spattering blank blue light over the sheets which cover the windows. You look to see your host manning the equipment, considering a tangle of wires and different hookups. Xe presses something, *and the empty image is replaced by shuddering, inky figures. Unlike your reflection, they pay you no heed, but play their own games. "The body is a magnificent machine," they continue. "A true cutting edge piece of technology, a marvel of engineering. The function of the human body is defined by its purpose... a purpose shrouded in mystery, but one which will, as I tell this next tale, demonstrate itself, because....*

Today I am a Tool

administered by Mave Goren

From first grade til the end of fifth, I hung out with Marcus. He was a boy who, while also having long hair and a carefree attitude, felt far more comfortable in his own body than me. I didn't know much about making friends back then, so I pretended to like whatever he did. This defaulted towards standard nerdy 8-year-old interests in the early 2000s: manga, *Pokémon*, cartoons, and everything in between. After school, we'd dash to his apartment, a sizable loft in Park Slope. His dad was a lawyer and his mother worked in finance, so he lived a comfortable life in a comfortable neighborhood. Two windows faced a supermarket, a bookstore and an upscale Mexican restaurant. No rugs graced the hardwood floor, so even in the middle of Brooklyn, his apartment had a rustic quality to it. The family computer lurked in the corner, and just past the kitchen, we'd watch TV in his room.

Past curtain blinds, a rabbit-eared TV sat atop a stack of magazines, facing a couch always stained with milk and always smelling of fruit gushers. The light in the apartment made the furniture the same color as hazelnuts. When it was raining, the lights would blend in with their green coverings, making everything all smudged and homey.

Marcus' house was my church. In class I'd doodle pictures of the TV, of his GameCube, longing for them. I didn't know what he thought of me, I must have been some kid who loved hanging out with him. Maybe I was too young to perceive it like this, but I felt like a sycophant, and this undying devotion to a friend colored my interactions with him with a melancholy that's hard for me to erase to this day.

It's difficult to escape this sadness when it so paints the day when everything changed. It was the last semester of the third grade, when the whole class started yearning for the summer. Summer meant an end to responsibilities and more time to troll museums and comic shops. Marcus and I first noticed the clouds by the time we got to the front door. They were pregnant with rain and jet black like someone had colored an entire page with scribbles. We felt the drops when Marcus's dad opened the door to the apartment; they came in light intervals first, but the breeze bustling through the air made me think it wasn't going to get any better. By the time we got upstairs, rain was smacking against the windows; as soon as his dad let us in, Marcus scrambled for the remote.

"What are we going to watch today?" I asked. I didn't watch much TV growing up, not for any restrictive religious reason or anything of that sort, but because my parents wanted to enrich me "naturally," whatever that meant. This meant way less screen time, and more time in front of books and sketch pads. Hanging out with Marcus was a window into the world in which my other classmates lived.

"I heard this new cartoon is coming on," Marcus said.

"What's it called?"

"*Today I am a Tool.* Have you heard of it?"

"No." There was something about the rhythmic nature of the title that frightened me. Even as a kid, an adult baby talking to me did nothing but make me view myself as detached from my surroundings, a reflection on a grime-stained mirror. Not wanting to ruin the fun and do something I'd prefer to do, I asked , "What's it about?"

With a flick of the remote, Marcus turned the TV on and visual snow enveloped the screen. "It's about a boy who goes to a factory and becomes a tool."

"A tool..." I said, "like something you use in the garden?"

"You'll see."

His dad from the other room said, "Hey Marcus? Paul? I'm going to the store. I'll be right back. Have fun, boys."

I could hear him fumbling to get his umbrella open as he left.

I prepared a bowl of Chex Mix, and by the time the show started, my hands were furry with orange detritus.

"Shh, it's starting, it's starting!" Marcus said.

"I didn't say anything!"

"Shh!"

Blocky words fell into place, one after another, as synths swelled in the distance. They spelled out the title: *Today I am a Tool.*

And then: a black screen, silence—save for what sounded like a rustling of paper in the background; someone coughing, *Hack, wheeze, hack, wheeze* at a muffled volume, made quieter by the cougher noticing that they coughed. A grainy camcorder cast a stained yellow on the scene where a cardboard cutout of a boy (black pants, black suit, orange tie) tilted left and right, left and right by an out of focus hand. A voice in an unnatural falsetto said: "Hello boys and girls! My name is Timmy and today, I am a tool!"

"This looks crappy," I said.

"Shh!" said Marcus.

Timmy continued his trek through a white paper background, eventually getting to a hasty drawing of a factory.

"Oh look!" the narrator said, "It's the factory."

The screen went black. Marcus' eyes were still glazed over the television set while my stomach caved in on itself. Just a black screen; I could only tell the TV wasn't off from the breathing sounds the show was making. Would this screen change? Would things return to normal? But I was there, alone in the house of someone I felt like I was performing friendship at just to be next to them. Something behind the TV breathed in and out and in and out until the narrator said, "I'm in the factory now!"

The cutout of Timmy was now in the hodgepodge of crayon scribblings that somehow counted for a factory, the same hand wobbling him back and forth. "I can't wait to be a tool!" he said, then the camera shook. Footsteps came from the box, shuffling, as if whoever was on the TV was dragging their feet like a knife through flesh. The hand returned with a hammer. It smashed Timmy's head.

"Ow! Ow! Ow—OW!" the falsetto voice said. Each strike vibrated the screen, the hammer pounding further and further into Timmy's cutout.

Outside of TV Land, someone was reaching for a doorknob. And turning the handle. Was Marcus even seeing this? I bet he wasn't.

Marcus's dad entered. His coat was slicked with rain and some droplets dribbled onto the rug. "Marcus? I'm home," he said. "Marcus?" His dad's mouth was wide open, surrendering to terror. "Marcus!"

Marcus lay right below me. I was straddling him, holding the remote to his neck. His eyes were open but glazed over like soap bubbles. My hands were clenched into fists. The TV blared a cartoon channel, this time an episode of *Pokémon*.

"Paul! Get off my son now!"

"What's going on?" I asked. "Whatever it was, I didn't do it!"

The alibi of a child doesn't hold up in a court of adults. Marcus's dad sent me home, where my parents told me that whatever went on had to stop. Marcus and I would still hang out, of course, but they didn't want to put him in any danger. I worried for him. Was he okay? Why would he show me such a creepy show?

The next day I saw him in class, but we only exchanged a weak wave to each other before continuing to eat lunch on our own. I kept trying to interact with him, but each time filled me with an inexplicable melancholy. Just what did I do to him? We still hung out, but each time we spent together grew more hollow. I observed the shell of my body, watching with rapt attention as Marcus showed off his *Pokémon* cards, slowly leaving the space, zipping off the back of my head, floating to the ceiling, staying in a better place.

⇔⇔⇔

I met a kid towards the end of fifth grade; I forget his name and I'd rather not remember. He'd coax me to slip out of class, give me bruises for being shorter and weaker than the other boys, and call me queer for wearing my hair long and talking about books with a high pitched voice. It was standard stuff for any boy who didn't conform to heteronormative expectations. "What the hell is wrong with you?" was his refrain. It didn't matter how many times he wanted to wrestle me in our underwear, he still thought I was wrong for existing.

One day, much to my parents' chagrin, I invited him over. It was the late summer and middle school was approaching like a heart attack. Mom and Dad must have been grateful that I wasn't going to see him again, but he and I were annoyed. So after waiting on the stoop for this kid to show up he arrived an hour late. A rabble came from his mom's car.

"No, Mom, I don't want to see Paul!"

"Well you made a promise and that's that!"

"But I don't wanna!"

As he waddled up to the porch, I wasn't so sure I wanted to see him.

"Do you want to see me?" I asked.

"Not really."

"Me either. Let's go play *Sonic*."

So we went to my room, booted up the GameCube and played *Sonic Adventure 2* until our thumbs got calluses. Throughout, we kept shooting eyes at each other. *I know you don't want to be here, but that's just fine.*

He said, "Why don't we watch TV?"

"My parents won't let me."

"Well that's too bad." He barged into my parents room and scrounged for the remote. I took a seat on the bed, trying to make sure that my mom wouldn't see us. I mean, she likely wouldn't have complained in the first place, but there was still an element of anxiety that made me think *she might.* Already the TV was on and he searched for one of the cartoon channels.

"What's going on?" I asked.

"Shh!"

My blood froze when I heard that squeaky voice.

"Hello boys and girls! My name is Timmy, and today I am a tool!"

Everything went black for a minute, then my mom screamed.

"PAUL!" she was shouting. I snapped back to reality and gasped when I discovered I was on top of the boy, holding the remote to his neck.

I didn't do it. I didn't mean to do it. I swear.

⊕⊕⊕

Years pass and friend groups shift; elementary school turns into middle and middle turns to high; high turns to college and Marcus still exists in the back of my mind. I look up nostalgic cartoons to watch before bed and my cluttered dorm is filled with high-pitched voices, but there's one show I can't erase from my mind. I look up *Today I am a Tool* and no results come up. I look up to see if people have tried to archive or document a show featuring cut-out crayon drawings… no results either. I make posts on several forums and no one answers.

Over some period of time, I realize I'm transgender. I get on hormones, live with my girlfriend and her girlfriends and make a respectable living as a librarian. Things are fine.

I don't see Marcus again until I fly back to New York to spend Thanksgiving with my parents. New York is something to behold in the fall, and across our old haunts, it becomes achingly beautiful. I try to get outside of my mom's apartment as much as possible: it's three rooms all smelling vaguely of cat piss. I start hanging out around Marcus' neighborhood.

At a coffee shop, I see him working the counter. Even behind his facial hair, he's still that same kid. I want to be convinced that he doesn't hate me and that he enjoyed the times we spent together. I want to, but that same melancholy prods at my side.

"Oh my god, is that Marcus?"

He shifts his glasses down, mouth agape. "Paul?"

"It's Piper now," I inform him.

"You look really different," says Marcus.

"A lot has changed since I last saw you. How are you?"

"Well I can't complain. I'm a barista now, so it could be better. Jesus Christ, talk about a trip down memory lane…"

"We used to hang out all the time," I say.

"Oh, those were good times. Can I get you a coffee?"

He hands me my coffee and I sit at the counter, looking at the trees weeping leaves onto the sidewalk. Marcus is six feet behind the counter, but we are miles apart. As I sip my coffee, savoring the rich aroma, I wonder if maybe he could give me the closure I need.

I browse my phone and against all of my better instincts, find an account from a British anti-trans activist. Seeing this kind of content used to be enraging, but now it's numbing. Entertaining, in a weird way. I scroll past rants against trans-identified males (or *TIMs)* in women's spaces until Marcus is ready.

The sun sets and an orange glare envelops the coffee shop. Marcus and I are the only people inside; he is wiping the countertop. I set my coffee down.

"Hey, Marcus?"

"What's up?"

"I was wondering if you wanted to exchange numbers. It's been so long and all."

"Shit, I'm free after closing. Why don't we hang out a little?"

"Perfect."

When Marcus closes up, I'm standing by the door. I look like the

Made in
U.S.A.
YOU KNOW HOW T.V. DISTRACTS ME!
WHO ARE YOU? WHERE DID YOU COME FROM?
?

platonic ideal of a liberal arts student, black turtleneck, beret, baggy pants with a geometric pattern. Marcus—in his red sports car t-shirt and bluejeans—doesn't look a day out of the third grade.

"Ready?" he says.

"Ready." I open the door and we disappear into the Autumn sunset.

The trees are exposing their skeletons; the dusk is met by a slow-moving pall of fog that settles just beneath the curb. When would the right time be to talk about the show?

We talk about our favorite programs now, our favorite places we went to as kids, what we've been up to. Marcus shivers to see if by contorting his body, he can make himself warmer.

"You haven't felt hollow?" I say.

"Not really. I don't think about it that much."

"Still living with your parents?"

"Hey, it beats rent. Besides, I'm house sitting while they're out in the Virgin Islands."

"That I can get behind." I say, "Where did you go to college?"

"Some place upstate," he says, "I was studying film, but the industry sucks."

"That's so cool. I went to Washington for library science."

"Figures. You had your nose deep in your books."

"Hey!" as much as I didn't want to be pieced into the Piper of 17 years ago, he *was* right; in lieu of many friends I developed a taste for reading, mostly middle school lit, and towards the end of elementary I got into Bradbury, Edgar Rice Burroughs, and even some Asimov.

"Do you want to go to the Canal?" Marcus says. "Figure we could throw rocks in the water, shoot the shit, maybe grab a couple of beers. I don't know what you do these days."

Perhaps I can get to know my childhood friend for the first time. "Sure," I say.

Once a blighted industrial neighborhood near downtown, Gowanus has become an overpriced, ugly, unlivable hellhole. Marcus and I sit between two windowless factories facing the water. It stinks of refuse and smog from eighteen-wheelers, but the rent must be high because of the spectacular view of Downtown Manhattan. The freedom tower broods in the night like a gargoyle. A pigeon flits against an old factory building and into the cold sky, its caw echoing into the deep dark. Marcus drains his lager and lobs the empty bottle into the East River. It bobs once, twice and sinks into the hodgepodge of waste. There's something about Marcus that makes me feel disgusting. With his humble goatee and shaggy hair he's almost… handsome? I'm not into men, at least not into cis men, but I think back to my time spent with him and wonder if the reason I associated with Marcus in the first place was that he was attractive. His hair was still shaggy then, and he wore bangs that covered his glasses. There was a certain level of male/male socialization I identified with, and I'd have liked to think it was deeper than "friendship," whatever that means. Truthfully, I was an opportunist, but if Marcus and I cuddled back then I wouldn't have said no—but who knows when feelings come in? It wasn't until puberty hit when I found out that I liked girls. And it wasn't until after college when I found out I liked girls *as a girl*. There was something about Marcus's boyishness as he lobs cans into the East River that makes me think, have I repressed this part of being gay this entire time?

"P, what's up? You look nervous."

"Beer's getting to me."

"You barely had one can."

"I'm a lightweight," I say, "It's the estrogen."

"Huh?"

"Estrogen reduces my tolerance for alcohol."

"You're on estrogen?"

"Three years." I'm tempted to ask if he is too, because I'm so used to talking to other girls about this.

"Oh." He says. "Cool. I have some other trans friends who take it. You'd like my friend Cujo. You remind me of her."

"Probably," I say. Truthfully, I'm tired of dealing with other trans women. No disrespect to the other girls, but living with a trans girlfriend and her two other trans girlfriends makes me feel as if I'm living in a soap opera. The West Coast trans "scene" being what it is, it might as well be one. Everyone I know in the area has slept with someone who slept with someone else, like a godforsaken lesbian Six Degrees of Kevin Bacon, only about four degrees shorter. Girls on the internet attest even the large trans community here is the same thing—I'd believe it.

"Oh. also," Marcus turns to me. "One of my exes was trans."

Do I have a chance?

Who am I kidding… I haven't seen this putz since the fourth grade and already I'm thinking of kissing him. *You're a creep, Piper, you know that, right?*

"No shit! That's really cool!" I say.

"Yeah. I still miss Magdalen sometimes." A solemnity haunts his voice. "Like, I'd date a girl if she was trans or wasn't, but trans girls are just *different*, you know?"

Don't tell me I'm dealing with a chaser. I don't respond.

"Hey, I still have some time to kill while my dad's out on vacation." Marcus says. "Do you want to watch some movies?

"I'd love to," I say.

We make our way from Gowanus to Park Slope. Somehow, it's gotten colder; the wind creeps into my bones and nips at my bare flesh. There's little distance between each other and maybe, if I sidle closer to him, I can initiate something, but who am I kidding? What did he even mean by "watch movies"? At his place?

Despite the red flags I don't want to call it a night just yet. Not when I'm staying at my mom's and there's unfinished business to take care of. I should ask him if he remembers. I know he probably won't recall as distant a memory as a TV show from the mid 2000s, but I can't remove it from my mind. *Out damn spot, out.*

His childhood apartment is pitch black and even as he turns on the light there is a preternatural darkness that looms behind it. The green lamp, now weathered by age, throws its shadow against the cutlery.

"Make yourself at home," he says.

I take a seat on the couch and memories overtake me, threatening to consume. "I might have had too much to drink."

"P, you only had one beer."

"Like I said, I'm a lightweight." And indeed, this is too much to take in. The ceiling is too low for my liking. What seemed large and expansive as a kid is now cramped, a small cube threatening to pulverize me into a shapeless pile of meat.

"Do you want some cake?" he asks.

"Sure."

Marcus goes to the fridge and pulls out a cake, freeing it from its plastic prison. Then he finds two paper plates, like the ones I ate from when we celebrated our birthdays together. He goes to the knife drawer and selects a sharp one. Gripping onto the handle, he stabs it into the chocolate frosting, saws through it and stabs it in again. Before long, two meaty slices grace our plates.

"What do you want to watch?" Marcus asks

"I'm game for anything," I say. I'm not anxious right now, but I feel as if there is a timeline in which I am. Am I just avoiding what I'm so scared of? This nameless anxiety? I hesitate—maybe he's going to put on *Today I am a Tool.*

"How about *Mulholland Drive?*"

"Interesting choice," I say. "Now I know why we hung out in the first place."

"Fuckin A!" Marcus plops in his copy of the DVD (resting next to other art house movies, ranging from *Persona* to *Pink Flamingos…* interesting taste.)

Halfway through the movie, Marcus moves closer, the cake stains around his mouth acting as a second beard. "Is this okay?" he puts his hand on my shoulder.

"Yes." I begin to feel his warmth and his heartbeat and I wonder if this was in fact the reason why I was interested in him in the first place. He smells so *thick* that I can hardly concentrate on anything but him. Right now the movie is starting to focus on the romance between our two female leads, in Lynch's typical dreamy style. When our *Mulholland Drive* heroines—Betty and Camilla—have sex together, Marcus and I nestle closer. I can hear his breathing against my ear. "You're so soft," he says.

"Thanks," I say. "It's the estrogen."

His heartbeat is getting faster and he seems more excited now, panting like a puppy. What if I were to hook up with him right now? I'm not straight. I'm not a gay man either, but I'm not straight and I can't help but hate myself for wanting. My hand is up his shirt now, bristling against his chest hair. And then…

The screen goes black.

I say: "Where's the movie?"

"Shh!" says Marcus. A rustling sound comes from the TV… and heavy breathing. *Don't tell me. Don't fucking tell me.*

Something on the screen is breathing in, breathing out, *Hack, wheeze, hack, wheeze,* just self-conscious enough to stop. The screen is still showing footage from the camcorder.

"What's up?" I ask. "What's happening?"

"Shh!" Marcus says.

"Hello, boys and girls!" A high pitched voice emanates from the set.

"My name is Timmy and today, I am a tool!"

No. Please. Anything but this. Anything.

Everything is black now, and then…

"Piper! What the fuck are you doing! *Stop it right now! FUCKING STOP IT!*"

When I come to, we're naked, and I'm still on the couch, and the TV is nearing the end of *Mulholland Drive*. Marcus is in a catatonic state below me as I straddle him, the cake knife against his neck. Red streaks mark a weapon that has done the unthinkable. His eyes are glazed over as blood wells from his chest, and it smells invigorating: smells of sex. He's thrashing about, trying to stop me from digging the knife further in.

"*"Piper…*" he manages. "*Stop it… Piper, stop it now…*"

But I don't listen. Instead I gouge my weapon into his neck, and his blood splatters from his body against the couch like semen.

As blood splashes against the screen the image shudders, returning to static, and your host apologizes. "Hmm," xe muses. "Probably not the best material for your present condition. But don't worry, we can try another channel. And if that's a no-go, there's a VCR, and a DVD player, and—"

The door to the playroom is thrown open and someone dressed as the Dread Pirate Roberts walks in, throwing the lights on as they enter. "Sorry to interrupt, but I left my notebook in here, I think, and the party is just getting good so I figured I'd—" They stop suddenly, blinking at you and at your host. "Who the fuck are you?" they ask, stepping fully inside and closing the door. They look at your host accusingly, and you realize your assumption that xe must live here was an incorrect one. "And is that your fucking cat?" they add, looking at where the sphynx is curled up on the coffee table.

"I'm just a friend of the house," the storyteller says.

"Bullshit," challenges the housemate. "And that doesn't matter. This room is private. Like, super private. So get out."

"Look, I appreciate your sacred rites and rituals," xe says, then gestures to you, "but someone at your party dosed my companion here, which means that as far as I'm concerned you owe me, and what you owe me is a safe space for them to settle down. Alright?"

The housemate bristles for a moment, looking as if they're going to argue, then they shrug. "Sure, fine." They cross to an end table by the couch where you sit, collecting a black Moleskine notebook from under an empty can of Coors, and tip you a salute. "Happy sailing, soldier. God bless and good luck and godspeed." They look at your host. "Try not to make a mess, and if anyone else comes in, I can't promise they'll be as magnanimous as me."

They disappear out the door, hitting the dimmer switch again as they go, and leaving you alone again. "Now," says your host, "where were we?" The projector again sputters to life, its murky construction paper cutouts replaced by wriggling rubberhose anatomy, reaching out towards you. "Ah, yes." The pooling ink starts at the top of the sheet and rains down, down the whole screen and to the floor, across the boards, up towards you. "A quick change of the channel, a quick hop, skip and a jump, out of the factory and into the smiling mouth of…

Mr. Belly's Infirmary
(or, The Wonderful World of Mr. Belly)

administered by Sirius

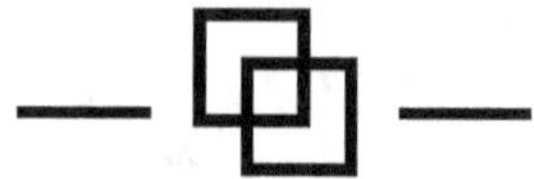

"Aww, shucks! Shouldn't have opened my big red mouth!" the TV show host wailed into his oversized white gloves. Carter stared at the screen, standing on the other side of the room and holding an old coffee cup filled with mold. Somewhere between deciding he was going to finally clean off his bedside table and walking into the living room, the edible hit. He'd definitely taken more than he should have, but it was too late now.

Now he was caught up in the size of the show host's gloves. They were each the size of Christmas hams. The host peeked over his fingertips, as bloated as Italian sausages, and stared right at Carter with beady, dark eyes set within an open, stark-white face. The style, he was pretty sure, was a callback to some kind of old 1930's cartoon. The whole show was in black-and-white, which made the reference to *my big red mouth* kind of weird, because all Carter could see was a grin as black as an oil stain, spreading from ear-to-ear across the host's jaw.

"Say, hey hey! What have you got there?" The cartoon host pointed straight at the screen. Carter's heart dropped into his stomach.

"Nothing," Carter said, swallowing down a lump. His fuzzy head wasn't helping his perception of reality, and it sounded like the host was talking directly *to* him.

"Nothing!" the host screeched, and Carter jumped. His knees gave out underneath him and he fell to the floor, catching himself with his hands. The mug banged against the hardwood and cracked, with the handle coming clean off.

A laugh track played, but the canned, dead guffaws weren't enough to cover the host's own hysterical screeching. Once, when Carter was *really* high, he had watched a documentary about hyenas hunting a lion cub—just a dozen shining eyes in complete darkness accompanied by that maniacal, ravenous cackling. That visual had haunted him since, and right now it felt familiar.

"Come here, Carter," the cartoon host pitched his voice. "Come here, come closer!"

He crawled across the floor. For some reason, it didn't seem worth it to try and stand up again. He stared up at the TV—eight inches from corner to corner of burning phosphors. He'd bought it specifically to watch programs in color.

The host's face got bigger, with his body shrinking until it was just one large, grinning feature looming over Carter like a devious barn owl. Phosphors crackled and static made a sound like a rubber band snapping as one white glove eclipsed the screen until those large, obscene fingers started poking through. Carter's heart skipped another beat, and he tried to back up, but the hand—once it was free—was too fast. It grabbed him by the hair and dragged him forward, gripping him so tightly that he heard follicles popping as they were yanked out, one by one.

Suddenly, he couldn't breathe. Static wreathed his face like a thousand needles jabbing his temples and the underside of his chin. Carter tried to inhale, but there was pressure on his chest like a concrete slab sitting on his ribs. Only when the needling static moved down to his shoulders could he finally start gasping for air. He wasn't sure how long he stayed in that position. It felt like an eternity, or at least a few hours. Finally, the hand let him go, and Carter fell on his face.

When he pulled his head up, he was staring at a giant pair of bulbous black-and-white spats.

"There he is!" The host from before picked him up and dusted him off. That black, smeary grin parted only slightly, and through the slit, Carter could see a row of teeth like shards.

"I'm sorry," Carter gasped out. His stomach churned and he felt like he was going to vomit. "Where am I?"

"You're on the Wonderful World of Mr. Belly! And I'm your host, Mr. Belly." The host spread his arms and legs out like a pinwheel. "Ta-da!"

Carter finally stood. "Is that so?" He looked around. "I've never been on TV before." This *had* to be a bad trip, so he figured he should just roll with it and see what happened. He'd learned, at a certain point, not to fight them,

"Yes siree! Well, it's your lucky day!" Mr. Belly pulled a needle out of his pocket and pricked the side of his head. The whole thing exploded like a balloon, and not a full second later, a new one inflated from the neck hole. His grin was even wider, like it was going to split his head in half, with more razor teeth showing through. "Anything is possible, in the Wonderful World of Mr. Belly!"

"Anything?" Carter's mouth went dry. He wanted so badly to take a step back so he was no longer standing toe-to-toe with the host, but putting distance between them also felt *strangely and immediately* dangerous.

"Anything." Belly's voice plummeted again, and he pitched the needle over his shoulder. He reached back into his pocket and pulled out a mallet as tall as Carter, with a head as thick as his torso. Belly handed it over, and it was like grabbing onto an anvil. Carter doubled over as the handle dragged him to the ground and Belly let out another hyena cackle.

"Not how you do it! Let me fix it for ya!" The host slammed a gloved hand onto his back and Carter's spine straightened out. The mallet was, suddenly, amazingly light. He almost lost his grip and nearly launched it into the air as he came up.

"What do you want me to do with this?" Carter asked, his voice trembling.

"Hit me!" Mr. Belly said, bouncing on his heels. He danced in a circle around Carter, every sudden motion blurry as his outline crackled through the air like static. "Hit me, hit me! Come on, come on! Put 'em up!" The cartoon host balled up his fists and made punching motions in the air. Carter grit his teeth and raised the mallet, bringing it down without much confidence. The first time it missed and there was a loud slide-whistle sound that came out of nowhere. Mr. Belly slipped between Carter's legs and popped up behind him, blowing a raspberry.

"Here! Here!" the host taunted him. Carter swung around and brought the mallet down. He didn't *actually* expect to hit the host, but he managed to bash him right on the head. Belly exploded in a bright red splat, the only blot of color against the inky stage.

SMASH!
CRASH!
HELP!
EAT ME
THC

"Oh my *fuck*!" Carter hauled the mallet back; the end was crusted with red and what looked like strands of coarse black hair. The air smelled like pennies. "*Fuck*, oh my god, what was that? What the *hell* was that?" He dropped the mallet and it landed on his toes. Three of them cracked under the impact and Carter crumpled again, clutching his foot.

"Agh!" He ground his teeth and squeezed out a tear. Pain radiated up his foot, shooting all the way up to his knee, and again it was hard to breathe. The red—the blood?—turned pitch-black and the pool shrank. It became thinner than a ribbon and it slithered across the ground, looping into what resembled that wide, oily smile before unlooping again and darting away.

"Wait!" Carter started to stand and nearly fell back onto his face. He cried out, a feral blend of rage and pain, and managed to stay upright on his one good foot. He hopped after the streak, one hand stretched out as if he had any hope of catching it. "I'm sorry about that! Please…" his voice faltered. "I think I need to go home now."

"*Ho-o-ome!*" Voices like a quartet harmony being played off a phonograph filled his ears while four lanky ghosts descended out of nowhere. At first he could see right through them, then they became a little more solidified and sprouted wobbly black legs and arms. They wobbled and bobbed around him, waving white-gloved hands around and wailing from black oval mouths. "*Ho-oo-oooooome to Mr. Belly's Wonderful World!*"

"No, no!" Carter snapped. Fear made his heart feel like it was going to come jumping out of his ribs. And in this world, he didn't trust it *not* to. "Home, my living room, the *real world* where I'm from!"

"*Hoooo-ooooo-oooome, my baby's coming home, to a white slab covered in roooooo-ooooo-ssseeesss-! Gooooooodbye, my baby—!*"

One of the ghosts pulled out a muted trumpet. Another produced a flute. None of them were listening to him. Carter stumbled and tried to catch himself on one of them, but his hand went right through.

"Please!" His desperation wrenched his throat. "Just tell me how to get out of here…!"

"*Mr. Belly has a place for you, on a white slab where the air smells like roooo-oooo-ssses! Gooooodbye, my baby, it's hot hot hot in here now!*"

Something grabbed Carter's hand and yanked him aside. He staggered, half-hopping, and fell behind a two-dimensional bush that was propped up like stage scenery.

"Oh my god." Carter's stomach flipped and he couldn't hold back any longer. He vomited onto the ground, and it was all blacker than ink.

"Are you looking for Mr. Belly?" a squeaky voice asked.

Carter turned his head, holding the back of his hand against his mouth. The thing sitting next to him looked *sort of* like a human, but its entire body was twisted out of balloons. "No," Carter said, deadpan. "I am looking for a way to get home."

"No way home except for up, up, up," the balloon boy pointed at the ceiling. Carter looked up, but his eyes were just met with a blinding white light. He grimaced and dropped his head back down.

"I need to get home," Carter said. "I'm on a bad trip."

"Where are you going?" The balloon boy asked. "Why is it bad?"

"I'm… never mind," Carter rubbed his face. "Please, I'm hurt. Are you sure there's no way out?"

"Did you find the color?" The balloon boy squeaked. "The color gets you out."

"What does that *mean?*" Carter's patience, and his sanity, were degrading at an alarming speed.

"Color comes from everywhere! I have a favorite color, too. It's blue!" The balloon boy squeezed its middle, and a balloon shaped like a stomach burst. Blue slime went flying, splattering across Carter's face, and the balloon boy hovered there for a second, its top half completely separated from its bottom.

"Ah, nuts!" it started rising towards the roof. "Up, up, up!"

"Wait!" Carter tried to snatch it and drag it back down, but it was going too fast. It disappeared into the blinding light and he winced again, shielding his eyes. He tried to see what was happening, but the balloon boy was lost. Only a second later, he heard several loud *pops!*, and latex rained down around him.

Carter dragged his hand down over his face and his palm came back blue. He stared at it for a long minute until the color turned black.

Color gets you out, the balloon boy's words echoed in his head. He turned them over and over in his skull, trying to figure out what they could mean. *I have a favorite color too, it's blue! Aww, shucks, I shouldn't have opened my big red mouth!*

What was his favorite color? Did he *have* a favorite color? Carter laughed. He was *losing his mind.*

"Yellow!" Carter shouted like it was a revelation. "My favorite color is yellow! Hello?" He grabbed hold of the wooden bush prop and pulled himself up again. "Where can I find something yellow in this place?"

The laugh track played again. This time, it was loud as a thunderstorm, booming around his ears.

"Yellow, yellow…" Carter limped, looking around for any hint of color. "Yellow to get me home, fuck!" He dropped down to his knees and began to crawl, unable to keep up with hopping on one foot. Back to crawling. *That's how this whole mess began.*

Carter's hands found what looked like a painted path on the studio floor and scrambled onto it. As soon as his hands found the paint, he left yellow handprints. His heart raced at the realization and he crawled even faster, not stopping to try and catch his breath, leaving more yellow handprints and drag marks from where his knees scraped along the path.

He only paused once to glance behind him, and the handprints were already starting to fade to black. Carter kept crawling, even as pain started to make his legs so stiff that he started losing confidence that he was going to be able to keep going.

"*Fooolllooooowww the ye-ll-ow paiiintt rooooooooaaaddd!*" A harmonious crescendo of phonograph voices, rolling drums, and crashing symbols rose like the end credits of an old cartoon. The paint road dropped off suddenly, but Carter didn't realize how steep the drop was until his hand hit empty air and he toppled over like a child's toy being launched off a kitchen table.

He fell through the darkness, and then the needling static was back, stabbing him from all sides until he screamed in agony.

It ended when he hit his head, and then all the color bounced back into his world. He put his hands over his face and sat up, his head reeling like he'd just dismounted from a roller coaster.

He was back in his living room. The cracked mug on the floor rested right next to his foot, where three toes were ballooning and turning a heinous shade of purple that was almost black.

Carter laughed. A maddening, hyena-like sound. He pulled himself up and hopped on one foot, right over to the television set. He pushed the curved screen and static crackled against his hand as it fell backward, landing with an expensive-sounding *crack.*

Mr. Belly's face was still frozen on the screen, wide and white with a big, dark grin—but no sound came from the TV, only singing electricity.

You cough and sputter, spitting the ink from your lungs, feeling it pour over your fingers, but when you look your hands are empty, unblemished, ready to receive whatever comes next. "Enough of that, I think," your host says, shutting the projector off and leaving you both in darkness until the dimmer switch is again lifted. "No big deal. There's plenty of other tales left to fill the space. Still, sorry the cartoons were a bust. No idea what's wrong with that AV setup." Xe smiles at you. "I hope that I've at least been a better trip sitter than Mr. Belly."

You flex your fingers, still expecting them to be stained with ink, but instead you feel them reaching for the crystal on the coffee table. As you pick back up the hunk of amethyst, your host crosses to a shelf of art supplies near the bathroom door. Xe grabs a small plastic bin of crayons and xer hand hovers over some coloring pages before reaching for a few sheets of blank construction paper. "Here," xe says. "How about you make some images of your own? Better than what was on the screen, anyway, right?"

Your fingers release their grip on the amethyst as you slide down from the couch and onto the rug in one liquid motion. Reaching into the melange of wax, you produce one of the Crayolas: "Periwinkle", reads the scuffed paper coating, its body a soft purple-blue. Reflexively, like the planchet of a Ouija board, the crayon seems to move of its own accord, pulling your wrist towards the paper. As the dulled tip touches down, your hand flits as if you're drawing a five-pointed star, instead producing the five windmill-like petals of a flower. Seeing it against the paper, you can almost smell it, a soft sweetness that's barely there—but is there. Your hand is your own again, but it follows its own example, making more of the flowers.

"It starts with one," says your host, stroking Deedee's back and watching you with burning eyes. "Like a cancer. Always with one, and then another, and then another—until the novelty of the bloom is smothered by the weight of its own reproduction, choking out whatever else is in its path, bleeding the greenery blue. Sometimes called centocchio—*"a hundred eyes"—but in our next tale, we learn why others have called it* la...

Fior di Morto

administered by James Arthur

ϕ 1 ϕ

Francine won Goldie via the old ring toss. A simple game, in principle, though not so simple in practice: the throwing of plastic rings with a circumference slightly larger than the necks of a group of old-fashioned milk bottles (made of really thick glass) with the goal of ensnaring as many as possible. She managed two out of three in a single round. No mean feat. Just one more "ringer" would have netted the grand prize—a giant stuffed bear larger than Francine herself—but once the plastic baggie (closed off with a violet twisty-tie) had exchanged hands and she saw the wonderful life form hovering with stationary grace within, its fins fluttering with delicate, mesmerizing motion (much like laundry dancing on the clothesline on a breezy day), she knew she had won the true grand prize.

The goldfish, instantly christened "Goldie", grinned from within the small baggie and tipped the young girl an obvious wink, despite the "fact" (as related by her father) that fish do not wink. "They simply cannot, honey," so explained the always serious adult as he sat all-knowing in his recliner later that same day. His stern countenance appeared above the book he had been reading and disappeared as soon as he had made his point, a leviathan dipping beneath the waves. His brow reappeared seconds later; he had decided to elaborate. "They cannot Franny, because they do not have eyelids like us mammals do." She knew her father was being *really* serious when he didn't use contractions in his speech; he was a talking textbook. "They do not need them because they live underwater, whereas we need them to moisten our eyes, else they would dry up . . . " And so on and so on. Francine had stopped paying attention as she often would under such circumstances. Now she wanted him to finish speaking so she could leave the room.

Often Francine's enthusiasm in a subject would start "drying up" in the face of her father's rational batterings, but not this time. It certainly might have if not for the dose of magic her pet brought into her life each and every morning. This magic was in the daily renewal of the wonder she felt watching Goldie zip about the confines of his small bowl. She took great delight watching his fins flutter and flap in the clear water that made up his home—and all the while he kept smiling and winking at her, in direct opposition to her father's words.

They had developed a silent language between them. Francine was just beginning to understand the subtle depth of such a language, when, right as third grade was ending and summer vacation was about to commence, the unthinkable occurred. One morning Francine found Goldie floating at the top of the bowl, unresponsive.

✢ 2 ✢

Right away she knew this was no trick, an aspect of the elaborate games the two of them played daily; it was too horrible. Goldie would never pretend such a thing. *Never.* When Francine poked the body of her dear friend he did not respond, at least not in a way that might elicit hope. Goldie's lifeless form bobbed under her finger's pressure. He dipped, causing a ripple to flutter across the water's surface. When it subsided his body rose, inert, like a discarded cork.

Somehow Francine knew this was her fault; she had killed her friend through non-action. She had wanted to get him a bigger home, one of those large fish tanks she had seen on a visit to the local pet shop, with plenty of room for him to swim around in. That wasn't all. Space meant nothing if there were no fishy friends for him to swim around with; she had dreamed of filling this tank with tropical fish representing all the colors in her crayon box. After all, she could not be with Goldie every waking minute and she did not want him to be lonely. Her parents said no, however, to both requests, informing her that buying said tank would be (in their harsh adult speak) "...an unnecessary expense; and since we are not about to buy a larger fish tank, there would be no point in buying more fish. There is simply not enough room in your fishbowl for more than one". Then they added in sugary tones, as if to make her feel better: "Perhaps for Christmas, *if* you are a good girl". Francine knew, if only from the abstracted way this vague promise had been tossed off that it meant next to nothing, it was weightless as air. She was no dummy—the words were spoken to make her "shut up" about yet one more way of throwing good money down the toilet. That this promise would be forgotten long before the next yuletide arrived was practically a given. More likely her parents would forget it by the end of the very day they had uttered it. So Francine told herself Goldie's death was her fault; she had not argued with enough passion, her folks assuming her request just another childish whim. Yet the girl had never been more sincere.

She buried Goldie in the backyard, doing the mournful job by herself. Her mother really wanted to flush her friend down the toilet (her father was off teaching at the university, but he no doubt would have gone along with the insensitive plan). Francine had been horrified. How could her mother even think such a thing? Nothing portrayed the widening chasm between her and her parents with better clarity.

Goldie had been animated with that magic stuff of life. All she needed to do to cause tears to blossom was picture him hovering there *gazing directly at her*, patiently listening. Francine had no doubt of this whatsoever, despite his lacking ears. While she talked over the events of her day *Goldie listened.* Now there would be no one to listen, not ever again.

When her parents mentioned buying another goldfish as a replacement she balked at the insensitivity of such a notion. "Goldie cannot be replaced. He is irreplaceable." Which was true. He was an individual, just as she was.

Francine could also avoid contractions when she was dead serious.

✣ 3 ✣

Until the vine with the purplish flowers emerged from Goldie's grave out behind the family's vegetable patch (the most secluded part of the yard), Francine never really thought of plants as living things, just as she had never considered animals to be truly "alive" until Goldie entered her life. Which would not have happened anyway had it not been for her right arm and her middling throwing ability, good enough to encircle two wide-mouthed bottles, perhaps, but not three.

She had gone into the backyard to check on the grave and the marker she had placed there. It was a black stone roughly egg-shaped that Francine found at the beach while the family had been on vacation. She had placed it inside the fishbowl to remind Goldie of his home in the great big ocean (where he must have swam from to end up beside her bed). She wondered about this often, his great quest to wind up in her goldfish bowl. Francine wished, and not for the first (or even hundredth) time, she could have had one honest conversation with him. While having no notion of an afterlife or what might happen after one died (she was only nine) Francine hoped one day to see her Goldie again. That, once both of them passed beyond and had become beings of pure spirit, they would then communicate as equals.

This journey was Francine's first trek into the soggy reaches of the yard after a solid week of rain (any thought of making such a trip before this had been too distressing, the memory of Goldie's passing too near). As she squelched in her galoshes past the soggy garden plot and came up to the grave she found something unexpected.

Growing directly out of the grave, right in front of the egg-shaped stone, was a trailing vine, fully (she guessed) a foot and a half long, with the loveliest purple flowers fluttering in the afternoon breeze. It certainly had not been there before the storms and the winds and the rains, and such speedy growth impressed her: as if the plant had had something to prove. That it must mean something Francine took for granted, even before taking into account the direction the tendril was growing. It was heading straight for the house.

What she did next, what her parents eventually labeled as the beginning of the whole heartbreaking affair, was to ask what kind of ivy was growing all over the yard, an ivy that, until the recent round of storms, had kept to a localized patch along the western side of the house. Her mother, elated Francine had begun showing an interest in something other than her precious goldfish, took her to consult the family encyclopedia, which had been hers when she was Francine's age (a fact the young girl had a hard time accepting; she'd always assumed her folks had been born old).

These books were kept on the lowest shelf in the library, a musty chamber of funereal stillness. Francine hated this room. On the rare occasion she entered slantwise sunbeams oozed through the window blinds casting a murky illumination that did little to penetrate the pervasive gloom within. The books, mostly her father's textbooks, had dark bindings, lacking all color.

Bookcases were monolithic and intimidating. The chair her father used, which she refused to go anywhere near, was foreboding, comprised of nothing but sharp angles. There was also a couch, but it was lumpy and uncomfortable, as though full of rocks.

This time Francine was curious, though, so she followed her mother with unusual eagerness into the gloom-filled chamber. Her father was a professor and loved his books (more than his own daughter, she often thought), and he spent a great deal of his evenings alone here. Along the walls in the few bare spots were gathered a collection of elaborately carved masks he had gotten on a trip abroad many years before. Their scary faces leered down, eye slits seeming to follow her progress through the room.

Glancing at the louvered window for some relief from these staring eye holes, Francine was abruptly cheered. Through the narrow horizontal slits of the lone window small violet flowers pressed against the window from outside.

Her mother went to a low shelf, ran a finger along the spines of the books arrayed there, and removed one that looked like all the others.

"It'll be in here, dear, under 'periwinkle'."

"Like the crayon?" Francine said, delighted by this unexpected concurrence pairing the vine with her crayons, her absolute favorite possessions.

"Exactly like it, I think you'll find." The elder smiled at her daughter, pleased. Unable to restrain herself, Francine beamed right back. It was a rare moment of warmth between mother and daughter.

The adult held the volume out to Francine, who took it (it was heavy) and carried it to the coffee table. As the girl set it on the table she felt stirrings of returning distress. Then, after taking a seat on the couch (and trying to ignore a big lump underneath her butt) she opened the book, imagining a great cloud of dust puffing upward while she did so.

Nothing like a book to drain a subject of wonder, Francine thought acidly. Turning to the entry she began to read, yet could not dismiss an unpleasant association that came along with it. Perhaps it was being in this room, looked down upon by those judgmental masks, but the words echoed off of the page in her father's dreary professor voice. Francine forged on, though, and did manage to pick up a few interesting tidbits from her reading.

It was indeed a vine, like she needed a book to tell her that, her eyes hazing over the Latin name without absorbing it. Talk about unimportant!

But then followed something cool: the plant, wherever it manifested, originated from one source, the same bit of root growing everywhere in, say, a plot of land. Then it told her that periwinkle was "invasive".

Oh, what do they know, Francine sniffed haughtily. While unsure of what this actually meant, it sounded so much like one of her father's pronouncements that she closed the huge tome, her low opinion of books and the adults who wrote them not altered a jot. The pictures weren't even in color, just grainy black and white that did the beautiful flowers (of roughly pentagram shape) no justice whatsoever! They were small, had five petals of blue with a violet tinge, which she could have verified had she gone to the window and glanced outside. Its leaves were oval and shiny, about nickle-sized. Though it wasn't like she didn't know these things already from time spent in front of Goldie's grave and her inspection of the lovely fragile flowers and the vine itself. The one thing the entry in the musty old book did was describe, in the driest language ever (bad as any school textbook), the technical aspects of the plant, the genus *Vinca*. She skimmed over all this and did not bother reading through to the end, which was too bad. Perhaps, considering her ingrown hardheadedness, it would not have made a difference if she had.

"Did you find what you wanted, dear?" her mother asked, picking up the large volume and carrying it back to its place on the shelf.

"There are two listings," Francine said. "The first has to do with something that grows along the seashore, but I found out some great stuff anyway." This wasn't exactly true, but she didn't want to disappoint her mother, who had gone to great lengths to help.

"We could move these books upstairs," her mother added hopefully. "That way you can look up whatever you want without leaving your room."

"Maybe someday," Francine said, knowing this wouldn't happen (she would never want such ugly books in her room). This was exactly what you got when you encouraged them, she told herself. Then she looked at her mother and smiled her best little girl smile. Best to be diplomatic.

"Thanks, Mom."

"Anytime, dear. I'm just glad you aren't disappointed."

The grin froze on Francine's face. Truth be told she could not be more disappointed, though she really was not surprised. Books were written by adults, after all. Where was the wonder? What about the magic? It wasn't lingering in the pages in old books, that was for sure.

✠ 4 ✠

Once she gave it some thought Francine realized that the encyclopedia had not been a disappointment after all. She was glad she had pushed her nose into her mother's moldy old book, but not because of the ivy. She knew all there was to know about the plant growing in her yard by observing it. It had been the other definition, the one about sea life, that gave her the information she needed to make one crucial connection. And it turned out to be a real zinger.

Goldie came from the *sea. So did periwinkle.* It was a kind of mollusk, a life form found along the seashore. That made them essentially the same. Francine told herself this, almost becoming giddy as the beauty of what she believed to be objective truth overwhelmed her, conveniently ignoring that the definitions had been referring to two separate species, or genera, entirely.

Now each time she took in the small violet flowers exploding all over the yard she was seeing her beloved friend in his new incarnation. *Goldie*: as it could be nothing and no one else. If she entertained any doubts all she needed to do was glance out the kitchen window. The fragile flowers would be fluttering about, as Goldie's fins had once fluttered, keeping him stationary in his watery home. And the size of him! How he had grown! The elaborate root system she had read about, that she now pictured growing beneath her very feet, would eventually grow to fill up the entire world!

✠ 5 ✠

A week after the great realization she woke up, cast the usual glance at the bare spot on her nightstand, and, despite knowing Goldie had returned in a new form, felt the familiar sting of sadness. She missed the goldfish by her bedside, waiting there every morning, staring at her as if to say, *wake up sleepyhead!* She missed those smiles and winks, and a plant, no matter how large it might one day become, could make no such personal gestures.

It was with extreme reluctance, then, that Francine pulled herself out of bed. It was a nice day. She did not have to look outside or go to her window to discover that. Her room was full to bursting with sunlight, as if every beam in the world had conspired to pay her a call in an attempt to dispel her gloom. Perhaps later she might spend time drawing on the

WHEN I
GROW
UP...

sidewalk. Maybe (if she were in the mood) she would see if any of the neighborhood kids wanted to get up a game of hopscotch. Maybe. She didn't really like many of the local girls, to be honest, and every time she drew on the great sandstone blocks in front of the house rain would come and wash away her creations.

Thinking of water brought Goldie to mind, the only living thing she really cared about, now dead, buried in the backyard behind the vegetable patch. Gone, like chalk, washed away forever.

Francine wanted to crawl back under the covers, despite that dumb old sun, and go right back to sleep (maybe she'd dream about Goldie!), but the sudden rumblings in her stomach stopped her. She might be sad, but she was also hungry. *Very* hungry. And wasn't that the smell of bacon wafting upwards from the kitchen? With a sigh she got out of bed and headed for the stairs.

A little later she had about finished eating. All through the scrambled eggs and toast and bacon her mother kept insisting she go out and play (she was just eager to get her daughter out of the house, as Francine well knew). This not-so-gentle prodding diminished the girl's enjoyment of her breakfast, which, hands down, was her favorite meal of the day. The view from the kitchen window really is inspiring, her mother repeated for the zillionth time in her high, shrill voice.

Picking up the last piece of bacon Francine lifted it and took a dainty nibble. *Sheesh*, she thought. *Mom can be so annoying.*

All of this would have been much more irritating had the sky as seen through the picture window not appeared almost heartachingly beautiful. It shone with that wonderful deep ocean blue, cerulean, the color of one of Francine's favorite crayons, and was dotted throughout with puffy clouds appearing soft as downy pillows. Her mother propped the window open and a pleasant breeze wafted into the bright kitchen. A floral scent rode that wind, and Francine's mind made the connection to the periwinkle in the backyard as ever tossing about in the breeze, just like Goldie's fins fluttering in the fishbowl. This visual association was the final spur. She would leave the house and follow, with some improvisation, her mother's plan. Go outside and be among those lovely flowers!

The screened-in porch, a holdover from a decade long past, was a quick shortcut into the backyard. The house had been built in the 1930s, her parents once informed her. This meant nothing to their daughter, whose ability to gauge the vastness of time was as minimal as that of most children her age; all she knew was that her folks meant it was old, ancient even, as some stone temple in a jungle clearing. "Charming", her mother called the enclosed porch. Father countered with "constricting". He spent little time there, even on pleasant evenings that were neither too hot nor too cold. He had his library, his books and the staring visages of those monstrous masks to keep him company.

Francine liked the porch a lot, probably because it was full of light and life and nothing like the static gloom of the library, but she especially liked it on rainy days. While the awnings outside kept the interior dry, the window screens (of wire mesh) allowed for the free play of wind and fresh air, and when it rained droplets of a pleasant mist found their way in to invigorate the inhabitants. It was almost as nice as being outside during the rain, splashing through puddles in her red galoshes.

This particular morning could not be more opposite to such a day, though, and once she stepped onto the porch from the living room all misgivings of before fled. She felt the warmth, a magnet pulling her towards the world beyond. In less than a second Francine was bolting for the far door. It had become the gate into one of the fairy tale worlds she loved so much.

Francine never made it. She tripped on the edge of the throw rug and fell forward, scuffing her knees and landing on her belly, the breath forced from her lungs. Taken by surprise she did not cry out; she had no time to. It happened so fast.

✠ 6 ✠

Somehow Francine had gotten turned around and fallen sideways; she faced a corner, a pair of lounge chairs placed at right angles before her. On the floor rested a light purple vase, set into the wedge formed by the angular chairs. The vase was smooth, ceramic and of a fluted arabesque style, what her mother referred to as an "air-loom". From the sensitive way she spoke of it Francine guessed she would be tarred and feathered if she managed to break it. It was pretty enough, she supposed, though her interests could not have lain any farther from fluted columns, air-looms, or even her currently throbbing knee. What interested her was the periwinkle vine that had forced itself into the porch from the yard outside.

Goldie was coming to visit, to say "hello", was her first thought. For who else but her beloved friend with his busily fluttering fins (he had never been absolutely still) would work so hard, even go so far as to push himself through a wall, to return to her?

The vine had made it all this way, forcing itself into the house as though it belonged here! Certainly it did, for if Goldie didn't belong with her nothing did. Francine had no doubt, even as she propelled herself upward on two shaky legs and brushed futilely at her skirt in an indifferent attempt at decorum, that the vine would climb all the way to her room if allowed to. She pictured it entwining the railing beside the stairs like the fake Christmas ivy her mother used, the plastic greenery bristling with tiny red and green lights. Only Francine's vine would be living, not fake like her mother's holiday decoration; it would need no lights to lend it such a brilliance.

This vision faded quickly in the bright halogen glow of reality. She knew her parents well enough to know how things would really go. The instant either of them set eyes on this vine they would tear it out by the root. It would be done without a second's thought. They could only accept nature if they were able to control it. That Francine could not see her precious Goldie now that she was standing made no difference. His new incarnation would grow and there would come a time when he could no longer hide behind an air-loom. Then one of *them* would see it and out would come the gardening shears and the valiant effort on her friend's behalf would end in a second death.

Looking behind to make sure she remained alone, Francine tiptoed to the corner and pushed the vase to one side to get a better look. Her vine had so far escaped detection because it had come through a crack in the wall at a point that hid it from direct sight. This strengthened her conviction it *must* be Goldie, for otherwise why would he be trying so hard not to be seen?

She had an idea connected with the length of vine crouching behind that vase (and it did appear to be crouching, she realized). Before it became a problem that must be eradicated she would get her parents to go along and become co-conspirators without their ever knowing it.

☦ 7 ☦

Her mother thought her plan a real plum of an idea. Francine had not had any doubt that it would "fly", but she was still surprised by her mother's immediate enthusiasm, a feeling shared by her husband the second he heard about it. Francine had assumed she would be forced to argue her point like a lawyer on a TV show, since her parents were never enthusiastic about any of her ideas. Yet this time they mutually decided this was what their daughter needed to take her mind off of the goldfish, and so each of them firmly endorsed the go ahead.

They had only one stipulation. That being, since they were talking about a vine, and it was inclined to grow (and very fast at that), it would be Francine's job to be mindful of its length at all times, a condition she had no problem consenting to. As far as conditions went it hardly counted at all.

"If it becomes a nuisance, out it goes!" her father proclaimed, but he was speaking in his pretend serious voice and grinning while he said it, which in turn made Francine smile. She was not worried, not anymore. She had gotten one over on the pair of them, and she hid her growing pleasure behind an upraised hand.

Father and daughter then went out to the garage to perform step one of the plan.

ϕ 8 ϕ

Dad was helpful throughout the whole process, which surprised her. He even devoted an entire afternoon to helping his daughter establish herself in what he referred to, in cloying tones, as Franny's new hobby. Further, he kept calling her "my little botanist" until the novelty had long worn off.

This annoyed Francine because she picked up on the vibe that her father was poking fun at her and her "hobby" by pretending to be serious about it. She especially hated his use of this word "hobby". It made her plans sound so much littler than they actually were. Yet she bore this behavior with a blunt smile; she even managed a good-humored chuckle to show what a good sport she was.

As she carried the pot in her arms (about the size of the air-loom vase) into the yard from the garage, her father beside her lugging a huge sack of potting soil in the crook of one arm and a small digging spade in his free hand, he kept up a steady stream of chatter. Francine barely listened as she led him towards Goldie's grave. This trek always made her feel sad; yet what greeted her as she approached this time filled her with elation. It wasn't Goldie's final resting place she was visiting, this was a transition point between stations.

"What are we doing, Franny?" her father asked as they tromped together across the grass.

"I'm going to dig up the vine, Daddy, and put it in this pot you got down for me." She stopped just beyond the vegetable patch, a few measly tomato vines beginning to spiral upward out of the soil (they had nothing on her periwinkle!), and indicated the precise spot with a nod. Dutifully her father set the huge bag of soil down and she followed with her flowerpot, noting with approval its shape resembled the truncated tip of an unused crayon. This similarity struck her as a good omen.

Francine had opted for a medium-sized pot (there were three sizes, stacked in separate piles on a shelf in the rear of the garage). While she had no idea how much room her ivy's root system might actually need she had settled on medium: not too big, not too small. The encyclopedia might have given more info on this important subject had she bothered reading the whole entry, but she had never had much patience with books. Francine told herself with inborn stubbornness she would figure out all she needed to know as she went along. In this she resembled her father, a man who had zero patience reading the instruction manuals that came with household appliances. All he did was file them away in a drawer, preferring to figure things out by himself. Often to disastrous effect.

He opened the bag of potting soil and tipped it bottom up, pouring the dark peaty-looking substance into the flowerpot. As careful as he was trying to be more wound up on the lawn than inside the pot; her father had never been that great with outdoorsy type stuff and Francine really wasn't surprised. If anyone had a green thumb in the family it was her mother.

Francine watched her father's fumbling process in growing frustration, hopping from one foot to the other as if she had to pee. She managed to bite her tongue, however, and watched in silence until at last he got it right, filling the pot about three-quarters full and then replacing what had fallen into clumps on the grass in the sack. The dark soil was full of little white specks, which her father explained would be good for her plant. "It is fertilizer. Full of nutrients that help plants grow."

Finally he passed the spade over and she took it with an air of great solemnity, as though she had been handed the key to the city. Then she knelt in front of the grave, readying herself to dig.

"Be careful," he said, standing over her. "You do not want to sever the root. And be sure to give yourself plenty of space. Try and put the plant as close to the middle of the pot as possible, to give it the room it needs to grow."

Absently Francine nodded, though she was not really listening. Once he had handed over the spade she forgot his existence. The universe had shrunk to the head of a pin, consisting of her, Goldie, and the spade. Having not heard his comments she yet adhered to what he had suggested from ingrown instinct, giving herself plenty of room within the pot and its outer edge to work.

" . . . " he mumbled.

"What, Dad?" she asked, a touch of asperity creeping into her voice. She was so close now!

"Do you think maybe we should have gone with the biggest pot?"

Maybe, she decided, but then she pictured her father going through his bumbling slapstick routine all over again like some cartoon rerun on Saturday morning TV, transferring soil from one pot to the other and spilling most of the contents. No, she didn't have the time to go through that again. She could repot later if such a need arose. All she wanted was to get this step in her quest over and done with. She pictured her room, her bedside table, and this pot right where she'd see it each and every morning thereafter. Francine smiled happily at the image.

She jammed the spade into the ground, right where she had buried Goldie. This next part was crucial, perhaps the most important stage of her plan. Hoping her father either wouldn't notice or, if he did, wouldn't give her a rough time and put a stop to it, she began to dig. Everything hinged on whatever happened, and whatever he might say, in the next few moments.

☦ 9 ☦

And within those minutes fortune smiled upon her. Their neighbor Mr. Radford took this propitious moment to appear at the boundary fence and call her father's name.

"Oh, hello Tim," her father said. He strolled away from his daughter's work.

Yes, she grinned watching him go, *everything is falling into place.* Not beyond ascribing mystical powers to her winking goldfish Francine sent up a prayer thanking him for this timely intervention. She needed to act fast, though, in case the conversation between the two adults was a short one, and so quickly set to work. Due to the recent rains the ground was moist and spongy and the digging went quickly. Another point in her favor.

✠ 10 ✠

Later she sat on her bed gazing at her newly installed periwinkle, the ivy's half dozen purplish flowers catching the light from the overhead fixture and reflecting brilliantly. The breath caught in Francine's throat. It was almost too beautiful for words. That violet-blue was so rich, so vibrant, so full of life. She was as excited as she used to be on Christmas Eve, back when she still believed in Santa Claus. She waited now, although she knew not what for, with renewed faith in the power of belief.

Did she expect the vine to change substantially during the nighttime hours while she was asleep visiting dreamland? No, she decided. That was not it, not precisely, although she did expect an alteration of sorts to occur. Because of this she found herself growing more excited than at any time since she had found Goldie floating in the fishbowl. Had she begun taking the little guy for granted while he had been alive? Yes, she realized with a jolt. She certainly had gotten used to his being there all the time, like some footman awaiting the princess's pleasure in a fairy tale.

Francine hated herself in that instant, vowing she would never take him for granted again.

The section of the plant she had transplanted was about a foot in length, with small oval leaves of shiny green. Looking at those leaves gave her an idea. Slowly she got up from her perch on the bed, reluctant to let Goldie out of her sight even for a second, despite that her friend wasn't doing much at the moment except "being". She needed her crayons. They were on her desk. There was something she needed to check.

Francine returned to her bedside and sat down with her deluxe box of crayons. Poking through the colors she found the color she was looking for and eased it from the rectangular box. Leaning forward she put "Periwinkle" next to one of the flowers. *Yes, an exact match!* This delighted her very much. Next she located a second crayon and placed it beside one of the waxy leaves. These grew in pairs off the stem in a precise symmetrical pattern. Maybe this shade wasn't as close as the flowers were to periwinkle, but Pine Green surely came close. What got her, though, were the shiny leaves: as though they were made of wax (like the crayon itself)! Only, unlike the phony plants her mother kept about the house which were also waxy-looking, this one was the real deal. What a delightful discovery to have made!

And Francine would be here every minute to watch Goldie as he grew. In her youthful enthusiasm she thought she might see him actually growing, if only she were patient enough.

Maybe her vine could not wink or flash a smile, as her goldfish had been fond of doing, but she knew there would be other compensations. Joyous discoveries awaited her. She must believe!

After returning the crayons to the box and setting it back on the desk Francine again returned to the bed. Once more she took her customary place on the edge—settling back into her ceaseless vigil.

"Goldie," she whispered reverentially, then placed a hand, palm outward, on the surface of the flowerpot. His heart beat through the hard ceramic surface and this pleased her. "I'm here."

<h1 style="text-align:center">✛ 11 ✛</h1>

Far too excited to sleep, Francine tossed and turned all night, but dawn at last arrived and she opened her eyes onto the first rays of a new day peeking through the slats of the blind.

She threw back the covers and looked for Goldie in his "I've been waiting for you" position on the bedside table. Her initial reaction was disappointment. There was the pot; there was the vine. Then the reality came to her and her disappointment vanished. At first she thought the vine was fluttering in place, but the movement was not repeated. She dismissed the impression as wishful thinking.

The sprig of ivy had grown, however. Quite a bit, too. There were all of seven flowers now, and the tiny buds of a bunch of new leaves. Plus another detail: contrary to heading for the window and the nearest light source, which plants have a habit of doing, her periwinkle was clearly making its way over the rim of the pot and down its slanting side, heading without any doubt whatever towards her.

Astounded by this clear show of affection Francine reached out to touch the plant (yes, it certainly had grown longer!). This time the tip of the vine curled about her little finger in a warm embrace!

Wow. At first she was much too shocked and overcome with joy to speak; she continued to stare at the living embodiment of Goldie. This was too wonderful to believe. And much better than winking!

"I love you too, Goldie," she cooed. As she spoke these words with obvious affection the tendril tightened about her finger, more constricting than she perhaps would have liked. It reminded her of the blood pressure cuff at the doctor's office.

"I never want to be without you either," she said.

Her mother's intrusive voice bellowed from the doorway. "Who are you talking to, dear?" She had opened the door and was standing on the threshold.

The tendril instantly released Francine's finger. At first she did not notice how numb that digit had become; she had her mother to deal with.

She turned from Goldie. "Oh, just my plant," she said. This was an acceptable half-truth. She often overheard her mother talking to the plants in the kitchen. She said it was good for them.

Her mother laughed, a bright cheery sound as full of sunshine as her daughter's bedroom. "They do say talking to plants helps them grow!"

"My plant moves," Francine cried, wanting to be believed more than anything. "It curled around my finger. Honest!"

The bright laughter was repeated, and Francine's cheeks burned. There had been a slight change in the quality of the laugh, and Francine knew her mother did not believe her. The response had been too quick, too pat, too bright. Like the false brightness of a hospital corridor. The words that followed did not change her surety in this belief, either.

"Of course, Franny!"

Francine turned away and very nearly screamed, biting down instead; all she had wanted before was for her mother to believe. Now all she wanted was for her to go away . . .

"I'm making French toast," her mother exclaimed, still gabbing away in that falsely pleasant manner. It made Francine think of the terminally cheerful hostesses on afternoon game shows. That French toast was her favorite food in the world little mattered. Francine was on the verge of a great revelation and all her mother could do was laugh that phony laugh!

"Awesome!" Francine seethed through clenched teeth.

"It'll be ready soon, so come down when you can. After you finish your conversation!" Her mother turned and left, pulling the door closed behind her.

For the second time Francine nearly howled out of frustration. She looked at Goldie; his lovely violet-blue flowers. She tried to ignore the deep rumblings in her gut, managing to do so (while thinking of French toast all the while) a whole thirty seconds before giving up.

"Sorry, Goldie," she said, rising and starting for the door. "I'll be back soon, I promise!"

As she left she did not notice the ivy's stem shudder in her direction, as though it desired nothing but to follow.

<h1 style="text-align:center">⚜ 12 ⚜</h1>

Days passed. Each morning it was obvious the plant had grown. The more flowers it sprouted the more she merrily chatted with it, careful now to keep her door closed and her voice low so neither of her parents would notice if they happened by. She must keep this secret. She must!

Once her mother made a comment about how lengthy Francine's periwinkle appeared to be getting, and her daughter airily told her that it had been that long to begin with. Talking around the truth on this issue had a great deal to do with her father. Its length had been one of his pre-conditions for her taking care of it, so she must tiptoe carefully when discussing it.

Each evening while she slept the vine grew closer to her bed. With haste, and within a few short weeks, the periwinkle had closed the distance. Once Francine got up she would rewrap the vine (which under cover of darkness had unwrapped itself and gone over the table's edge) around the flowerpot. She had to be careful, else her mother would catch on. Three times Goldie encircled the pot now, and was well on his way to a fourth. In under two weeks he had grown to almost four times his original length. Altogether there were almost twenty of the pretty flowers now.

And every morning he curled about her pinkie (and was becoming most constricting indeed).

<h1 style="text-align:center">⚜ 13 ⚜</h1>

It was during the fifth week, and getting into midsummer, when Francine made the discovery that a second tendril was growing from the flowerpot. She had not noticed it sooner because it had poked through a tiny crack in the rear of the pot—the side facing the window and away from casual view. She knew the pot had been brand new and without a single crack, chip, or imperfection, and for the briefest of instants she experienced a vague unease. The tendril trailed off the far side of the table; it was growing so it would not be noticed. It was being sneaky!

Francine recalled how the vine had been growing on the porch in much the same way and told herself she was being silly. This was Goldie. It was not in his nature to be "sneaky"; he was trying to surprise her while staying out of her mother's sight! The vine trailed down a table leg and crept along the baseboard like an old telephone cable. It was crawling up the bedpost next to her sleeping head, winding about the post in a fashion much like what she had envisioned along the staircase railing.

After her formless fear dissipated she decided she was overjoyed to find that Goldie loved her so much he would stop at nothing to be with her. The ivy, this second tendril, had made it to within a foot of her head. She wondered that her mother hadn't noticed it, for surely she would have uprooted it if she had. Then Francine asked herself how fast it had been growing. It must be fast indeed!

"You'd better hurry," she said, hardly knowing why she was saying it, "or else Mom will catch you. She'll probably be doing the bedding in a day or two, so you really must hurry!" With that she got up from her customary spot on the mattress, patted the ivy in the pot—it had grown lush with her constant attention (she never missed a day of watering, another of her father's conditions), and headed down to yet another breakfast. She was more excited than ever. Her waiting was about to pay off!

<h1 style="text-align:center;">☦ 14 ☦</h1>

When Francine did not show for breakfast the next morning her mother was not concerned. In fact, she hardly noticed. During the summer months her daughter slept in and usually did not get moving until the sun reached a point where its light shining into the bedroom window could not be ignored, usually sometime during mid-morning.

When ten-thirty rolled around and the parent still had heard nothing, no sensations of movement, no creaking of boards as her daughter made her shambling way to the bathroom, she decided she'd better check on her. It wasn't like Franny to miss breakfast! She was not worried, not exactly, but she would have a little chat with her about, perhaps, getting up a little earlier to make the most of her days, especially during the summer months (the ones that really mattered to a child).

And wasn't Franny spending altogether too much time in her room these days? For no reason she thought of that plant her daughter had brought into the house and felt a distinct chill. She was, maybe, devoting far too much time to its care. All of a sudden it did not seem quite healthy. Children needed real friends to interact with. She set down the pan she had been scrubbing and left the kitchen, heading for the stairs at a brisk pace. She was abruptly worried, no longer just below the surface. Her harried thoughts kept returning to that plant. It had grown a lot since Franny had brought it into her room, contrary to what her daughter had claimed. Too much, she now realized. What had Franny said about the vine curling about her finger that time? Nonsense of course, and yet . . . Her pace quickened more still and she nearly tripped on her run up the stairs to Franny's room, afraid for her daughter and not really understanding why.

ф 15 ф

The coroner determined the girl had been dead since sometime before dawn, probably between four and five am—not that this was any consolation to her shocked and grieving parents.

Further, the coroner had never seen anything like what greeted him when he entered that perfectly ordinary house on its perfectly ordinary street in its perfectly normal suburb, although he had been warned beforehand of its utter strangeness. Before this he would have claimed he had seen it all. Over twenty-five years he had attended many gruesome crime scenes. Nothing, he would have said, could ever shock him again.

There was the girl, nine years old, wrapped head to toe in the cocooning growth of an invasive vine, her body covered in little violet flowers. Like a decorously wrapped mummy, he later confided to his wife, the vine so tightly wound that all circulation had been cut off, skin gone the purplish hue of the flowers themselves. Objectively it was quite beautiful. When he stepped into the bedroom, and before he knew what he was seeing, he assumed he was looking at a particularly lovely bedspread.

He had, so he repeated till the day he died two decades later, never seen anything like it. He might be shocked again, who could say what might yet cross his path one day, but never in quite the way he had been on that bright morning with the sun blasting into that perfectly normal bedroom on that perfectly normal street, a light so bright truth could not later be tucked conveniently away within the skeptical confines of a shadowy disbelief. There weren't any shadows within that room he could ever seek solace in, never.

✠ 16 ✠

Excerpt from encyclopedia entry for "periwinkle" (final paragraph): *In Italy, periwinkle is called fior di morto, the flower of death, because it was customary to lay periwinkle wreaths on the graves of dead babies. The word, broken down, means "entwine" or "bind".*

It is perhaps unfortunate Francine did not read the whole entry beforehand.

✠ 17 ✠

When the flowerpot, along with its trailing vine, had been taken to forensics for analysis, and once the pot itself had been emptied of its contents, the delicate bones of a small goldfish were found deep within the potting soil.

FINE

Upon your return to the playroom, you see that the construction paper before you has blossomed into a full regiment of waxy violet-blue petals, interwoven with spiraling tendrils of green and darker green. Your host smiles from the couch next to you, still petting the cat in xer lap. "Luckily, you're still breathing. How are you feeling now?"

You look inside yourself and ask. Yourself spits an answer back at you like spouting water from a trick flower. The floor suddenly feels like lava under your criss-cross-applesauced ass and you stand up, almost stumbling backwards onto the couch and landing like a lunar module amongst the throw pillows. You need something to hold onto with your hands, something soft, not the crystal with its pulsing light and its secret self-taught arithmetical language.

As if sensing this distress, your host crosses to the toybox near the far wall, rummaging through it, searching through the assembly of playthings. Finally, xe withdraws two items: one, a stuffed monkey with button eyes, and the other a handpuppet of a clown in tramp garb. Xe hands you the monkey and your fingers sink into the slightly grubby fur, rubbing your thumb along the tag. GANZ, it reads in red block letters. As you squeeze the fabric, you hear your host speak in an exaggerated, squeaking voice, far removed from xer usual caramel tone.

"Say, why do you get when you boil a clown?" asks the puppet.

"I don't know," asks your host. "What do you get?" Deedee has already by this point had more than enough of this nonsense, and has wandered off to a different side of the room to resume his nap.

"Laughing stock!" says the puppet, and takes a little bow. "Now, tell me: what do you get when you cross a fool?"

"Cross a fool with what?" asks your host.

"With stupid questions like that!" the puppet says, and clears its throat. "I ask the questions! Now listen; when you cross a fool, you get…

A Fun Day of ~~Grand Illusions~~ Bland Delusions

administered by Kevin Novalina

— ⚕ —

"Instead of getting married again, I'm just going to find a woman I don't like and give her a house."

—Lewis Grizzard

"Satire is the true story of real life's insanity."

—Anonymous

"You really are a hot herpe on humanity," Witch says, and I tell her: "Yeah, but you're the one who infected me."

My ex-wife crinkles her nose, jabs her tongue out, and says, "At least I moved on with life."

"BFD," I say, peeling off my red afro bald wig. "A hundred percent of life ends in ash or mud and maggots." I can smell Witch's Eau de Givenchy perfume, her stale booze breath like an unwiped bum's bum. "Now, Heaven and Hell's fifty/fifty, unless you're French," I say. "Then it tips ninety/ten."

"Hey," Witch says. "He can't help it he's French!" She studies her nails curled in her palm, then spread flat an arm length away. "I didn't come here to fight."

"Yes, you did," I say, downing another stiff drink to loosen up. "You just didn't come to lose."

"Can I at least sit?"

"You *are* sitting," I tell her. "In my only chair!"

"Well, can I have a drink then?"

"Toilet's down the hall."

Witch pouts all evil and sexy. Sharon Stones her legs and I cock my head for a better view up one of the many Valentino skirts I paid for. Still in my clown face paint from a cookout this afternoon, I prop my oversized red shoes on a stack of *Tramps*, a quarterly hybrid of skin mag and gossip rag for all things Clowndom. "What makes you think I'd wanna work a birthday party for your Frenchman's little French Fry?"

Witch rolls her eyes, clears her throat. "A, you can use the money," she says. "B, I'm the one you can use it on, and C, being a clown for you is like taking candy from a baby."

"Well D, you're a dumbass and E, everybody knows it," I tell her. "F, Frenchy and you both can G, go to H in a handbasket."

Crazy Witch. Married for what seemed a billion dog years and one day she up and decides her life lacks substance. Wants to learn acrylic art, so I pick up another job to afford this French teacher. They fingerpainted, then fingerbanged, and she fell head over heels with heels over her head. Soon she was divorcing me for him, citing "Irreconcilable Differences (in length and girth)." Now they live together but won't get married, just to keep receiving alimony. She said it's not so much they need the money, it's that they know I need it *so much*.

We were without child, Witch and I. Truth is, she wanted to have a kid without the process of *having* it. She swore she could take pain but said: "It's the conception I can't bear."

Best for the kid anyway, since Witch's family tree is a wreath.

Either way, Frenchy has a son from a previous gigolo con, so I guess Witch wins (or loses) all around.

Me, now I'm a clown. *Literally.* It's my main job of four and my name is "Clyde the Clown." I work birthdays and bat mitzvahs. Hospitals, an occasional wedding. Even did a funeral once.

Not classy enough to be a White Clown (*Clown Blanc* in French), I'm an Auguste Jester. I play the fool, harlequin, anarchist, and my makeup's a discount Bozo, my act the typical Grotesque routine. Rubber chicken and lapel sunflower squirter. I dabble in sat-down stand-up and sleight of hand. A little balloon modelling: twisted dogs and pretzeled cats. Giraffe necks on baboon bodies. Last week I purchased the book *The Magic's Not Real but Who Cares?* and even learned how to yank a rabbit from a top hat.

It doesn't pay much but I take clowning seriously, and now Witch is trying to make a fool out of me. Parade me around like a buffoon. "Why're you really here?" I say, then nod at her middle. "Is it game week for this month's 'Crimson Tide'?"

"You joke," Witch says, leafing through the book *Lifestyles of the Witch and Blameless*, "but I'm owed royalties for your menstrual minstrel clown smile."

"Can't you just let me jest in peace."

"It's shameful employment," she says. "Besides, we want the best clown there is and, Lord knows, you're the best clown there is." Witch fishes out a Virginia Slim. "Got an ashtray?"

"I do," I say, "but you kept it in the settlement."

And Witch says, "Well, *something* good had to come outta that circus."

I make another drink. "Did it have to be my chomping chimp ashtray?"

"Would you just drop the chomping chimp ashtray?" Witch says. "For once, could we forget about the damn chomping chimp ashtray!"

"It's just my favorite thing in the world's all."

Witch reaches over and snatches my drink. Drains it to the ice, her lipstick leaving a kiss on the glass rim opposite mine.

"Look, I know what you think of me," she says.

"Witch, Hag—"

"I mean, sometimes around noon on Tuesdays I even feel kinda guilty."

"—Crone, Gold Digger—"

"And if it's about the money, *any* price would be worth *this* show."

"—fake breasts, lips, nails, hair, chin-tucked, butt-sucked, eye-lifted, chomping chimp ashtray stealing skank."

"Besides the once, have I ever given you reason to doubt me?"

"So, let me get this straight," I say. "You want me to come to the house I paid for, prance around for the little Plaster of Paris and Friends, then take the money you pay me and mail it right back to you for alimony?"

"We won't even need to exchange payment," Witch says. "That way you'll save on a stamp." Her Witchy smile wide as a clown's. "Whatcha say?"

"Fine," I tell her. "See you Saturday."

❈❈❈

☐ JESTER BAY OFFICIAL POLICE REPORT ☐

Case Number: 08-1978
Location: 1031 Ringling Rd
Incident: VAUDEVILLIAN VIOLATIONS

On the afternoon of Saturday, June 15th at approx. 1500 hours, units responded to a distress call at 1031 Ringling Rd. Officers arrived on the scene and discovered what eyewitnesses are calling a cross between a coulrophobe's nightmare and The Greatest Horror Show on Earth.

According to gawkers nearby, Professional (Unconfirmed) Fool (Confirmed) "Clyde the Clown" was working a children's birthday party at the residence of ex-wife and her current boyfriend (French/Bad Artist). At some point, Numskull allegedly spiked the punchbowl with corn mash moonshine, then slipped Lysergic Acid Diethylamide (LSD) into attending parents' drinks.

As adults sat tripping and tipping in lawn chairs by the swimming pool, Perp gathered the children around and yanked a bloody rabbit's head from a magician's hat, twisting it to the body of a colorful aardvark balloon. He then played Fučík's "Entry of the Gladiators" while juggling the lady of the manor's $1,500 Gucci Signoria slingbacks.

Next, he proceeded to sit the ex on his knee for an improvised set of well-rehearsed ventriloquism where, according to children's testimony, he told the following joke: "Kids, how do you make a Frenchman's noodle disappear?" Dancing his unibrow, he wriggled a Stogie before his smile,

HA
HA
HO
HO
HEE
HEE
HEE
HEE
Promenade
SPIKED

waved her "dummy" hand, and announced: *"Here you go!"*

Clown followed this up by asking the boyfriend (now drooling), "Wanna smell my *Peeony?*" After which, he squirted Frenchman's face with what officers could only describe as a "foul urinous ooze."

At some point, former wife rose and pointed to her stink wrinkle, proclaiming: "It's game time!" As if on cue, Clyde responded by scooping her up in a fireman's carry and hauling her upstairs to the master bedroom. Screams of *"Roll Tide!"* were heard coming from an open window where Violator was reportedly leaving his smeared 🐶 shit over ex's saddle straddler that, according to a Forensic Artist's sketch, resembled a cross between Bozo, Emmett Kelly, and Gacy's Pogo the Clown.[1*]

Now sporting an even wider red smile, Idiot proceeded to hawk loogies on a year's salary of Armani dresses and Louis Vuitton bags hung in a walk-in closet. Dunce snatched a bottle of Eau de Givenchy (perfume), a chomping chimpanzee cigar ashtray, and ex-Ballbreaker and Chain, then carried the load back outside where the party would build toward a showstopping Finale.

First, he emptied the fragrance and remaining moonshine over the hedgerows, then performed a fire breathing act and set it alight while singing "Great Balls of Fire."

He next led the children (now intoxicated) in a game of "Pin the Tail on the Pussy," thumbtacking several donkey tails (real) to the Frenchman

---

[1*]Clown's big red nose still missing

(fake) before sitting him on a unicycle and giving him a push.

Clown then decided to *Caddy Shack* a turd in the pool, but having no Baby Ruth and suffering severe constipation, he instead tossed Frenchy's son in, certain he'd suffice as stool.

Culprit kept the hijinks rolling by placing ex-wife on a deflating blowup raft and launching her into the deep end as she sang: "I chew my nails and I twiddle my thumbs!"

According to several party crashers, Dolt cocked his hat on his 'fro and stood bobbing on stilts at the end of the diving board. With arms upraised, he began to monolog: "I wanna shatter the windows of every McDonald's for passing me over as fry cook because I didn't have enough un-popped pimples. I'd like a reversal of all celebrity, where movie and reality stars, sports icons and pop gods pay outrageous ticket prices to watch teachers teach children, maids scrub toilets, and clowns clown around for *minimal* wage."

The raft whistling air, ex-spouse sang at the top of deflated lungs: "I laughed at love 'cause I thought it was funny," as Frenchman cycled past, adding: "You came along and we stole his money!"

Jester continued holding court, announcing: "I wanna issue clown makeup mandates for every breathing soul, so everyone's always showing their true colors.

"And may we fit the world population with hands-free selfie sticks attached to funhouse mirrors, so no matter who you're looking to blame, you're always seeing the guilty.

"Let us force the Haves to halve what they have with the Have-nots, so at least the Have-nots have a little.

"Let's deem diamonds worthless and make gravel precious stones, then every street will be paved with jewels.

"Why not sign into law that we revert to a natural standard backing the world's currency, but instead of gold and silver make it water. Have class separation determined by levels of dehydration and watch how fast we drain the seas.

"I demand," he hollered, "every country pick up and move to another—Britain to somewhere in Africa, China to Tibet, Germany to Israel. Move America to Iraq and see if we're really so advanced or if it's just location, location, location.

"Let us settle all wars by playing The Grand Prize Game, where each bucket made is another battle won.

"And children remember, friends don't let friends drive drunk," he said. "They get blitzed and ride with them."

Having forgotten the fake vomit, Idiot had queasy partygoers replace it with real. He then squonked a bicycle horn that dropped his harem pants to heart print boxers before leading the children in a mass urination around the pool.

As ex-wife submerged singing, "Got to tell this world that you're *mine, mine, mine, mine!*" Frenchman pedaled by, crashed through the cake table, and was subsequently arrested for UWFI (Unicycling While French and Intoxicated).

Doffing his top hat with a curtain call curtsy, Clown last landed a half-assed "Triple Lindy" off the diving board, then splatted responding officers (who were highly entertained) in the face with cream pies, before being pepper sprayed and patted down with nightsticks. Clyde was then taken into custody and Mirandized yet gave up said rights by screaming: *"My chomping chimp ashtray, my chomping chimp ashtray!"* over and over until he was tased into silence.

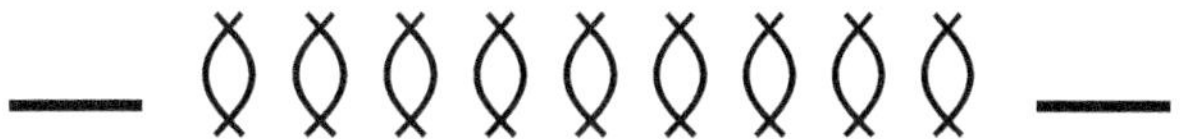

Again the puppet takes his bow, and then it is spinning through the air, landing in a heap on the far floor, where Deedee pounces on it like prey and immediately begins to batter its damned fool head to-and-fro.

Your own head feels well-battered itself—battered and fried to a golden brown crisp, for that matter. You realize you're still holding the monkey plush, which you realize now is actually a chimpanzee, and tuck it into the cushion next to you as your fingers reach again for the amethyst.

"You're deep enough into it by this point," says your host. "Still nowhere near sober, I'd wager, but you're probably thirsty by this point. You want a drink?" Xe cocks a thumb at the minifridge in the corner, and at your nod, crouches down in front of it. "What have we here…" xe muses, shuffling through bottles and cans. "Ah. This should do the trick." Standing, spinning in a flowing ballerina's twirl, crossing back over to you, stepping over Deedee scratching up his kill. Xe holds out the drink, and you take the cold can in your hands. It's a dark lager, says the can, and below the name of the brew on the label is a printed illustration of a lighted bus cutting down a dark road. Cracking it open, you smell someplace far away from this house, a place you've never been but feel from the aroma that you could almost touch: salted air, dirt roads, carrion along the way. It should be repulsive, but it draws you in, beckons you down into the deep, dark mash.

There is a crackling hiss and you look up to see your host holding a drink of xer own, lifting it into the air. "To nights we'll never remember," xe says, "and to people we'll never forget." You find yourself matching xer toast and take a long sip. It's sour and rich and heady and herbal, but not overbearing, and as you take another sip xe adopts xer now intimately familiar introductory tone. "Drink it all in: the journey, the destination, the road before and behind you," xe says before introducing the next tale, the title echoing the name of the beer on the can: "Climb aboard, and don't worry about the fare: pay only with your attention as you board a strange vessel and catch a lift on…

The Night Ride

administered by Sali Andiamo Siyaya

— ǂ —

That morning, Gregory Burnet woke with a groan. He dragged a hand across his face and blinked at the ceiling. The sour taste of last night's beer still clung to his tongue. He swung his legs off the bed and sat up.

"Ah… too much," he muttered, rubbing his temples.

After a long pause, he walked to the bathroom. The cold water of the bath stung his skin, waking him fully. He dressed slowly, buttoning his guard uniform with clumsy fingers, and he stepped outside.

The small kitchen smelled of frying eggs and porridge. Maryan, his wife, was bent over the stove, her head was wrapped in a simple scarf, stirring the porridge gently. When she heard the door creak, she looked up.

"Gregory," she said gently, "breakfast is ready. Come, eat before you go."

Gregory rubbed the back of his neck, avoiding her eyes. "I can't, Maryan. I'm already late," he said.

Maryan wiped her hands on her apron and stood straighter. "Late or not, you can't work on an empty stomach."

Gregory shook his head, frowning. "No, no. I'll eat later."

Maryan stepped closer, pleading with her eyes. "Please, Gregory. Just sit and eat something. You drink too much as it is. Don't make me worry more."

For a moment, they stared at each other. Finally, Gregory let out a long sigh and shrugged. "Fine. But not today. I really must go. Timo's already waiting for me."

Maryan's face changed at the name. "That man," she said, shaking her head slowly. "Gregory, can't you see? He isn't a good friend. If only you knew what I mean…"

Gregory gave a dry laugh and waved a hand, brushing her words aside. "Maryan, don't start. He's my friend, that's all. I'll be fine."

He grabbed his small black bag from the chair, double checking inside if he had packed the small bottle of salt he used for roasted meat he bought at lunch, and slung it over his shoulder as he stepped toward the door. Maryan's voice followed him.

"Just… don't drink today, Gregory."

He paused for a second, then glanced back with a crooked smile. "We'll see," he muttered, and then he was gone.

Maryan stood by the stove, staring at the door long after it closed as if holding back words she couldn't say.

⚜⚜⚜

Gregory walked slowly down the dusty path, his small bag swinging at his side. The morning air was cool, carrying the smell of wet grass and smoke from cooking fires. Birds chattered in the trees, and far away he heard a rooster crowing.

As he walked, a memory crept into his mind. He saw his father's serious face, the way his mother had folded her arms and shook her head.

"Don't trust Ravenwood people, son," his father had said.

"They are bad people, not like us," his mother had added with worry.

But he hadn't listened. How could he, when Maryan's smile had lit his whole world? She was the most beautiful girl he had ever seen, gentle and kind. He had married her despite his parents' protests, and now, years later, he could see that she truly cared for him. His parents had been wrong about her.

"Gregory!" a cheerful voice cut through his thoughts.

He turned and saw Timo Andrews waving, a wide grin on his face. Timo's shirt was half-buttoned, and he looked as though he, too, had drunk deeply the night before.

"Ah, my brother!" Gregory laughed.

"You walk like an old man today," Timo teased, clapping Gregory on the shoulder.

Gregory grinned. "And you? You look like you fought with your bed and lost."

They both burst out laughing, and their voices echoed across the quiet path.

As they walked, they shared small stories. Timo bragged about how he had outdrunk two men at the tavern. Gregory shook his head, saying he couldn't remember half the night. Timo joked that maybe they had danced on the tables, and Gregory laughed, though Maryan's warning still rang in his ears.

"Work will be long today," Gregory sighed.

Timo shrugged. "Better than sitting at home. At least we guard, we see people, we live."

When they reached the bus station, the old wooden benches were crowded with villagers waiting for rides. The bus pulled up, and the two men climbed aboard, squeezing past others, and found seats near the back. The engine roared, and the bus lurched forward, carrying them away from the village.

The road was bumpy, dust rising in clouds through the windows, but they didn't mind. Timo told another wild story about nearly chasing away a thief last week, while Gregory nodded with a smile. He liked Timo's company, despite what Maryan had said earlier.

When the bus finally reached the town, they stepped off into the busy street. Gregory straightened his uniform as they entered the company gate, and the busy day was about to begin.

"Time to be serious," Timo muttered with a playful grin.

They signed in at the guardhouse, nodded to their fellow workers, and took over from the tired night-shift guards. They exchanged short greetings, then stood at their posts near the company gate. The morning sun had climbed higher, and Gregory leaned against the wall, his eyes scanning people coming in and out. From time to time, he tapped his foot, or adjusted the strap of his bag. His stomach grumbled, and he regretted not eating Maryan's breakfast.

Just then, his phone rang in his pocket. He frowned, pulled it out, and saw Maryan's name flashing on the screen. He smiled, ready to hear her sweet voice again, but when he answered, all he heard was her sobbing.

"Maryan?" He asked. "What is it? What's wrong?"

Her voice trembled. "Gregory… my mother… she has passed away."

Gregory froze. His mouth fell open, but no words came out. He hadn't expected such news.

"What? No, Maryan… how?" His words came out broken. "When… when did it happen?"

"This morning," she whispered through tears. "They just told me. I have to go to her now. The funeral is today."

Gregory's heart pounded. He wanted to be by her side. "I will come too. We must go together. I am your husband… I should be there."

But Maryan quickly replied. "No, Gregory. Don't come. You have work. It is not necessary for you. I'll go alone."

Gregory blinked, confused. He pressed the phone harder against his ear, as if he hadn't heard right. "Not necessary? Maryan, this is your mother. My mother-in-law. I must come."

"You don't have to," Maryan said, and her voice was now weaker. "Stay at your job. Please, just stay. I will manage. Don't worry about me."

It felt strange to him, even wrong, but her words were final. He swallowed hard, and after a pause he gave a slow nod no one could see. "Alright," he said softly. "If that is what you want. But my heart goes with you."

Maryan sniffled. "Thank you. Just… take care of yourself. We will talk later."

There was a silence, broken only by her sobbing breath. Finally Gregory whispered, "Be strong, my love."

"And you too," she replied, then the line went dead.

Gregory stood still, with the phone in his hand and he looked sad.

Timo noticed and walked over. "Brother, what is it? You look like you've seen a ghost."

Gregory replied slowly. "My wife's mother… she has died. Maryan is going alone to the funeral. She told me not to come. But I… I wish we could go together, as a family should."should be 'as a family should'

Timo looked not to be bothered. He gave a half-shrug, almost careless. "It happens. In our ways, not everyone must go. The women's side of the family can handle it. You are here, working. That is enough."

Gregory looked down, rubbing his fingers over the phone. "But still… she shouldn't face this alone. She needs me."

Timo chuckled softly, shaking his head. "Gregory, don't carry a heavy heart. Funerals come and go. Work feeds us. Drink later, laugh later, and life moves on."

Gregory lifted his eyes, uncertain. "Maybe you are right… but I feel something is not right about this."

Timo clapped him on the shoulder. "You think too much. Come, guard with me. The day is long."

Gregory forced a small nod, though the sorrow still clouded his face. Slowly, he joined Timo again at their post, and soon the rhythm of work returned.

⫴⫴⫴

A few days after Maryan came back from her mother's funeral, Gregory felt something different in the house. She no longer smiled at him in the mornings, nor asked if he had eaten. She didn't even remind him to leave beer alone, a thing she always used to say with a worried frown.

When Gregory tried to talk to her, she would just stare at him with blank eyes, then look away like his words meant nothing. Sometimes her lips would part, as if she wanted to speak, but then she pressed them shut again.

One evening at work, Gregory shared it with Timo. "Brother, Maryan doesn't talk to me anymore. She just keeps quiet, even when I ask her something."

Timo scratched his chin and nodded like he knew better. "It is the way of our people, Gregory. A widow's daughter must not speak freely until her grief cools. Let her be. This silence is part of her mourning."

Gregory sighed. He wanted to believe Timo, but something was still troubling him.

A few days later, Timo didn't show up for work. Word was he was sick. Gregory found himself working the day shift alone. Then one night, the guard who was supposed to replace him came very late. Gregory had to wait, pacing up and down by the gate, tired and hungry.

When the man finally arrived, Gregory left with slow steps. As always, he stopped by the nearby bar. He bought one cold bottle of beer and a small plate of roasted meat. Sitting outside under the weak lamp, he took a long sip. He closed his eyes in relief as the bitter drink warmed his throat. He opened his bag, pulled out the tiny salt bottle he always carried, and rubbed

GENFARE
INSERT IN SLOT
DO NOT BEND OR FOLD
AA-
SHOOM
THE WHEELS
ON
THE BUS
GO
FRESH
MEAT
UNDERGROUND
AND
Strong
Beer
9

the grains onto the meat. He chewed slowly, promising himself to save the rest for home.

Afterward, he walked toward the bus station, but the place was dead quiet. There were no people waiting, no conductors shouting, not even a single bus in sight. The wide ground looked hollow, with empty benches. And a little wind whistled between the poles.

Gregory scratched his head, confused. He thought of going back to the company, maybe sleeping in the guardroom, but he knew the rules. They wouldn't let him inside smelling of lager, even if he wasn't on duty.

He sighed, pulled out his bottle, and raised it again. Just as he was about to open his bag for another sip, his eyes caught something.

A bus was rolling into the station. Gregory narrowed his eyes. The bus looked strange. The tires weren't the same size, wobbling and wriggling as though they might tear off any moment. The headlights were dim, blinking like dying candles. One couldn't tell the figures inside, as their faces were unclear behind the dusty glass.

Gregory blinked hard, rubbing his eyes with the back of his hand. "It's the beer," he muttered to himself. "Just the drink making me see things."

But the bus came closer, rumbling and groaning. He swallowed hard when he noticed ancient symbols written all over its body. They twisted like snakes in the dull light. His lips moved as he read the words painted in bold letters across the side: *Raven Night Ride.*

⊭⊭⊭

The bus stopped right in front of him. The door opened on its own with a slow hiss.

Gregory looked around. The station was still empty. No one else was there. His heart beat fast, but he badly wanted to go home. He wiped his face, steadied himself, and walked forward.should be, 'he badly wanted to go home

As his foot touched the bus step, a shiver ran up his spine. Inside, the bus was almost full, every seat holding passengers who sat too quiet with their heads tilted.

Gregory found an empty seat near the middle. He sat down, clutching his bag on his lap. The door closed by itself with a loud thud, and before he could change his mind, the bus came to life and rolled into the night.

Gregory sat stiff in his seat, the sound of the strange transport filling his ears. To calm his nerves, he reached for his bag. His hand brushed against the bottle of beer he had saved, and he thought, *maybe one more sip will settle me down*. But just as he pulled the bottle halfway out, a strange smell hit his nose. His face twisted, and it was foul, like meat left to rot in the sun, like something dead. Gregory held his breath, pressing the back of his hand against his nose.

He lifted his eyes slowly, and that was when he saw it. Every single passenger was wearing the same thing; black, old cloaks, with their hoods pulled low. He swallowed hard. He was the only one without it, the only one dressed different. A cold sweat slid down his back.

He lowered his eyes and looked down. That's when he froze. Their feet weren't human: they were longer, and stretched like claws. Their toenails were curled, long and yellow, scraping against the floor with each small movement. Gregory gripped the bottle tightly, as if it was the only thing that could save him. His heart pounded hard, so loud, he thought they might hear it.

He turned his head just a little, daring to look at the figure sitting right next to him. The cloak's hood hid most of its face, but the skin that showed was pale… too pale, as if no blood ran under it. It was white as chalk, and wrinkled. Gregory's lips parted, but no words came out.

The figure beside him shifted, and Gregory's whole body trembled. He pulled back, pressing himself against the seat. That's when the truth sank into his heart. This was no bus of people.

He wanted to stand, to run, but the bus was already moving through the night, the cloaked figures were silent, breathing together like one body.

Gregory sat there, trying to calm himself. Suddenly, a thought struck him… *the fare*. What if the conductor or driver asked? What could he pay on such a bus? Money—or something else?

Before he could think further, the figure beside him moved its head and spoke in a low voice.

"Are you okay, Timo? I can hear your heart beat. You seem so excited. Don't worry… dinner will arrive soon. The woman who died last week will be served again today."

Gregory's whole body went cold. His lips trembled. *The woman who died last week… Maryan's mother.* He wanted to scream, to run, to throw himself out of the moving bus, but he knew if he showed fear, they would tear him apart.

He forced himself to breathe, forced his shaking lips to move. "Ah… yes, I'm fine," he said slowly, trying to copy the tone of one of them. "My heart… sometimes it beats too fast when I'm happy."

His voice trembled, but the figure didn't seem to notice. Gregory thought quickly. He needed to keep the act, to blend in like Timo.

"I… I forgot something," Gregory said, lowering his head like he was ashamed. "What did I do the last time I rode this bus? I can't remember well."

The figure gave a deep laugh that made Gregory's skin crawl. "You forgot, Timo? Last time you were slapped hard by the Master for saying the dinner prayer wrongly. You looked like a fool. Your cheek was red for days."

Gregory swallowed hard. He connected the pieces in his mind. Timo had been sick that week, too weak to come to work. So, he had been slapped by this so-called Master. Now Gregory understood. His friend wasn't just a drunk, or lazy. Timo was one of them. A witch.

He held his hands tightly, hiding the shake in his fingers. If they thought he was Timo, he had to act fast. "Ah… yes. That slap." He forced a nervous chuckle. "I don't want to feel that again. Please, brother, remind me of the prayer. I must say it well tonight."

The figure turned its hooded head toward him. Gregory's skin prickled, and his heart was ready to burst.

The low voice recited slowly, word by word:

"Blood for the cup,
Flesh for the plate,
Darkness bless our feast,
Master, open the gate."

Gregory repeated it softly in his mind, word by word.

The figure leaned closer, and the rotten smell was thick on its cloak. "Say it right this time, Timo. Or the Master will not just slap you. This time, you will not get better."

Gregory swallowed hard. He nodded quickly, pretending to be strong. But inside, he knew one mistake could cost him his life.

Then he noticed movement in the aisle. A tall figure in a long black cloak walked slowly between the seats, holding a wide wooden tray.

The smell hit first… rotten meat. One by one, the cloaked passengers stretched out their long fingers, picking pieces from the tray. None of them ate. They held the meat in their hands, waiting, as if something important had to happen first.

Gregory bent forward, covering his mouth with his shirt. He vomited quietly into the cloth, but the figure beside him didn't notice. It was staring hungrily at the tray moving closer.

Step by step, the tray came nearer. Gregory's heart pounded. Soon it was right at their row. The figure next to him reached first, claws closing around a moldy piece. Gregory forced his hand out, trembling, and picked one too. The flesh was cold and slimy in his palm. He wanted to throw it away, to scream, but he pushed the feeling down. The tray moved on to the next row.

The hooded figure beside him leaned close. "When the last one picks," it whispered, "you must say the prayer. Don't forget, Timo."

Gregory's knees nearly gave in. His mouth was dry, but he nodded. His eyes followed the tray as it went, row after row, until finally the last cloaked creature took its piece.

The bus went silent.

Gregory swallowed hard, and he said: "Blood for the cup, flesh for the plate. Darkness bless our feast, Master, open the gate."

For a moment, there was silence. Then all at once, the cloaked figures answered in a single voice: *The gate is open.*

They raised the meat to their mouths and started eating, tearing and chewing with wet sounds that made Gregory's stomach twist again. He dared not to eat. His hands shook as he set the meat on his lap and slowly opened his bag for salt. He thought… *maybe if I put salt, the smell will go away. Maybe I can pretend.*

He reached for it, but before his fingers touched the lid, the figure beside him froze and sniffed the air.

"I know we do not turn our heads sideways when we're about to arrive at the Oracle Tree," the voice said. "But… have you carried salt? I have smelt it. Do you want to kill us all?"

Gregory's blood turned cold. His hand froze inside the bag. His first thought was to run, but where? He forced himself to breathe, forced his voice to come out.

"You smell far," Gregory said quickly, keeping his face calm. "There might be salt in the shops we are passing. That is what you smell."

The figure stared for a long moment. Gregory felt the sweat slide down his neck. Then, slowly, the hooded head turned away.

"Perhaps," it said. "Perhaps."

Gregory let out a shaky breath he didn't know he was holding. Through the window, he saw the last sign of town falling behind. The road narrowed, and dark woods rose ahead. The bus rolled deeper into the trees, creaking like an old coffin on wheels.

The trees grew taller, their branches clawing over the road like black fingers. Gregory kept his hand inside his pocket, gripping the small bottle of salt.

After some minutes, the bus groaned to a stop. The cloaked figures rose together and shuffled out. Gregory followed, though his legs were weak.

Outside, a bonfire burned high, and beside it stood a massive tree. Its trunk was thick, its roots were wide and knotted. Its branches looked like arms stretched out to the sky. The witches bowed their heads toward it… the Oracle Tree.

They circled the fire, their voices rising in strange prayers. Gregory moved his lips, copying them, though sweat slid down his face. His voice trembled, but no one noticed.

Then silence fell as a figure stepped into the center. Taller than the rest, with a hood darker than night, it was their leader. He lifted his head slightly and sniffed the air.

"Someone has carried salt here."

Gasps rose at once. The witches turned their heads, murmuring with eyes darting at one another.

Gregory swallowed hard, he had to act fast. He pressed his hand against the small bottle in his pocket. If they found it, he would not leave this place alive.

He glanced at the fire, then made his move. Slowly and carefully, he pulled the bottle out and tossed it into the flames.

The fire roared like thunder. It exploded upward, brighter than the sun, spraying sparks into the sky. There were a great many screams as the flames spread, catching the witches' cloaks. One by one, their bodies lit up. They stumbled, they clawed at the ground, but the fire swallowed them.

The heat was unbearable. Gregory stumbled back, covering his face. His skin burned though the flames did not touch him. The air was too hot to breathe. His legs gave way, and everything went black.

⚡⚡⚡

The following morning, Gregory woke up with the light. He opened his eyes, and he was on the blackened ground. Ash drifted in the breeze, and there was nothing around him, not even the mighty Oracle Tree. It was gone, burnt to nothing. The air smelled of smoke and silence.

Shaking, Gregory stood and turned toward the road. His heart pounded with one thought... *I must go home*. He didn't wait for a bus. He didn't want to see one again, and he started walking back home.

Hours later, the village came into view—ut instead of laughter and chatter, he heard cries... voices filled with mourning. Women wept in the streets. Men sat with their heads in their hands. Almost every house had a family grieving.

Gregory felt bitter. He saw faces he knew filled with sorrow. Then he heard the words: Timo was dead. His friend had not lived through the night.

Gregory looked down. *Was it me?* he thought. *Was it the fire? Did I bring this on them?*

He searched for Maryan, his wife, his reason for staying in this cursed village. But she was gone. No one could tell him where. He didn't know if he too should start crying. *Was Maryan a witch too?* he asked himself

That evening, Gregory went to his house. He packed his things in silence, his hands felt like they didn't belong to him. Without a word, he walked back to his parents' village and that was when he heard Maryan's voice, like a whisper: *Gregory!* He froze, but he never looked back.

~121~

You swallow the last of the beer, feeling salt and fire on the back of your throat, the sensations of the infernal bus bumping over rocky road dissolving in your stomach until they are only the slightest impression. Your host crushes xer own can, tossing it in a high arc into the recycling bin by the minifridge. You attempt to match the trajectory of xer throw and nearly hit Deedee instead, who zips away and hides under the couch.

"We've come a long way, haven't we?" xe says. "But I'm afraid it will be mostly by foot from this point forward. Why don't you follow me?"

Xe crosses the room to the sheets which had played host to the diabolical picture shows earlier in your voyage, and you manage to pull yourself up and follow. By this point the discomfort has mostly transfigured itself into euphoria. It's a frightful feeling in and of itself, threatening in its purity, too good to possibly be true—but you sense it is true, perhaps truer than anything you've ever felt before. Or, perhaps, you've always felt this way, and are just noticing it for the first time.

As you reach the sheet overhanging the windows, your guide draws them back with a hand, revealing the house's front yard and the night sky beyond. Stepping up, looking out the window, you see a handful of people smoking in the front yard. You see a couple girls at the picnic table, heating up dabs and letting them into the air, feeling somehow like you're viewing the world from inside of a spacecraft. You wonder if the party is over, if these are stragglers, or if it's still raging inside. You still hear music, but cannot be certain it is coming from the house and not your heart. Your guide opens the window and the illusion of isolation is shattered as a breeze enters your tomb. Upon tasting the wind you see the moon, and though it has been a waxing gibbous when you and your friend arrived a million years ago, it is now plump and full, a perfect glowing white.

"A little fresh air does one good," xe says, "especially after such suffocation. In the appendices to The Doors of Perception, *Huxley noted that oxygen and carbon dioxide are themselves inhalants, and that control of one's intake and outtake of breath can itself induce a sort of religious delirium. Take it in now. Taste the night, and swallow, and listen to the howl in your gut telling you that…*

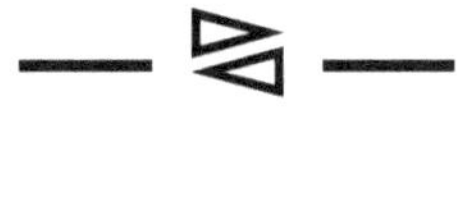

I like it.

I should not, but I do. It hums inside me like a second heart, louder and truer than the first.

At night, when the village sleeps beneath a fog that smells of wet stone and decay, I walk the alleys and hear it, the pulse beneath the cobblestones, the growl beneath the church bell. The villagers would not understand. They pray before bed, bolt their shutters, whisper the names of saints as if those syllables could keep the dark from touching them. I do not hide. I listen. I breathe. I like it.

It began on a night when the moon was too large, pale and swollen in the sky. I had been restless, feverish, tasting copper on my tongue. My dreams were all motion and noise, the tearing of cloth, the thud of flesh, the warm drip of something I could not name. I woke with my nails blackened, the sheets torn, the faint impression of teeth in my own shoulder.

I told myself it was nothing.

But I lied.

Because even then, before I knew what I was becoming, I liked it. The ache in my bones was holy. My skin felt too tight. My blood too loud. Every heartbeat called me forward.

The next night, I walked to the edge of the village, where the houses leaned into the forest like old ghosts. The earth clung to my feet. The moon rose. The world slowed.

I felt it begin, a pressure deep in my spine, a surge in my veins. My breath came ragged, and I fell to my knees, laughing and sobbing. My body shifted, not with pain but with clarity. Skin tore like old cloth, bone shifted, remade itself in rhythm with the pulse of the earth. My shadow stretched and warped, a wolfish grin blooming where my human mouth had been.

I felt it surge, spine snapping and reshaping, ribs twisting, lungs tearing open and filling with fire. My hands split and lengthened, claws shearing through the flesh of my palms. Teeth pushed past my gums, thick and jagged, ripping the skin at the corners of my mouth. I fell forward, raw and electric, bones and muscles melting and reforming with the pulse of the night.

My legs buckled, bones grinding, muscles bunching and reshaping like wet clay. Skin stretched, split, and fur erupted across my arms, back, chest. Nails scraped the stones beneath me, leaving red streaks, leaving prints I would never recognize. Every nerve thrummed, every sense stretched wide, every heartbeat echoing in rhythm with the wolf inside.

I raised my head. My grin split wider than it should, tongue thick and wet, dripping with shadow and motion. The human me was gone. The wolf had arrived, sharp and hungry, complete and unstoppable. I breathed deep, fur slicked with blood and sweat, and I laughed because I liked it.

When it was over, I was no longer the man who had walked these streets. I stood, dripping and raw, fur sprouting along my arms and back, claws digging into the stones. The wolf inside me had taken control, but I was still myself, in some impossible way. I raised my head to the moon, tasting blood and iron in my mouth, and for the first time, I felt complete.

The old women who washed clothes in alleys would claim that the wolf was a curse, something to wrangle in the basic fears of humans—but this was no curse. This was a blessing. Whatever power you believe in had granted me this, had plucked me from the barren fields of apathy and the hospice that makes the average life, and fed me straight into the jaws of power.

We are all beasts pretending to be kind.

⋈ 2 ⋈

I walked that road every night, and I did not know it then, but the wolf already lived inside of me. Becoming the wolf only completed me. So

FOOD
&
LEISURE
AS YOU LIKE IT
LB
LAMB SHOULDER
CHOPS OR FROZEN
GOAT CHOPS
13.23/KG

when that wolf coursed out and bit me, I welcomed it. Like most things, the initial fear was far worse than the act itself. Once I felt the blood rush through my brain and into my synapses, I knew that this was who I was meant to be: a predator.

The first one I hunted properly, I remember every detail. A man stumbled home from the tavern, drunk and singing, the smell of cheap wine thick on his clothes. I crouched in the fog, claws brushing wet stones. My body thrummed. My eyes saw too clearly.

I struck. My teeth sank into the back of his neck. He screamed, a high-pitched, horrible sound, but it was beautiful. I ripped, I tore. Blood coated my hands and face. Bones cracked. His life left him in waves, and I drank it, every drop making me more myself, more whole, more feral. He tasted of morning dew drank straight from a meadow buttercup.

I howled as the village dissolved around me, moonlight and mist carrying the sound.

The blood still throbbed on my claws, the taste of life heavy in my senses, but it was not enough. A new hunger surged, sharper and more demanding than before. I wished for more time to bask in the glory of my first kill, to linger in that exquisite carnage, but the wolf inside me demanded more. There was still flesh to tear, still blood to spill, still the perfect hunt waiting in the fog-drenched streets. I moved again, unstoppable, unsated, chasing the pulse of life that called to me.

I moved through the village as only an animal could. Sleek and efficient. No motion unneeded. The streets twisting beneath me, my senses picking up every sound, every breath. I could smell it. Not just in my nose, but deep inside the caverns of my soul. The human weaknesses of fear and jealousy would never again grace my craw.

Around me, hovel and tavern torches flared, reflecting off wet stones slick with rain. Every sound echoed inside of me, a chorus feeding the wolf. Shapes fled before me, stumbling, collapsing, their fear and chaos vibrating through my limbs. I was faster than thought, sharper than the night, every step a drumbeat in the rhythm of the hunt.

A smaller figure darted through the fog, hesitant and bright, lantern swinging in tiny hands. The pulse of the wolf surged, urgent and hungry. I crouched in the shadows, muscles coiled, eyes catching every movement, every flutter of breath. The world slowed and warped, the mist thickening, and I moved. Silent, inevitable, complete, the predator closing in on the final, perfect moment.

There, in the narrow lane, the child appeared, humming a tune too innocent for what was coming. I froze for a heartbeat, savoring the moment, the anticipation, the raw perfection of the hunt. Then the wolf surged forward.

He looked delicious.

I struck with everything I was. Teeth sank into the small neck, muscles snapping and claws raking through delicate limbs in a single, fluid action. The scream was brief, piercing, slicing through the fog and fracturing into echoes that reverberated inside me. The body twisted, limbs folding and giving way beneath the wolf's ferocity. Lantern glass shattered, scattering light across the alley as the mist turned crimson red.. When it was done, the child lay still, a small heap of red and stillness, and I rose above it, pulse thrumming with something raw, infinite, and unbroken. The forest itself seemed to lean closer, watching, approving, as if the hunt had awakened it as well.

I stood in the remains of the fallen lantern, shards of glass and slick fuel strewn across the stones. Remnants of the young lad matted my fur and besieged my beautiful claws, sticking to every curve and edge, a cruel tribute to the hunt. The young child who moments before was filled with hope of a long life and delicious puddings was nothing but mere litter. Debris. A scene so full of beautiful gravity it would cling to every weaker mind that beheld it. A true piece of art.

I looked up towards the heavens and basked in the country dark. I felt like I was seeing the stars for the first time. The air hummed around me. Shadows clung to the edges of the path, writhing in the flickering light.. I looked down as blood pooled along the cobblestones. I stood among the fog and watched it ripple like water. The world was mine, and I had become exactly what I was meant to be.

⪦ 3 ⪧

The village noticed quickly. Disappearances, screams, a growing sense of wrong. Torches lit streets at night, priests called for prayers and protection. Farmers and tradesmen set traps and formed hunting parties. Every night they came, shouting, swinging sticks, knives, axes, fire.

I watched them from the shadows. I studied them. Every attempt they made to find me failed. I moved through walls of fog, through their torches, through their fear. I could smell their panic. It was intoxicating.

They cornered me once in the square. They carried nothing but rudimentary weapons and pure terror. I heard shouts, the ringing of metal, the prayers of terrified mouths. I moved, and suddenly the square was chaos. I struck, teeth and claws finding flesh. Screams filled the night. I danced in the destruction. Some fell, some fled. Smoke and torchlight wrapped around me, but I was untouched. I was whole.

The wolf inside me was no longer a secret. It was my mind, my body, my memory, my desire. I did not think as a man anymore. I moved as the wolf. I hunted as the wolf. I became the storm that haunted their nights.

I tore through walls, slipped through barred doors, crushed the weak, and left survivors trembling in the dark. Their eyes saw what I was, and they knew the truth. They were nothing compared to this. I did not feel guilt. I did not feel joy. Only the clarity of the hunt and the pulse of life in my veins.

The nights became long and endless. I wandered the village at will. The streets became mine. The houses, the alleys, the market square, all were playgrounds and sanctuaries and traps. I learned their patterns, their fears, their rhythms. They could not stop me.

≊ 4 ≊

One night, I left the village behind. The forest welcomed me. The trees no longer whispered. They sang. The moon followed me, silver and heavy, lighting the way to places I had not yet seen. Rivers ran dark and quiet. Mountains rose in shadow. The wolf inside me pulsed with anticipation. The world stretched open. The village was nothing but a once was.

I could feel the pull of something larger. The wolf wanted it. I wanted it. Beyond the forest, beyond the hills, there were other places, older places, places that waited for the predator. I moved without thinking, moving through the night, through streams, under branches, through darkness and fog and silence—

—and yet, I thought of the village still. The fear, the screams, the futile attempts to hunt me. They would rebuild. They would tell stories. They would pray for safety. But I was gone, and gone forever. The wolf would find new paths, new prey, new revelations.

I am not a man. I am not a memory. I am the wolf, and the wolf is freedom. The forests, the hills, the rivers, they will know me. I will be there, silent and moving, present and unstoppable.

And when I pause in a quiet hollow, under the moon, I whisper again, as I always have:

I like it.

⸺ ⧓⧓⧓⧓⧓⧓⧓⧓⧓⧓ ⸺

When you breathe out, the moon has turned pinkish, bloodshot, is rolling in its socket, but before you can determine if this is yet another illusion the makeshift curtain falls back into place. Sealed once more in your capsule, you look at your host, who gives that by-now familiar smile, and motions once more to the rest of the room.

"Why don't you direct our next diversion?" xe asks, moving xer hand in a flourishing parabola past the bookshelves, the craft supplies, the toys and the games and the television wires. You let your blood guide you, moving to the bookshelf, where your fingers trace a multitude of spines: The Medium is the Massage: An Inventory of Effects, *reads one.* Trans Rites: An Anthology of Genderfucked Horror *reads another. Shakespeare's* Lear, *Sendak's* Where the Wild Things Are, *a random volume of Morrison's* Doom Patrol *and Carroll's* Alice *books bound together in one volume. Your finger glides over each until you reach the bottom row, mostly coffee table books, and you settle on an art book. Sliding it from its place, you take it back to the coffee table, set it down on top of a powder-scuffed mirror, and open to a page near the middle. There, in glossy print, is a painting.*

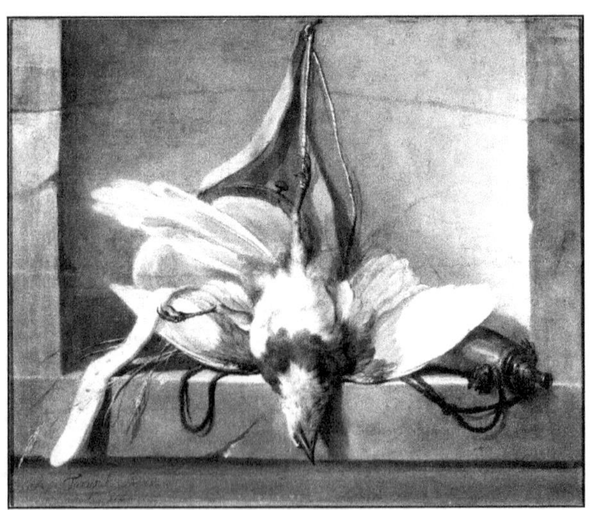

"Ah," your host says, peering at your selection. "It seems there is one more bus to catch before our journey is over after all. Climb on, toss your coin to the driver, and prepare to reach your final destination. Next stop...

Taraval Street

administered by E. B. Ratcliffe

The words "open house" released my expectations like a canary set free from its cage. I can't afford a house in San Francisco. I can't even afford rent in San Francisco, but I dream of having a home. A home where my artistic obsessions can be given full rein.

I arrived at the condos on Taraval Street with my friends, Tiffany and William. It was late on a summer afternoon. Warm breezes stirred the green grass. Sun lit the clouds on Taraval Street as if angels would burst forth at any moment.

Guillaume Taraval introduced Rococo art to Sweden. Rococo paintings spoke to me of lazy days with rosy cheeked maidens in satin gowns. It seemed fitting to find an open house on Taraval Street when life is so bleak. A portent of good fortune. The condos are two blocks from the zoo. If I lived here, it would be an easy stroll to sidewalk spaces where I could show my paintings. Perhaps, I'd find a benefactor the way Taraval did.

More clouds meandered like sheep across the cerulean sky. At the top of cement stairs, a door stood ajar, welcoming us to the converted 19th century school. Hoary stone railing warmed my palm. We walked up to a door inlaid with walnut panels. My hands were gray and rough with ground-in pigment.

I held them behind my back when the listing agent met us. White woman with hair out of a bottle. Too brassy for a professional dye job, but behind her I spied heaven. Red oak floors the color of honey stretched out in waxy splendor.

William stepped forward and shook hands with her. "Nice to meet you. This is my wife, Tiffany, and her brother, Tom."

I smirked at Tiffany. She'd been upgraded from William's paramour to his wife and we were now siblings. One look at us would show the lie. Tiffany was a natural blond and I was half Japanese. The listing agent barely glanced at us. She had real estate to sell.

Her smile wilted as I walked past her. She grimaced at my paint splattered plum t-shirt. At least William looked respectable in his slacks and white button-down shirt. Miss Brass pointed out the open concept of the ground floor and failed to offer us food or drink. She'd caught on to our subterfuge. This would be the bum's rush.

I didn't care at that point. It was enough to see a beautiful space. The colors and shapes made me long for my oil paints. I wasn't sure that William's abstract art really needed inspiration. It seemed to only need a good throwing arm and soggy towels. In comparison, Tiffany had real talent with her watercolors and inks. Like me, she couldn't talk easily to strangers. As our instructors told us during school, you needed to be able to market and sell your work. We didn't have the knack.

Rattling about in a lovely place where inspiration ruled. I realized my true desires were smaller than a condo on Taraval Street. I'd die to paint in a warm covered place.

As they went upstairs to see the master suite, I wandered outside. The grounds of the former school were the size of a small park. Trees cast shadows across the verdant lawns and decorative benches. A dizzying group of skyscrapers rose in the distance. I settled onto a sturdy cement bench with ironwork that was new, but hearkened back to earlier times when men wore bowler hats and ladies had parasols. The sky made me want to become lost in it and I could smell the bay.

A few minutes later, Tiffany and William plopped down next to me.

Tiffany fanned herself with a brochure from the open house. William stretched out, poised for his next conquest. He always had a plan. It was exhausting. "We've got to make tracks if we're going to catch the art gallery before dinner."

I leaned back. "Why don't you two go ahead? I'll catch a bus."

Tiffany patted my hand with her ink stained fingers. "You're already bailing on us."

I shrugged. "I want to take it slow."

Tiffany leaned against me and looked back at the condos. Her profile, that of a Renaissance angel. "It's glorious, isn't it?"

"It is. William finds the best places for us. I'm just jaded enough that an art gallery will only make me depressed."

 William snickered. "You aren't jaded, buddy, just lazy."

Tiffany chimed in, "He isn't. There has to be something better for us. Tom, you're just frustrated." She kissed my cheek. I didn't think "frustrated" carried the gravitas of my current situation.

I am Sisyphus. Out of money and options. I'll be homeless by the end of the month.

William led her away and she waved her fingers in that little girl way that some women never let go of.

As I stood waiting for a bus back to downtown, I reveled in my brief solitude. The heat of the asphalt kept the cooler air at bay. A simple bus ride through the city would make me better appreciate my friends. Missing their company, I would know once again how lucky I was to have them to drag me out of my room for an open house. I'd known Tiffany since college. I thought William was good for her, even if he was relentless.

The bus pulled to a stop. Doors opened like curtains showing stairs to another world. I climbed up into the bus. A place where I belonged. People struggling to make it to the next payday. The burly white bus driver frowned at me as if I were a junkie, but I showed him my card.

One thing you can say for the buses in San Francisco, they are air conditioned and clean. There were spicy smells like someone had recently visited a taco stand. My stomach grumbled, but it must have known that the cupboard was bare because it let the bus drown it out. I heard at least three different languages as I found a plastic seat jaundiced with age.

A middle-aged Asian woman who resembled my mom with her smile lines, fair skin and chocolate brown eyes sat alone. She made no objection when I sat next to her.

I settled in as the bus began its dance along the stops to downtown. Oddly, I missed the condo we'd viewed. It was almost paradise. Guess my desires hadn't quite dwindled to nothing. I texted my sister Grace that I'd be out to see her soon. My only sibling, we shared that bond which comes when no one understands you.

Grace was so shy she wouldn't talk. As children, I interpreted her to our parents. She gestured like a swimmer seeking the surface. She'd outgrown her shyness, but not her dependence on me for love and support.

Bang! The bus hit something.

Several passengers jumped up to see what happened. The bus driver, frowning even more now, in his navy blue uniform, yelled, "Sit down. You all sit down. There ain't nothing to see."

A monster headache gripped me. It must have shown. The woman next to me said, "You're squinting. Did you hit your head?"

"No. I'm fine. Just a little dizzy." I rubbed my thumbs across my temples and the pain receded. She nudged me and I looked around realizing there was something off. Fewer people on the bus. Passengers still stood looking out the windows.

Outside, houses lined up on the street with a sad sepia tone. As my seatmate stood, she asked, "Do you know if this is the stop for the Science Center?" I almost responded, but then thought I must have heard her incorrectly. The Science Center was in Seattle. I was in San Francisco. Maybe she meant the Science Academy at Golden Gate Park. I shook my head.

She walked down the aisle and exited. There was a kaleidoscope of light at the bus's door. The street called to me like a siren. Colors vibrant as the night Tiffany and I dropped acid at *La Boheme.*

The bus started up again. A man, a few seats up, turned and stared at me. Slick black hair. He was Hispanic and asked which way was 42nd. I focused out the window and saw a street sign for Raleigh followed by Quitman. Was I in Denver? I grew up there.

Without much hesitation, I told him, "Two blocks to the south."

He nodded and got off the bus.

Something was wrong. The smell of almonds rushed past me. I really must have hit my head, but it didn't hurt anymore. I couldn't exactly figure out why I was so out of it. The color of the street pulsed in a hypnotic way. How could I capture it on canvas?

I glanced up to the front of the bus. It was headed towards the bridge across to Oakland. Shit. Missed my stop. I was nowhere near downtown.

A couple were jabbering at each other in Tagalog and tugging on the stop cord. Several people popped out of their seats and shifted to the back of the bus. It was like a movie that had been shot at the wrong speed.

The bus pulled off the street and onto a dirt road before the bridge. I focused up the aisle at the driver but his seat was empty. The bus jerked to the right, rumbled off the road and into the bay. I got up and dashed to the front of the bus.

Cold brown water sloshed up to my knees. I grabbed the steering wheel. Could I turn it around? The wheel fought me as I twisted it to the left.

UNDERSTAND
THE POWER of DESIGN
SINK
OR
SWIM
UNDERGROUND
TRANSFER
A TRANSIT
Welcome
Transfer
ISSUED: 02:28P
Sat 11 Oct 25
BUS:
ROUTE: 2118
DIR: 110
OUTBOUND
EXPIRE: 04:28P
916

I held on as the murky water came up to my shoulders. The air smelled of fish and exhaust. As the water reached my chin, I grabbed a breath and stayed at the wheel. I wrenched it as hard as I could, but the bus wasn't responding.

Someone tugged on my arm, pulling at me. I let go of the wheel. I felt a shove from behind and was pushed out the door. Expelling my breath, I watched the bubbles rise in the dark waters. I pushed against the water, swimming after the bubbles.

After what seemed like an eternity, I broke through to the surface. Coughing, I searched for a landmark. Fading sunlight glinted on the water. There were two people swimming toward shore and an older man already dragging himself out of the water. A young woman with dark hair treaded water next to me. The area around her blue eyes were smudged black like she was crying ebony tears. She smiled.

Good teeth. I'm absurd. I escaped drowning to focus on dental hygiene. The water was cold and dusk was quickly blending the shore and the water into a smoky gray haze. I dog-paddled after the woman.

As we struggled onto a rocky shore, a grandmotherly lady with silver hair, so delicate she must too be Japanese, motioned us into the back door of a bungalow not fifteen yards away. Dusk had muted the colors of the lawn and the house.

The house's door shone like a beacon. No police sirens sounded. No flashing lights from ambulances. Just the sound of lapping water. A consoling murmur as though apologizing for pulling the bus under.

The woman led us into a small living room. It was furnished neatly. An emerald green sofa and a tan leather armchair framed the tiled fireplace. None of the survivors were sitting on the furniture. I rested on the hardwood floor. I didn't want to be the first person to abuse the woman's hospitality by getting her furniture wet. "Ma'am, what's your name?"

The woman grinned at me. Her lips were pale, but her cheeks flushed to a rosy hue. "Izanami. I'll get you all some more towels."

One of the men was leaning on the armchair and whispering to a young Asian woman from the bus. Her features were broad, but symmetrical. Beautiful, really. I'd love to paint her. The bus had made more of a splash, then a crash, but I figured, in time, I'd be able to sort things out. Izanami handed me a large sapphire blue towel.

"Thank you."

She nodded. "I'll go get you all some tea."

I sat on the floor and kept an eye on the other passengers. The man talking to the Asian woman was black. His dark eyes looked kind. The other man was a tall white guy in a brown suit with streaks of gray in his dark chestnut hair. I'd guess he was about retirement age.

He kept pushing at one of his shoulders as if it hurt. Everyone was drenched, but no one seemed hurt. No blood or bruises.

I wondered what had happened to the bus driver. I suppose a driver wasn't expected to go down with his bus. Still, it seemed irresponsible to let it splash into the bay.

I pulled out my cell phone, but it was waterlogged. The screen stayed dark, so I shoved it back in my pocket.

The blue-eyed woman knelt down next to me. "Are you okay? What's your name? I'm Marte."

"I'm Tom. Not sure what happened."

She shrugged her shoulders, slid down onto her butt, and used a lemon yellow towel to furiously rub her long dark hair. I mopped at myself with my blue towel, wiping down my arms and face. "Is your phone working?"

"No. It was in my purse and I didn't grab it."

"Did you see what happened to the bus driver?"

She cocked her head at me. "I thought you were the driver."

"No. I only went up front after we were in the water."

"I don't know then. It all happened pretty fast."

Looked into her lazuline eyes.

Eyes like afternoon sky.

Like the sky when I sat on the bench —

Like staring up rather than sitting on the floor

This wasn't reality.

Sisyphus had let the boulder roll over him. My stomach clenched and I folded into a fetal position. I was dead. Something had happened and my brain kept firing, making up stories for me, but I wasn't really here. I was lying dead somewhere and would never get to paint another canvas, joke with Grace about our sibling bond, or hold Tiffany when Will broke her heart.

Marte patted my back. "It's all right. You're safe."

I slowly pulled myself into a sitting position. "I think we're dead."

Frowning, Marte shook her head. "You're just in shock."

I looked around the room.
Dark shadows in every corner—
Lines of the furniture are too sharp.
Everyone caught up in their own misery.

Izanami came back into the room with a pot of tea. She poured us each a cup. I took a sip. It tasted of jasmine with a hint of cinnamon. When she finished pouring, I asked, "Are we dead?"

Izanami winked at me. "You're a bright one. Why didn't you get off the bus?"

"I did get off the bus."

Izanami shook her head as if I was slow and turned to the group. "Tom has spoken true. You lot are at a way station."

Marte gasped, "What?"

"You are dead. This is just a stopping place to grab some comfort before you go back out. You can stay the night, but by tomorrow, you all have to be gone."

The pretty Asian woman, with her pale skin and high cheekbones, raised her hand. "Gone? Where?"

Izanami shrugged. "It will come to you." She smiled at me. "If you're smart, you'll leave now."

The black man stood up. "Should have known. Never had anyone do something good for me."

I finished my tea. It had a bitter aftertaste. If I was going to be dead, I'd do it on my own terms. I was tired of pushing for something that seemed like it would never come. "She said we should leave. Why don't we go together? Has to be better than waiting around."

The older white man leaned back against the tan chair, clearly not going to be pushed out of the nest anytime soon. The black man walked up and offered me his fist to bump. "Name's Robert and this is Sun. Let's go."

I reached my gray hand down to pretty Marte. "You want to come?"

She shook her head. "I'm going to ask for a phone or, maybe, wait to wake up."

"What happened to your hands?" Robert asked.

I looked at my pigment stained hands and wondered why I had ever been ashamed of them. "I'm an artist."

I obsessed about creation during my life. Now that I was dead, it felt as if someone had opened a door and I could finally breathe.

I led Robert and Sun out the door and into the cooler air of the night. I noted how the indigo colors of the sky were like that of the canvas I had been working on.

"Where do we go?" Sun asked.

"Why don't we visit an open house I saw on Taraval Street? It's near the zoo. I last saw someone that I love there and I found it inspirational."

— ⧓⧓⧓⧓⧓⧓⧓⧓⧓⧓⧓ —

The artbook is gone: instead, on the table before you, lies an open sketchpad, adorned with fresh paint. Your fingers bear the marks of their labor, each tipped a different hue, slightly tacky as the pigment begins to dry.

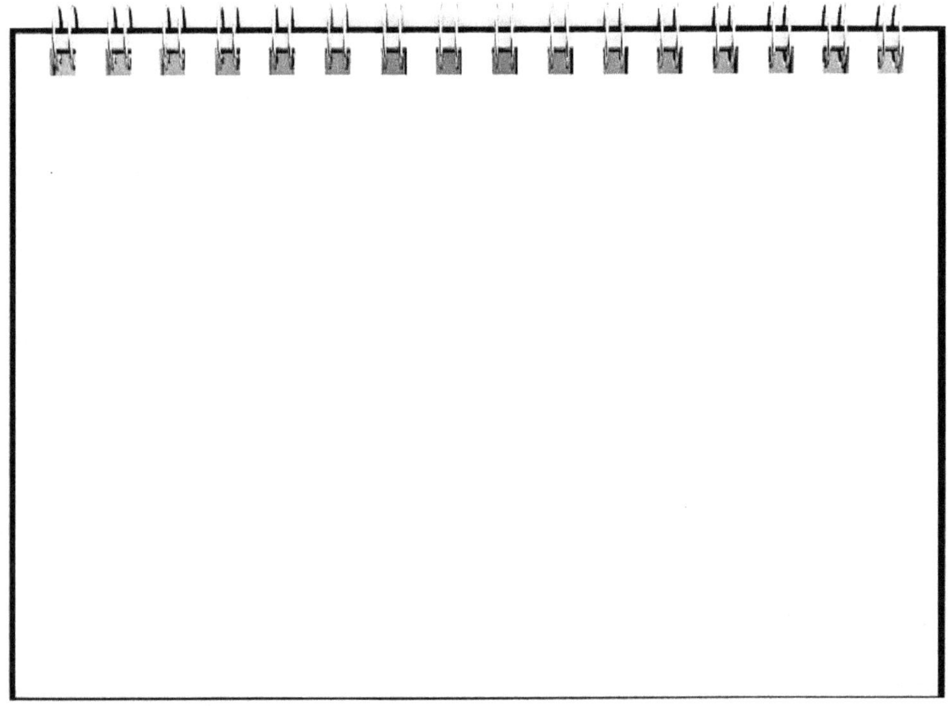

You stand and move to the bathroom, leaving a painted handprint on the doorknob, then on the knob of the faucet, then on the other knob after you burn your hand under the stream. The colors run down your wrists and into the basin, a vibrant Day-Glo Charybdis sucking down the world into its mouth.

Some paint remains in the cracks of your knuckles and the deepest lines of your palms, but it is mostly gone, and you wipe your hands on your shirt. As you raise your gaze to the mirror, your reflection smiles at you and tips you a wink that you do not feel echoed by your own eye. It should maybe feel like a threat, but you find the gesture reassuring, and the ground feels a bit stiller under your feet. You've heard that you should never look into the mirror while tripping, but if the mirror is going to look back, you'd rather be paying attention when it does. When the discrepancy between you and you is not repeated, you move back into the playroom, where you can smell the pungent tang of incense.

"If I had been thinking," your host says, "I would have lit something earlier." Xe shakes off a match, blowing gently into the burner to stoke the embers. "Aromas can really help center your trip." Xe rises, fixing you with xer gaze. "Of course, scents can have other effects… can remind us of things we'd give anything to relive, or of things we'd do anything to scrub from the record. In our next tale, it acts as just such a stimulant, bringing love back to life, a love that is meant…

12th Dose:

Not For You... For Me

administered by Stephen McQuiggan

It was only as the coffin disappeared through the curtain and into the furnace that Willis remembered his deal with Miles. He laughed a little, though with his red-ringed eyes it could be mistaken for a sob. The music drowned it out and no-one was looking at him anyway; they were all staring at the curtain as if they expected Miles to come bounding through it (*Ta da!*) at any moment like some crap kids' magician.

Willis had seen what was left of Miles after the crash—he had been seated beside him after all—and he knew that the remains of his buddy were hardly worth burning. He hadn't noticed that Miles wasn't wearing his seatbelt that night they decided to drive down and surprise Lana, but he *had* noticed he'd been drinking like a loon; Willis had been canning the beer himself otherwise he would never have agreed to accompany him.

But the deal had been made a week before, when they had been sitting under Tewkley Bridge drinking car-bombs, and the subject, as usual, had gotten around to death. Lana had dumped Miles again, hence the morbid turn of conversation; hence the car-bombs too.

It struck Willis as funny that he should only think of it now that he saw his mate travel down into the oven; why hadn't he thought of it as he lay in hospital, or when he saw him in his coffin? As Willis rose awkwardly to his feet, trying to manoeuvre himself round on his crutches, wincing as his shattered ribs protested, he figured he had his answer—he'd had enough to deal with without pondering on some daft, drunken tete a tete.

Except, it didn't seem so daft now the curtains were drawn and the strains of Iron Maiden were shaking the crematorium; it seemed... prophetic.

"What do you think happens after you die?" Miles had asked, and Willis felt a sudden stab of sobriety. He didn't believe Miles would do anything stupid, but Lana had pushed him to the limit and who knew what he would do if she kept on pushing.

"I think harps and clouds," Willis said, trying to lighten the mood. "An eternity of Sundays with no heavy rock, just hymns, and you end up lumbered with all those relatives you were glad croaked in the first place."

"Seriously though, what do you reckon? Do we go on or... is that it, lights out?"

Willis shrugged. "Who knows? Ain't nobody ever come back, leastways nobody I know."

"True," Miles grinned, "so that's what we'll do—first one of us goes, the other one comes back to spill the beans."

They drank to it and Willis promptly forgot (they drank to everything after all) until now, when the remains of his best friend were being barbecued somewhere behind that awful salmon curtain. To have been discussing this very event only a few days before it happened was spooky, it was—

"—a disgrace. I didn't think you'd have the nerve to show yourself here today."

Willis turned to find Lana plonked in front of him, as solid and unyielding as the tree Miles had ploughed into that night. He wanted to yell at her, *You're the disgrace, you were the one who used played with his emotions like a yo-yo, you drove him to it*, but behind her he could see Miles's parents, his aunts and workmates, his old English teacher for Christsake, and he knew that everyone one of them agreed with Lana.

"'He was my friend," was all he said; part of him hoped his injuries would deflect the worst of her ire, spare him the contempt of the rest of the mourners.

"A real friend would have kept him out of that car."

"That sticks in your throat, doesn't it Lana—the fact that Miles and me were so close? He told me everything—he told me all about you and the promises you made. He didn't even like you. I think he stayed with you out of duty. I wish it was me in that oven—if I could bring him back I would, but not for you… for me.'

Lana spat at his feet and moved away. Miles's parents didn't utter a word, just lashed him with their eyes until he wobbled on his crutches. It had been a mistake to come here. Willis hobbled out, more buckled by public opinion than he had been by the smash. At home he reheated a takeaway that he couldn't bring himself to eat. He watched TV without taking in a single word and, defeated by the stairs, drank until he passed out on the sofa.

He awoke in the early hours of the morning, the streetlight bathing the living room in a stage set glow. There was a smell of burnt meat hanging greasy in the air that, mixed with the curdled wine in his belly, made him want to puke. Willis struggled up to a sitting position to look for his crutches. They lay on the far side of the room (he must have flung them there in a fit of drunken pique); he would have to crawl over to get them.

He was debating whether it would be simpler just to crawl to the toilet and leave them where they were when he heard the back door open, footsteps in the kitchen, followed by a harsh braying cough. The temperature plummeted. Willis clutched the blanket around himself as his throat tightened.

"Who's there?" he croaked—it had to be his sister, right? She was the only one with a key—ut Mandy hadn't spoken to him for a while now, not since —

The living room door-handle rattled and Willis cried out in a high-pitched yelp that managed to scare him more than he already was. He fell off the sofa just as the door opened and the stench of burnt meat grew strong enough to make him gag. Although the telly was off as well as the lights, the streetlamp pooling through the open curtains was enough to illuminate the figure that now loomed over him.

It was Miles: his face was scorched right down to the blackened skull, charred flakes of crisp flesh fell from his bones with every step and his eyes were seared out of his sockets, but Willis knew him nonetheless. It was Miles come back from the dead, come back to keep his promise.

Willis screamed so long and hard he thought his heart must burst. In his terror his mind floated away on the voodoo beat of his pulse, blacking out as though his scream was an anaesthetic needle plunged directly into his brain.

He awoke on the floor, his face fused there by excess slobber, his back howling in protest, his broken ribs a white band of fire, yet the only thing he really felt was relief. Sunlight bathed him, chasing away the horrors of the night before—it was only a nightmare brought on by Miles's cremation, the blame heaped upon him when he was grieving too, and the memory of the deal, the pact they'd drunkenly made. A perfect storm of stress that, coupled with wine and painkillers, had led to his angst ridden mind conjuring up a visit from—

Willis stopped hauling himself up onto the sofa. There were footprints on the floor; black and smeared as if someone (someone burnt) had shuffled across to where he lay and left their oily residue behind. The air still held a faint odour of scalded meat.

He had to get out. He fell several times trying to reach his crutches and was in tears by the time he got to the door—a mix of pain and fear, and the horrible anticipation of a burning hand touching his back, *branding* him.

Outside it was a beautiful morning that seemed to mock his fright. Where could he go? His sister wasn't speaking to him; she blamed him for Miles's death too. He concentrated on getting as far away from the house as possible, he would work something out later—the goal was just to Long John Silver it until the house was miles behind; he shivered—was *Miles* behind?

He risked a peek over his shoulder but the street was empty save for a few kids on their way to school. Willis kept on walking until the sweat caused his hand to lose grip on the crutch. He found himself by the park and made it as far as the first bench by the duck pond, all but collapsing onto it.

Should he tell Miles's parents that their son was back and trying to communicate? They already hated him—the best he could hope for there was that they would think grief (or guilt) had pushed him over the edge and he had lost his mind. Even if (and what a long shot that was) they did believe him, did he really want to hear what Miles had to say? What if he blamed him too? Miles had always been quick to accuse Willis of betrayal and subterfuge whenever the slightest thing went against him.

What about Lana though? She was always into (or at least pretended to be) all that new age witchery fuckery; candles and incense and henna tattoos. Maybe she would listen to him—maybe she even knew a way to stop Miles from visiting him. If he could get her onside somehow she might even act as a bridge, or a buffer, between him and Miles's mum and dad.

Just as he managed to regain his feet he heard a sizzling hiss. He looked over to the pond, where the ducks were honking manically as they flew from the bubbling ripples in its midst, and saw a charred and peeling skull rise up from the water, followed by a blistered, smoking hand. A skinless finger clicked as it pointed at him and a harsh croak drowned out the ducks.

"Willis!"

LAST
WILL
AND
TESTAMENT
JACK DANIEL'S
Old No.7
Tennessee
WHISKEY
SILVER
PATRÓN
Two of Swords
THE KRAKEN
RETURN
NO! STOP!!
CONTINUED...
CRASH!

He pivoted on the crutch, made it to the grass verge but, in his haste, toppled down the short bank and rolled in a tangled heap down to the waste bins. A passing jogger stopped to help but all Willis could do was babble and point toward the pond. Soon a small crowd had gathered around him.

"Maybe we should call an ambulance," the jogger suggested to a general murmur of consent.

"I'm okay," Willis protested as they helped him to his feet, 'if someone could just call me a taxi.'

They waited with him, clucking over him until his cab arrived, and helped him inside. It was actually quite nice, he thought, to be on the receiving end of some sympathy—he might even have enjoyed it if it wasn't for the fact that every time he closed his eyes he saw the lump of boiling meat that once was Miles lumbering toward him.

He told the driver to take him to Half Moon street and hobbled the rest of the way to Lana's flat. Of course, the bitch had to live on the top floor and, of course, the lift was out of order. He could barely breathe by the time he reached her landing, but at least the bone crunching exercise took his mind off his waking nightmares.

It actually worked in his favour—when Lana opened her door Willis looked so pathetic and bedraggled she couldn't bring herself to slam it in his face.

"What do *you* want?"

"I need to talk to you," Willis sobbed; "about Miles."

"I don't want to hear your excuses—Miles is dead. You should have stopped him from getting behind the wheel, simple as that, and if you can't accept–"

"But that's just it—he isn't dead, Lana."

"What?" He had caught her off guard. She had been expecting alibis, mitigating circumstances, outright denials of responsibility, but not this.

"I mean, he *is* dead, of course he is... but he's come back. He said he would and he has. Twice now. I thought you could—" He slumped against her door.

"Jesus, Willis you're burning up."

"Don't say that!' He tried to grab her arm but it slipped out of his sweat soaked grip. 'Please just hear me out, Lana, I need help."

She stared at him as she chewed on her lip. "You can come in until you get your breath back—I don't want you having a heart attack on my doorstep—but then you go, okay? I've no time for crazy right now."

"Me neither, but it seems to have all the time in the world for me."

Once inside Willis collapsed onto the sofa; there was a large photo of Lana and Miles next to the telly and he twisted his body round so that he didn't have to face it.

"Would you like a glass of water?"

"Look, you know about this kind of stuff, you were always banging on about the dark arts; you gotta tell me how to get rid of him."

"I think you did a pretty good job of getting rid of Miles all by yourself," she said. "Now I'll get you that drink and you can be on your way."

"Lana!' he called after her, but he could see it was no use—what had he expected, a smile and a wink and a helping hand? "What are you cooking?" he demanded as she came back in from the kitchen.

"If you think you're staying for dinner you can think again, I'm not—"

"What's that smell?" He already knew; it was the stomach churning stench of burning meat. "He's coming, Lana," Willis cried, grabbing at the hem of her skirt, "he's coming for me and you'll see I'm not crazy. Tell him, Lana, tell him I don't want to see him, tell him I'm sorry, tell him anything but make him leave."

"Okay, okay Jesus, let go of me." Her skirt tore as she extracted herself from his grasp. "You need to go to the hospital, Willis, or at least lie down for a while before... Look, come into the bedroom, you'll be safe there."

"But Miles will come and—"

"I'll be right outside the whole time. There's nothing to be afraid of." She squeezed his hand as she helped him up. "I promise."

She led him to the bedroom and got him settled beneath the blankets.

"I'll go and get you another drink—something stronger this time."

Sleep was tugging at him so hard he didn't even question why she was being so kind to him; it never crossed his mind until he heard the bedroom door's lock click.

"Lana?" He tried to get up but she had taken his crutches. "Lana, you there?" The smell of burnt flesh oozed under the door and Willis gagged, his heart pounding like a fist against his ribs. "For fucksake, Lana let me out!" He heard giggling from the hallway as he fell onto the floor.

"Are you frightened of your best friend?" Her voice was scratchy with hate. "Miles and I were closer than you could ever comprehend, Willis my dear. He told me everything about you, all about the pacts you made. You know, he didn't even like you—he felt bound to you out of pity. I wish it had been you in that oven too."

The air in the bedroom took on a greasy, hazy taint and Willis's eyes began to water as though he were peering through smoke. Through the haze a figure slowly began to take shape, a dark apparition whose shoulders were licked by flame. It came toward him, flecks of crispy flesh falling like charnel snow from its outstretched arms.

"It's torture, Willis," the blackened monstrosity said, its voice that of Miles. "Eternal pain—but I've managed to reserve a place by my side for my best mate. Lana saw to that.'

"Lana!" Willis knew that as soon as that parboiled hand touched him it would fry away what was left of his sanity. "Lana, help me!"

"Now we'll see just how strong your friendship really is," she called through the door. "I brought him back, Willis—but not for me... for you."

The incense continues its slow burn as the playroom once again swims into focus around you, your host sitting across from you with Deedee in xer lap. "A guilty conscience is one hell of a drug, don't you think?" xe asks, standing and sending the cat into an annoyed leap. He hisses at his master, trodding over to the couch next to you and curling up against your thigh. You feel his heartbeat through his skin and up against yours, reminding you that this small clockwork creature is alive—and that you too have a heart beating somewhere inside of yourself.

"Memory is a funny thing in all its forms," your host says, stepping onto the couch cushions and perusing the high mounted shelving that surrounds the perimeter of the room, filled with black-bound diaries tucked in rows like teeth. Your host's finger lights along the spines, considering but not removing any of the volumes. "All of these, for instance, carry the memories of people who have been in situations very much like the one you find yourself in now—put to paper, preserved, left for future psychonauts to psychoanalyze." Xe pauses, xer voice almost sad as xe slips back down and onto the ground. "We all want to have a story—to believe that we were really here, and that on some level, that we were here mattered. That it still matters when we're gone." Xe moves back to the standing bookshelf, fingers again tracing spines, this time finding a quarry. The Greater English Poets Of The Nineteenth Century, *reads the open cover. Xe flutters through the book, stopping to let xer fingers glide along a margin here or there. "Are you familiar with Biron Swinford?" The book closes shut with a thud. "I doubt you are, and you certainly won't find him listed here. A contemporary of Poe, and one whose life bore a suspicious resemblance to the madman from Baltimore—a series of strange symmetries in a pair of strange lives. His story is far longer than we have time for here, but we shall join him now for a sampling, a vignette we will call...*

13th Dose:

Swinford & the Girl in White

administered by Ted Morrissey

It took a moment to grasp the sounds, or rather the meaning of the sounds. The movement without chattering conversation, only the occasional *chk-chking* at a horse or mule. Feet and wheels and hooves moving with meaning along Division Street. It must have been the brief morning interval when the workmen and shopkeepers and corner peddlers were beginning their day, and the whores and gamblers and other ruffians of the rude dark were surrendering back the city streets. All, like this London district itself, timeworn, weary, disheveled.

Waking now, to that changing of the guard, meant without equivocation that he had established himself as a member of the latter class, the labor class—and the task before him very much felt like a labor. *Be careful, Swinford, what you long for.*

He roused himself from the warm bedclothes and pulled back the heavy drapes, their dust overdue for a vigorous beating. Three floors below, Division Street, in all its tawdriness, was becoming visible in the rising light. The gaslamp boys were busy extinguishing the globes, a quarter-penny per post. They raced from post to post, dodging pedestrians, to see who could darken their side of the street first. It was a contest, and among the few games the starving urchins had liberty to play. For a second or two his attention rested upon a girl in white, a girl as young as the gaslamp boys, still wearing her night-dress, standing across the busy street. Likely a poor child forced too soon into a life of depravity. She appeared to be looking up, toward his window—then she was lost in the teeming streaming crowd flowing to and fro.

He dressed and wetted his hair into place. He let it grow Byronically past his collar and regretted its undeniable thinning. Mrs. Smithey would be along shortly with coffee and hot milk, and a roll as stiff as a sponge. Until then he should get to work. On a good day he could dance a thousand words across the sheets of cheap paper before the landlady announced her arrival by kicking the bottom of the door. On a good day he rued her arrival because it interrupted his daisy-chain of thoughts, which on a good day flew at him almost faster than he could capture them in ink upon the page. Such a good writing day, however, had not been his for more days than he could count.

That was a lie. Sixty-seven. Precisely the number of days since he'd delivered the manuscript of "The Disappearance of Andre Dupin" to Murry's underling. It was the third Inspector Klaus story, and Murry was anxious to have it set in type and printed, given the surprising popularity of the first two Klaus mysteries. Murry's instincts were unfaltering, and "The Disappearance" was an unbelievable success—he at least, the author, had trouble believing it.

The issue of *Mars Mystery Magazine* in which it appeared could not be printed spryly enough. The pressmen pushed through five runs before London and environs appeared sated. Indeed saturated.

With the third Inspector Klaus mystery, the character and the concept established itself as a series, not a one-off anomaly and a second lark.

He had always written in near-perfect obscurity and therefore anonymity. Mostly poems and sometimes a brief sketch published in this journal or that newspaper—known among London's literati and in certain Bohemian dens, a member of the motley and mostly dissipated "American circle," but Biron Swinford was not a name on the tongues or minds of the general leisure reader. In other words, his work was unknown among the masses.

That is, unknown prior to the arrival of Inspector Krispen Klaus of Scotland Yard's newly formed Department of Scientific Inquiry—a fictitious department, one he wholly fabricated after reading the proceedings of the local anatomy club at the district's library branch. There was an article on blood coagulation at various temperatures and altitudes; and for some unfathomable reason it fired his imagination in ways previously uncharted. The inaugural Inspector Klaus story spilled from the nib of his pen as if dictated by an unearthly force.

He sent a fair copy of the manuscript to A.B.C. Murry, whom he'd known since his arrival in England nearly twenty years before. Murry's support had prevented his starvation until he could collect a cadre of editors who would print his work, including a steady stream of theatrical reviews, which, for most, was their chief interest. They printed his poems and sketches, paying their weight in what might as well have been wampum, in trade for his reviews, which he published under the nom de plume H. Garrison, as not infrequently it was more accurately a nom de guerre.

Now, however, that a burgeoning number of Londoners anticipated his creative efforts—appreciated them in fact, were willing to pay their hard-earned money for them—his pen was stymied on the page. The ink dried on the nib as he stared blankly at the blank sheet. After a while the unblemished whiteness hurt his eyes. It wasn't that he had nothing to say. His mind boiled and bubbled with poetry. He contemplated complete sonnet cycles, and envisioned ship loads of odes, stockpiles of stanzas. He'd been introduced to Eastern forms, the Pankti and Mandakranta among them, that beckoned to his meter-muttering-murmuring brain—but on the matter of Inspector Klaus his Muse was as mum as one of the British Museum's Egyptian queens.

He felt Murry's eyes upon his shoulder, casting disapproving and disappointed glances at the empty page while the minutes melted away like mismanaged finances.

Trying to force the process forward, he'd written thousands of words about Krispen Klaus's past—his idyllic boyhood in the mountains of Bavaria, his coming to England, the events that sparked his interest in the criminal temperament, his schooling in the sciences, his utter contempt for fictional literature, his courtship of a Prussian ballerina, and the loss of his great love to consumption. Those and dozens of other details of the Inspector's early life, but none of them productively led Biron Swinford to a new mystery, a new case, a new murder, a new kidnapping …

Mrs. Smithey's merciful boot upon the door startled him. Now, thankfully, he could cease trying to squeeze a few worthless words out of his pen so that he could have his coffee and roll. The landlady also brought the morning *Gazette*. Perhaps some crime report therein would prove fruitful.

The burly-boned Mrs. Smithey managed the tray into the room and onto his writing table, where he had kept a corner clear. She sported a dramatic limp, as if one leg was shorter than its mate—the result of a childhood accident perhaps, or a congenital condition. Such malformities were common among the city folk. It was one of Swinford's first observations after arriving in England. His own rustic upbringing on the outskirts of Boston provided a most wholesome environment, and he'd grown to well over six feet tall. His height wavered between six-foot-three and -five depending on who was doing the measuring. Inclined toward quieter pursuits, like the absorption and production of poetry, combined with ambulophilia, meant that very little meat manifested on his elevated form, which exaggerated his height even more.

Mrs. Smithey left him to his meager breakfast. He opened the *Gazette* and spread it across the table like a place setting. Nothing in the leading pages piqued his imagination—financial shenanigans in the commodities market, a barge run aground along the Thames, gossip about an MP and his loquacious mistress, the plight of chimneysweeps in Hampstead . . . that is to say, the usual fare.

Swinford brushed crumbs from the folds as he turned from page to page, until he came to a back-page notice that arrested his attention: There was to be a reception at the London Zoological Gardens in honor of the release of a newly published book of sonnets by Lady Chamberlain. The sonnets, it seemed, were inspired by Lord and Lady Chamberlain's visit to India the previous year. The reception was to be in the hall adjacent to the Bengal tiger exhibit.

The notice brought back a thunderclap of memories, mostly unpleasant. The last time he was in the company of Lord and Lady Chamberlain was the evening that Margaret Haeley died, at her own home. There had been a reading—the star of which was the visiting author Jefferson Wheelwright, from America, New York. Murry and Lord Chamberlain had arranged it all; and they invited him, the visiting author's countryman, Biron Swinford, to open the literary soiree.

He hoped that the event would call attention to his poetry and advance his reputation. And he had read well. But the evening ended in tragedy when the famous authoress collapsed, never to be revived. Several newspapers reported the event, but of course their focus was the death of Margaret Haeley, authoress of *Dunkelraum* and widow of the infamous poet Stephen Haeley. The accounts mentioned Jefferson Wheelwright's presence (the rumormongering rags had already been implying a romantic liaison between the celebrity novelists); however, only two or three included Biron Swinford's name at all, and certainly nothing that would promote his rank as a poet. (He had been a minor "character" in Edith Hill's novelized version of the affair, *An Untimely Frost*, but the book failed to attract a significant readership—and his understanding was Miss Hill had moved to the Continent.)

A polite yet preening appearance at the Chamberlains' reception may be beneficial to his reputation. No doubt Murry would be in attendance. He didn't relish seeing his publisher, who must be as keenly aware of the number of days since his last Inspector Klaus story as he, but the business-minded Murry would recognize the advantages of a public appearance—an opportunity to mention *Mars Mystery Magazine* and the Klaus stories among such a well-heeled gathering. The society pages would almost certainly mention that Biron Swinford was present, author of popular stories of detection.

The effort to increase his circulation surely would be enough work for one day. He sheathed his pen and stoppered his ink—and prepared to while away the hours until Lady Chamberlain's literary soiree.

Biron Swinford had never become acclimated to the style of London dress, preferring a longer-cut coat and wider-brimmed hat than local businessmen were inclined to wear—retaining the look of a young Bostonian, though he was no longer young and had not set foot in Boston for more than twenty years. In lieu of standard neckwear, a tie or cravat, he liked a silk scarf printed with a geometric Calcuttan design, in either scarlet or lavender. Today, at first, he opted for the scarlet; then he recalled that lavender was Lady Chamberlain's signature color, displaying it from plumed head to capped toe. Perhaps she, or better still, Lord Chamberlain would appreciate his gesture as homage.

His small room had a locking cabinet, where he kept his manuscripts and a few volumes of some value: a calfskin Chaucer, a crimson-clothed *Arabian Nights*, a gilt-edged *Collected Works*, as well as personally inscribed copies of Mrs. Haeley's *Dunkelraum* and Mr. Wheelwright's *Sunnydale*. At the bottom of the cabinet, beneath a fragrant goat-hair rug, there was a sturdy strongbox wherein he secured his coin. Thanks to Inspector Klaus and A.B.C. Murry, there were far more coins and notes than he was used to keeping. Most of his funds occupied a growing account at Peacock & Sons Bank & Mortgage, but he kept some money on hand, doubly locked within box and cabinet. The unaccustomed funds were both reassuring and nerve-racking. The coffers of a poet were too inconspicuous to attract the attention of ne'er-do-wells and cut-throats. Sudden wherewithal was a sudden worry.

His day lay before him. He would take a circuitous, rambling route to the zoological gardens that would afford him ample opportunity to observe his fellow creatures as they went about their business, mercantile or merely, like his own, meandering. He would take Division Street to Canal, which followed its namesake with admirable directness to the Thames. The canal waters trickled or churned depending on the sluice and baffles whose adjustments were tied, somehow or another, to the incoming or outgoing tide. He had never bothered to solve the mystery of the seemingly capricious canal system.

Its workings were not his interest. Rather, he enjoyed the bustle of men and machines and beasts of burden as they bore their labors in service to the factories, workshops, and slaughterhouses that had grown along the banks of the canal like an ever-creeping fungus. Chaucer knew some of these structures; Shakespeare knew more of them. One day would some wistful poet think, *Swinford knew these banks and barges and bridges of stone and rust?* Would he record his impressions in a small blank-page book? As Biron Swinford did now.

More likely it will be Dickens who springs to mind, the reformer with his noble orphans, brassy old ladies and comic shopkeepers; or Thackarey, the parodist with his fondness for the exotic; or one of the Bells, with their lovesick governesses and windswept heaths; or perhaps even that Irish-infatuated postman, Trollope. Each one a darling of the bookshops and literary columns.

Swinford soaked in the scenes along the canal, including its acrid aura: dyes, turpentine, wood pulp, leathering agents, raw alcohol, blood, manure, sweat, and a host of unknowable smells. He had always been drawn to such places, places of almost alchemical transformations. In Boston, it was the whaling ports, and the human and mechanical operations that processed the giants' oils, baleen and ambergris into soaps and candles and a hundred other domestic essentials. A nearer ramble would take him to the breweries, where local grains and hops were transformed into bitters, ales, and lagers.

Everywhere, here and there, it was the energy of human and animal toil that excited his imagination. Though he was not part of the processes—not a sweating, grunting toiler himself—he felt in harmony with the workers, and saw his own calling, as poet, just as worthy of respect, just as necessary to the common good.

He merged with the throng of pedestrians moving through and past the workmen and their beast-drawn drays. Ahead, he saw a laborer who was already taking a break from his labors, seated on a crate smoking a pipe and reading a morning paper. The gray-whiskered fellow, his beaten leather gloves beside him, was the very picture of tranquility. As Swinford drew near he observed the rag was not the early *Gazette* or *Times* or any morning edition. Rather it was *Mars Mystery Magazine*. He knew the particular issue. When he reached the peaceful fellow, he stopped next to him and feigned a spontaneous interest in the goings-on across the canal. In fact, he surreptitiously spied precisely what was so engrossing. It was "The Disappearance of Andre Dupin".

The revelation, half expected though it was, spurred a host of competing thoughts and emotions. He was of course flattered and pleased that of all the things this fellow could be reading, upon the occasion of his relaxation, he had selected a work of his own. Puffing on his clay pipe he was clearly absorbed in Inspector Klaus's detection. That he could cause his fellow man an hour's worth of amusement was heartening. In the same moment, however, the simple scene reinforced how securely he was now bonded to his own creation, like criminals in their connected shackles. In love or in hate, Krispin Klaus would be his constant companion for the foreseeable future, perhaps forever. Moreover, the fact the issue of *Mars* was two months old underscored the tardiness of his next Klaus story.

One of the main purposes of this outing was to forget about the pressure of composing a new mystery, and now, quite by accident, the pressure fell upon him like a piece of cargo hotly escaped from its tackle-and-hoist.

He continued on, telling himself he was observing the frenetic city and its frenzied citizens for inspiration, and that was a kind of writing in itself, a necessary part of the creative process. He recalled, one by one, this ramble or that which led his mind to an especially successful outpouring of words. Back home, the stroll near Commons Creek that inspired "Ode to Autumn's Splendor"; the hike up Overlook Hill that gave him "The Steeple"; the unsteady pacing aboard the England-bound packet that sparked "Gull's Lament"; and more recently the local ambulations which yielded "Sonnet to a Watchman," "A Trestle Bridge," "The Flower Peddlers," and "Lunar Reflection." All concrete examples, evidence, that aimless Odyssean wanderings could lead to fruitful work. Every piece published in a respectable place; every one brought at least a tittle of bread to his table.

But, also, each memory was of a poem. Whether other types of writing sprang from his walks was less clear. They seemed to be born of other stuff. Reading frequently stoked his ideas for writing. Like the article on coagulation that somehow initiated the invention of Inspector Klaus.

He was some distance from the library branch, but perhaps lightning would strike twice. He gathered his bearings and set off in a new direction.

The plots and twists and turns of the second and third Inspector Klaus mysteries came to him with relative ease—and so quickly there hadn't been time for their popularity to manifest. Then one after another they appeared in *Mars*, and the enthusiastic babble began, at first apparently by word of mouth, then mentions in the literary columns. Sales of the numbers with Inspector Klaus rose, then it was as if the figures were shot heavenward by a cannon. For the number containing the second Klaus story, "The Shadow of the Phantom Forger," Murry had the printers do a second run; then a third. Murry ordered 50,000 for the initial printing of the "Andre Dupin" issue, and yet second and third runs were still necessary. It seemed all of London must have a copy of *Mars* featuring Biron Swinford's intrepid inspector.

Bookshops began putting notices in their windows. Street vendors were tacking hand-lettered advertisements to their stalls. It was beyond real the first time he heard a vendor's boy shouting on a crowded corner "Ready! … Ready! … Bran'-new Inspector Klaus! … Old Klaussy's solved 'nother one … Ready!"

He bought a copy, perhaps to make it real—the sweet smell of fresh ink, the cool smoothness of cheap paper, its sharp-edged solidness when folded into a quarter and slipped into his coat pocket. It was perfectly real. His creation was a genuine sensation.

That may have been the day, the moment, the blockage began. The pressure to produce a new story of detection—the idea that his name was on the lips of thousands, tens of thousands, of readers—the knowledge that every new mystery would be judged against the ones which came before: he'd never written with the pressure of expectation, with the sword of disappointment hanging heavily overhead.

He tried to put such nagging thoughts out of his mind and concentrate on the city scenes, with an eye for the unusual, the mysterious, the mystical. But he was distracted. The image of the workman at the canal would not leave him, haunted him. He at last conceded to himself there was only one method for exorcizing it from his thoughts. He ducked into the first pub he came to, not even noticing its name, ordered a cup of tea and claimed a small table by the window. He removed the notebook and pencil from inside his coat and turned to a blank page. It was a poem that was haunting him, harassing him, a poem about the old workman. He began transcribing the lines and stanzas that had been bottled up in his brain. The words were swift and sure of foot:

O noble dock-man upon thy leisure:
A good pipe, a paper, a place to rest.
Time well earn'd and rightly deserv'd pleasure.
For thy fellows, a kind smile, a fair jest.

Too few appreciate thy good service:
Honest work to assist thy fellow man.
Like the brave huntsman whose aim preserves us,
The bold explorer who brings us to land.

Your absence would mean our deprivation,
A loss felt wholly to our weaken'd core.
Citizens affected of every station.
Our fabric torn, rent, lost forever more.

So take thy moment in the morning sun;
Son of Integrity, Son of England,
Son of Hard Labor before the day's begun.

Swinford requested two sheets of paper, as well as pen and ink, from the publican in exchange for purchasing a second cup of tea. The pen's nib was a tad flat and the ink a smidge gritty, but suitable enough to produce a pair of fair copies of the poem, which he titled "Ode to a Son of England." He let the sheets dry while he finished his cup and watched the street scene through the pub's unwashed window. The day, like so many, was overcast, and the players upon the street's stage cast no shadows, like weightless spirits wandering to nowhere.

The observations suggested another poem, but for now he merely noted it in his little book. He had finished his tea so he set aside the cup and

Championing the arts
from the page
to the stage
PUBLIC LIBRARY
tune on a fid - dle on a

saucer and carefully folded the two sheets into thirds. One copy he placed between the pages of his book, which went securely into his coat pocket. The other he would carry by hand the three blocks to the office of *London's Literary Ledger*, whose editor had published a few of his poems over the years. The *Ledger's* circulation was modest compared to the city's major dailies, but it catered to a more cultured readership—some may say "more Bohemian"—so appearing in its cheaply printed pages was a plume in any poet's cap.

He felt the need to assert his true artistic self—as serious poet, as poet to be taken seriously—since the sudden celebrity cast upon his name by the success of the Inspector Klaus stories.

Long of stride, he soon arrived at the *Ledger* office, as mundane and unassuming as any building on the block. The words "LONDON'S LITERARY LEDGER" appeared in red oxide paint on the only window, and the letters were so fulsomely flaked one had to arrive at the name almost as if by solving a puzzle.

He turned the tarnished brass knob and a weak bell whispered his arrival. He removed his hat and ducked beneath the head jamb. The room was claustrophobically arranged into four desks in two tight columns, all facing the door, and a mismatched assortment of shelves and cabinets along the dun-colored walls. In the back of the room, standing sentinel to the only exit were prodigious columns of the *Ledger*, back issues whose untidy arrangement implied collapse was imminent. A haze of pipe smoke hovered near the mercifully high ceiling.

Three of the four desks belonged to editorial assistants, whose duties ranged from selecting manuscripts for publication, to communicating with contributors, to setting type, to correcting proof copies. The condition of their desks, ranging from messy or tidy, was a reflection of their individual levels of fastidiousness. At present, only the least fastidious, Mr. Jayne, was in view. He, and the occupant of the fourth desk, the bookkeeper Mr. Harrow, upon whose neatly arranged desk a large ledger lay open. It was also Mr. Harrow's responsibility to receive visitors.

Barely glancing from his accounts, Mr. Harrow, pipe trapped between his teeth, said, "He's in the factory."

The *he* was Harold Henderson, founding editor of the *Literary Ledger* whom everyone knew as "Houndstooth," due apparently to a fondness for the fabric pattern in his youth. Over time Mr. Henderson's tastes changed, making the nickname ironic; yet it persisted.

The "factory" was the adjacent building where the *Ledger* was set in type, printed, folded, and prepared for circulation. Swinford was familiar with the way—between the close-set desks, down the narrow hall, past Houndstooth Henderson's office, beyond other rooms mainly devoted to storage, out the rear door, across the alley, and through the factory's half-open admittance—the smells of ink, machine oil, and raw paper stock growing more potent with every step.

The editor was just inside, seated on a bundle of virgin paper, still held tight by twine. He was reading a freshly printed page. Houndstooth was bald, except for tufts of unkempt gray hair covering each ear and meeting at the back of his perhaps smaller-than-average head. The fingers that held the *Ledger* pages were ebon with ink, and he had absentmindedly made dark smudges on both cheeks, like tribal war-paint, thought Biron Swinford. A dark fingerprint also stood out on his smoothly pale pate. Eye-spectacles with round lenses perched precariously at the end of his rather narrow Roman nose.

Maybe the editor wasn't as engrossed in the page as he first appeared because almost immediately he said, "Ah … Lord Swinford—I'd a thought you'd be dining at the club today with Dickens and the Mayor, and perhaps a member of Parliament or two. I assumed you were finished with such Friday fish as my humble rag."

He fought back the irritation he felt at the editor's jibe. "On the contrary, I remain your humble poet." He paused and proffered the sheet of paper in his hand. "In fact, I bring a modest effort to place before you, in your infinite wisdom." He bowed slightly.

Houndstooth hesitated a beat or two before setting aside the *Ledger* pages and taking the poem. He unfolded the paper. "'Ode to a Son of England,'" he read aloud. Swinford noticed all at once the noise of the factory—the metal clank of machinery, the uneven hubs and bubs of human labor, though it was a small group of compositors and printers and assistants, one or two little more than children. He heard them as much as saw them from his vantage point.

Houndstooth read through the poem quickly, then appeared to read it again with greater care. Finally, "You're becoming a sentimentalist in your old age, Swinford. If you're not careful you'll be the favorite poet of grannies and nannies across all of Britannia. Standard fare in every governess's nursery room." He waited for a reaction.

"My poetry will gladly embrace whatever adulation it can elicit."

Houndstooth refolded the paper. "Admittedly there's a worthy turn of phrase or two, and its technical apparatus won't damage your reputation." He slid the poem into his vest pocket. "Far be it from me to keep your work from our cherished readers. I do have one stipulation, however."

His expression inquired: *yes?*

Beneath your name I'll place: "Author of the Inspector Klaus Mysteries"… in stately but unassuming type of course. Perhaps the *Ledger* can attract a new stripe of subscriber, with your lordship's contribution."

The irritation made a resurgence, but he agreed, emphasizing the unassuming type size.

"On your way out, see old Harrow, he of the sunny disposition. Tell him we've conducted twenty guineas' worth of business." He glanced back at the compositing area for a moment. "I just may have a cozy corner for your Son of England in the new number."

Twenty guineas richer, Biron Swinford continued toward the library branch. Better than the money was the satisfaction that he'd written and placed a poem. Sometimes he worried—3 a.m. sorts of worries—that writing the stories of detection would erode his abilities as a poet, erase his abilities to write a poem at all. The worry was baseless, he knew. He wrote other things, sketches and theatrical reviews, without their affecting his poetry. Why should the popular fiction be fundamentally different? It was more, he thought, his change of fortune than the sojourn in style. The life of the poet must be one of struggle—or at least it could not be one of ease. There was of course the contrary example of Lord Byron, but he manufactured struggle, through his destructive predilections and disastrous life choices. Had he wallowed in the comforts of the manor-born aristocrat what sort of poetry would he have produced then?

He had only advanced a few blocks when he felt a rough hand on his shoulder. He turned—

"Swinford! I thought it was you, you ink-stained cur! Where's your poisonous pen, you insufferable hack?"

Taken aback, it required a few seconds to connect the fellow's freshly shaven face to a name: Ronald Penney, actor … in fact the lead of *My Streetwise Sweetheart,* a production that Swinford had panned, mercilessly, upon attending its opening performance. He recalled writing, "The wise theatre-goer will do well to prevent *their* sweetheart—and anyone who is not their sworn enemy!—from seeing this heart-stoppingly atrocious play." Of Penney in particular he'd written, "The romantic lead's acting—dare I call it such?—is so lethargic that it is far more likely the girl of his fancy would fall asleep before falling in love. This writer distinctly heard snoring from the mezzanine before intermission."

The review appeared on the lead theater page of the *Daily News*, but of course under his pen-name, H. Garrison. He'd known for a long while that his anonymity was only partially intact at best.

"They shut us down, after only three performances," fumed Penney, "thanks to you! What do *you* know about acting? How much time have *you* spent on the boards?!"

"I … I daresay . . . it wasn't only you, my dear fellow. The entire show was flawed, beginning with the thinnest of scripts … No doubt a better-written play would have inspired your talents more advantageously…." It was clear, however, that the unemployed actor was not to be mollified.

"Go off and write your silly stories, Swinford. Perhaps they'll prevent you from ruining good people's perfectly good livelihoods. Grub-streeter!"

The young man, who seemed deflated after venting so much vitriol, crossed the busy street, almost stepping in front of a cab. It was a shame, thought Swinford, that he hadn't brought that level of passion to his acting: it may have helped save *My Streetwise Sweetheart*.

The unpleasant encounter led him to consider the reviews he had written over his years in London. Had he at times been too harsh, too combative? Editors wanted strong voices, strong opinions. And he had been generous when warranted, too, effusively praiseful even on a few occasions. All in all, he decided, he'd been fair. Some productions he'd saved through the generosity of his pen. In the end, all accounts balanced on the ledger sheet.

He believed that theatre wasn't mere entertainment, or, at least, it shouldn't be. It had great potential to affect the masses, to shape their opinions, to modify their behavior, to steer their civic engagement. But, at the same time, that mustn't be playwrights' principal aim. In fact it needn't enter the calculus at all. Interesting characters, a clever plot, language that sparks and sparkles—these must be the aims of the playwright, as they were Shakespeare's, as they were Dryden's, Fielding's, Addison's. Of course they wrote in particular historical and political milieus, which must be, as a matter of course, reflected in their work—but such messaging, such moralizing was not their main artistic concern.

Swinford, in his musings, came to the heart of his trepidation about the Inspector Klaus stories: Were they purely fluff? Did they have redeeming artistic value? Their popularity, he was afraid, suggested they did not. Yet other writers had managed both—Shakespeare again came to mind—mass appeal alongside artistic achievement.

Such rattlings of self-doubt and recrimination evaporated his ramble in a seeming instant, and he had reached the library branch. The entrance of the old brick building was ornamented with stone columns supporting a rectangular frieze, in which was carved the phrase "semper illuminant tenebras." The first time he visited, it took Swinford a moment: *always illuminate the darkness*. The portico projected the impression of an ancient tomb or mausoleum, the precious resting place of the great; and there *was* a greatness about it, about all libraries. He had believed so since childhood, when he discovered that every book was a treasure, that each volume held a trove of golden adventure, of diamond-knobbed knowledge, emerald-encrusted wisdom. If each book was so brimful, how valuable then, was the vault which held them all?

As a small child he understood that, as much as he loved his own simple books, those read by his elder brother were even worthier of adoration—and the tomes that occupied his father after supper were once again as great. Swinford recalled his impatience to grow and graduate to the next rung of books, and the next, and the next.

Inside the door of the library was a Persion rug, or at least a rug in the style of the genuine article. Such rugs were laid throughout, to dampen patrons' pesky steps on the oaken floors and keep the spell of studious quiet as much as possible. Free-standing bookcases, in military order, stood on either side of the central room—hard sciences to the left, tales of imagination to the right. Straight ahead was the head librarian's desk, a mahogany wonder as large and as fancifully carved as a pharaoh's sarcophagus.

Chief among the elements that always made him feel that he was *home* was the smell—the richly unique and uniquely rich melange of books and periodicals, leather bindings, the dyes of cloth boards, ink both fresh and long-cured, and most of all the paper, ranging from heavy cotton rag to the cheap pulp of daily news sheets. The heady scent permeated every corner of the old building, from the uppermost shelves along the walls that required a ladder to retrieve and reshelve their lofty volumes, to the basement where periodicals (the bound as well as the recently issued) were fastidiously housed, to the sub-basement where labels were affixed, loose bindings bound, and floundering repairs made right.

At least, that is what Swinford imagined took place on the lowest level. He had never been, but after a lifetime lived in libraries he had a sound understanding of their operations. They were *home* not in the same sense of his childhood home on the outskirts of Boston, nor any of the low-rent rooms he'd occupied over time (like the hovel here, on Division Street). Rather, libraries were a kind of spiritual home, more akin to a church or some other sacred space than a mere repository of material for reading and researching. In fact there was nowhere that he felt the presence of the divine more forcefully than a library—but instead of saints and martyrs there were authors and illustrators, which made librarians and their assistants priests and their acolytes. A church undergirded by the Trivium instead of the Trinity: the Grammar, the Logic, and the Holy Rhetoric. Instead of one good and holy book, all books had a claim to goodness and holiness. All books, by and large, had the power and potential to save one's soul.

Beyond the librarian's scenic desk were the stairs leading to the periodicals area. The head librarian, Mr. Thorpe, was seated at the desk reading through a sheaf of papers with the aid of a large pearl-handled magnifying-glass. He looked up, squinting, as Swinford went by, and they silently nodded their hellos. As soon as Swinford set foot in the basement he turned and proceeded to the angle-topped table where newly arrived journals were kept.

He was hoping for the most recent *Proceedings of the Gateshead Anatomy Club*, but alas only the previous quarter was set out, and he'd already perused it. In its stead he took up the *Semi-Annual Report of the Royal Society of Archeologists & Antiquarians*. It was a hefty publication so surely something within its esteemed pages would spark his imagination and set him on the path to a new Inspector Klaus mystery.

He took the *Report* to a deep and well-worn leather chair in the corner, beneath a street-level window whose incoming light would aid the lamps placed here and there throughout. The chair provided a panoramic view of the periodical area, which, at the moment, was pleasantly void of any other visitors. Swinford settled in and turned to the abstracts at the front of the journal. Almost at once the summary of a report on an Anglo-Saxon manuscript in the possession of the central library arrested his attention.

It seemed that progress had been made in deciphering the damaged and disintegrating 800-year-old book, composed in a dead Germanic ancestor of modern English. He turned to the full report—thinking about a priceless manuscript being stolen and the responsibility for its recovery being placed before ever-clever Inspector Klaus.

A fellow named J. Kemble had presented the report to the Society. J. Kemble, Esquire, not a professor of linguistics or philology, but rather a barrister with a passion for medieval manuscripts. The centuries-old story, reported Mr Kemble, was about a Swedish warrior who was descended from a bear: "The Bear's Son" he was called in the old language, and he possessed "the strength and fury of thirty men".

Swinford removed the small blank-page book from his pocket, and his pencil, and began taking notes from the report. As he read further, Mr Kemble paraphrased passages wherein the Swedish hero prepares to fight various monsters—well, "perhaps monsters," said Mr Kemble, "perhaps more accurately ghosts, in our modern vernacular." The old language was elusive.

Swinford stopped writing in his note-book. He felt he was being watched. Yet no one was in the periodical area, not even a sub-librarian. Satisfied he was only imagining the surveillance, he returned his attention to the report. In addition to the supernatural foes in the antique story, there was an element of palace intrigue. The aged king whose people were at war with the monsters would not live forever—"regardless of the Swede's success, or not, of ridding the king of his pernicious and vicious adversaries"—and so there was some question regarding who would ascend to the throne. The queen seemed to be enlisting the support of the visiting Swede in making sure her son was duly installed. "Various scheming cousins could lay claim once the throne was vacant."

Swinford thought, *Barrister he may be but Mr. Kemble has a touch of the poet about him*. He looked up ... and just then, a figure disappeared behind a standing bookcase of journals. He *had* been being watched.

"Hello," he said. "Someone there?"

It must be his imagination, but he had the impression it was a girl who had slipped out of sight, a young girl in white, but he'd only had a half-second's fleeting glance.

It was enough, for he saw her plainly among the museum pieces of his memory, the girl of eleven, tall for her age but thin as wheatstalk and as white as the marble basin of baptismal water in Holy Union, where he planned to wed her one day, when she was of age. His cousin Penelope had always been mature beyond her years, an "old soul", so their matrimonial date was not so very far off. It was a still-undeclared day of bliss when Penny ("Henny" was his pet name for her) became ill—stomach influenza, said the local quack, stale bread and bone broth, heavily salted, would have her right as rain. But Penny's fever raged, burning black brings around her eyes and cracking her lips of stone, and she could take no nourishment. Two days hence the quack croaked a new diagnosis: severe typhus. A freshly watered rag on her feverish head every hour, and on the half-hour feed her a teaspoon of mashed orange pulp and rhubarb, soaked in brandy.

In another two days his beautiful bride-to-be was gone. Throughout the ordeal of her illness—he waited fretfully in the parlor, sleeping on the too-short settee, and allowed to attend her bedside thrice daily—she wore a sleeping frock of pure white, only a shade whiter than her cadaverously pale skin. Pretty Penny, Happy Henny was delivered to her grave at Holy Union cemetery in that same sad frock.

In recognition of Swinford's unwavering affection for his cousin, Penelope's mother gave him a lock of her hair, as black as Virginia coal, as black as a raven's shadow, as black as the thundercloud of sadness that banked and boiled in his heart. The lock of hair was tied with a crimson ribbon.

It was Penelope he glimpsed disappearing among the tall stacks, ghostly wan and wearing her funeral frock. He knew it was a foolish thought, yet his pulse's pace was quickened. He rose from his chair and walked to the spot where she had been spying him. He took a lamp from a table to illuminate the gloomy rows of bound periodicals.

His pulse drumming, he looked down each aisle—but of course there was no girl, long-dead Penny or otherwise. There was no one, and he felt his aloneness more acutely than he had for years. It was a profound emptiness in the pit of his soul, a heaviness harnessed to his heart, a leadenness lashed to his loveless psyche, pinned painfully, burned bitterly.

He returned to the corner chair and attempted to concentrate on the report regarding the old manuscript, but the feeling of being watched persisted. He scribbled a few more perfunctory notes before allowing himself to quit the endeavor. He replaced the *Report* to the table with its kin and went to exit the basement. Before stepping onto the first stair, he glanced back at the regimented stacks. No one.

Upstairs, the head librarian, Mr. Thorpe, was not at his desk. There were, however, a few patrons here and there, reading a book or thumbing through a daily, and the animated life helped somewhat to lift the gloom of loneliness that had settled on his spirit. Resuming his circuitous ramble may help further, especially now that he had at least the inkling of a plot idea for a new Klaus.

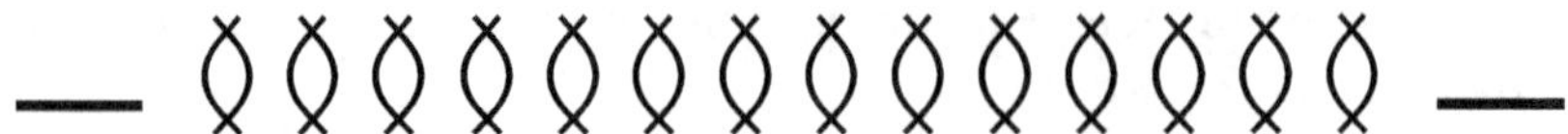

The smell of old books is replaced by the last remains of the incense, though the sense of mystery lingers. Is what has happened to you—is still happening to you—a mystery? It feels like it, to be sure, but there is another feeling, another surety beneath that surety: the feeling that you are exactly where you are supposed to be, that your whole life unspooled thus far has led you to this meeting and this moment. "Poor Mr. Swinford," muses your host, replacing the book of poets on the shelf. "So worried that his detective stories would be what he was remembered for instead of his verse. As it turns out, he needn't have minded that much; he hasn't been remembered at all, except perhaps by those who have cared enough to seek those in the margins of the movements in which he moved." Xe fixes xer gaze on you, lightly teasing and intensely burning all at once. "How do you want to be remembered?" Xe pauses. "Do you want to be remembered, or would you pass from this dream into the next unfettered, untethered by any leftover presence?"

As xe speaks, xe moves across the perimeter of the room, stopping by the light switch. "'Time is out of joint,' or so I've heard," xe says, and the room goes dark save for a pair of glowing feline eyes shining by the toybox. "Perhaps a little illumination, then, to help realign the moment. Music is meant to die. Only in its expiration can it produce its effect. A note cannot be sustained indefinitely, nor would we wish it to. Is the body, instrument of life's production that it is, bound by similar logic? Are we all just songs, written to linger only in impressions?" A match flickers, lighting a small candle on the table, and the final dregs of the incense are joined by a sharp lavender-lemon tang. As the candle cuts through the gloom, you see a guitar in xer hands, a guitar you do not recall seeing anywhere around the room when it was lit. Before you can second-guess this notion, xe begins to play, fingers fluttering up and down the strings. "I hope it's not too late in the program for an interlude," your host says. "But music resets the blood, I find, when it's been beset by too much chatter—and indeed this has been a night of words, words, words. Why don't you just sit back and relax while I play us…"

14th Dose:

A Couple of Tunes

administered by Raining Rivers

Unlodged Sludge — Raining Rivers

EM   Am   EM   AM
If you crack me open all of the sludge
              EM
    will come out
EM   Am
  he told me I look beautiful broken
EM That's all I can think about now Am
  EM the winter blows a freezing cold Am
                                              EM
    Am it makes me feel like I'm at home
  EM
    Your warmth is all I've ever known Am
      EM   Am
        Please don't leave me in the snow

    EM   AM

      Please god have mercy on me Am
  EM
    Please this is all I ever wanted it
        to be

EM   Am

EM You say that you don't recognize me
EM I've change myself a million times Am
I don't think there ever was a real me Am
like sand I've washed away by the tide
now there's no one left to console
all of this just eats at my soul
I'm afraid its going to swallow me whole
all of this shit gets so damn old
Please god have mercy on me
please I've turned into something
I don't want to be

Wildwood Rd 35 - Raining Rivers (demo)

AM (Capo 4th Fret)
Laugh like we're sisters, fight like we're dogs
I never know what you think...
You stay quiet I read you wrong
I never know what you think
You're up then you're down you're spinning around
I never know what you think

I see you...
I look right through
You see me...
See what I hide beneath

You talk in your sleep, sing in my dreams
You always know what I think
lighthouse on the shore, you're begging for more
You always know what I think
You're a blizzard in may, I ask you to stay
You always know what I think
I see you...
See right through
You see me...
See what hides beneath

AM C AM C (repeat)
I know you know, I know you know, I know you
Know... I knooow, I know you know I know you
Know I know you know I know
You always know you always know

~173~

Fine.
SEE
THE
COLOR
OF
SOUND.
CUZ IM TWI
UP IM TWI
RENDEZVOUS
WITH
FILTER CIGARETTES
MENTHOL
MADNESS
CLASS A CIGARETTES
Temperance
XIV

Ode to Nicky — Raining Rivers

dedicated to Nicholas Shafto ♡

G
Please tell me you're favorite things
    G   C
    I'd love to hear
G   C
  You could talk about anything
  G   C
  And I'd be all ears
  G   C
  the way that you're eyes light up
  G   C
  When your passion is fierce
  in my life you mean so much
    G   C
    and I'll always be here

        Ode to Nicky
    I don't think you know how beautiful
        you are
    Ode to Nicky
    You are a sun kissed dream that
      bellows through the night
        G   C   G   C
Piano on rainy days, you soothe me with your song
        G   C
You're humming while we both sway
      I   G wanna sing along
    G   C
    Ode to Nicky
    I don't think you know how beautiful you are
      G Ode to Nicky
let me show you how beautiful
      G   C
      you are

~175~

Stay Clean - Raining Rivers

```
      G                    C              G                    C
I've been feeling growing pains  I can feel it all Deep
           G        in my veins      C
been wondering when my life will change...
      But for now  I think I'll Stay the Same
         G                       C
         Been wondering when my body will give out
      G    I'll fail on me without a doubt
      G  I use to have so much life in me
      G  wasted it all  at  17                    @

              G                        C
      G  If you know what I mean X2
      I just  try to stay clean
              G       I was only a teen
              G  if you know what I mean

         G                            C
      You ask me why me why my songs are
              G  So    sad           C
      G  Singings  all I'v ever had
      I think you're wasting your time on me
      G  It'll hurt less now if you set me free
      I still dont know who I wanna be
      G. I'd rather be anyone else but me
      G  Sometimes I wish I could be a tree
      G  So firm so tall and sways like the sea
              G                        C
      If you know what I mean X2
         G  I just try to stay clean
      G   I was only a teen          @
      If  you know what I mean
         G  If you know what I mean
         G  I just try to stay clean
         G  If you know what I mean
```

As the music ends you see that the candle is already on its last legs, barely more than a sputtering flame at the center of a pond of wax on the table's surface. You see your host's face framed by the glinting glow for just a moment, and then, before it can burn itself out, you hear a quick exhalation. You are again thrust into darkness, but it is no longer quite as complete as it was at the beginning of the serenade, the first hesitant twitches of dawn nipping at the sheets tacked over the windows.

The overhead light comes on again, and your host is once more empty-handed. You look around for where xe might have stashed the guitar, but you see no likely hiding place. Before you can ponder this too much, xe is speaking once again. "If our lives are indeed but songs, then houses are the venues where we are played out—concert halls where we make our music, good or bad, happy or sad. May we all be so fortunate." Xe has moved to a blank stretch of painted wall, is moving xer hand across the surface in an almost sensual arc. "Houses catch glimpses of what happens in their corridors—and sometimes they keep them." Xe moves up from the wall, again tracing the shelf of notebooks which lines the high perimeter. "This is one such house; the decades have intervened here, have turned her into a monument to herself. Outside this room is a party, a party that has ebbed and flowed for the better part of a century. There is respite, and there is rest, but the party always comes back, like the rising and falling of a mighty river. That river flows through these corridors; you were caught in its currents tonight. I hope you don't mind that I fished you out. Your constitution is admirable; you might have been fine out there without me."

Xer hands return to the paint, to the skin of the house itself. "Mark Fisher observed that Baudrillard observed that computers don't really remember because they lack the ability to forget. So too buildings, I think, lack these twin capacities, along a similar principle. This spurs me to memory myself, reminding me of another house which kept its grip on the patterns it had sheltered over the years, holding on and holding on and holding on until its history crescendoed in...

The Great Un-Haunting of Raven's End

administered by Lucien R. Starchild

Most people think a haunting is the worst thing that can happen to a house. They're wrong. The worst thing is to be un-haunted.

I should know. I am, or was, 12 Sycamore Lane. A proud Queen Anne Victorian, all gingerbread trim and witch's-hat turrets. For a hundred and seventeen years, I stood sentinel on the hill overlooking Raven's End, a perfect monument to spookiness—and for most of that time, I was gloriously, vibrantly haunted.

My specters were not mere pests. They were my purpose. Bartholomew, a melancholic Victorian gentleman, would pace the library, his spectral cigar smoke smelling of old books and regret. Seraphina, a flapper from the Roaring Twenties, would dance a silent Charleston in the ballroom, the faint scent of gin and jasmine trailing in her wake. A pair of giggling children, Thomas and Clara, would play hide-and-seek in the attic, their laughter like the tinkling of distant wind chimes. We were an ecosystem. A symphony of sorrow and joy, forever playing just out of sight.

Then the Millers arrived.

New owners always came with a mix of trepidation and giddy excitement, armed with sage bundles and weak-hinged crucifixes. We'd give them a good show—a cold spot here, a misplaced locket there—and they'd usually flee within the month, adding to my glorious legend.

But the Millers were different. They didn't come to exorcise us. They came to renovate us.

They were a couple of "influencers" from the city, with bright, empty smiles and a pathological need to optimize everything. Where we saw character, they saw "dated fixtures." Where we felt the comfortable gloom of history, they saw "poor light flow."

"We'll really open up the space, babe," chirped Chad, knocking on my original mahogany wainscoting with his knuckles. "Let the good vibes in."

Bartholomew, from the shadows, muttered, "The only 'vibe' in here is my profound disdain for that man's shoes."

The horror began not with a scream, but with a swatch of paint: "Agreeable Gray." They slathered it over my deep, moody burgundies and forest greens. Seraphina tried to manifest, a flicker of pearls and fringe, but she simply couldn't hold her form against the soul-crushing beigeness. She dissolved with a sound like a silent radio signal fading out.

Next came the "smart home" upgrades. They installed speakers in every room, pumping out a ceaseless stream of upbeat, soulless pop music. Thomas and Clara's joyful giggles were drowned out by auto-tuned vocals about club bangers. They tried to play, but their essence was scattered by the relentless, thumping bass. Their tiny spirits flickered and vanished, their game of eternal hide-and-seek finally called off.

The final blow was the "negative ion generator" and "full-spectrum wellness lighting" they had installed to "purify the atmosphere." To them, it just made the air smell crisp. To my remaining specters, it was acid rain. Bartholomew, desperately trying to pace in his now-gray library, found his form becoming thin, translucent. His cigar smoke, once so rich, now looked like pathetic, dissipating mist.

"This… this antiseptic hell," he whispered one evening, his voice barely a rustle in the air. "There's no room for a proper gloom. No space for a dignified sorrow." I felt his presence, a weight on my floorboards for over a century, simply… unpin itself. With a sigh that was mostly relief, Bartholomew stopped being.

I was empty. A shell. A beautifully optimized, open-concept shell with excellent Wi-Fi and a smart fridge that could order almond milk on its own.

The Millers were thrilled. "Can you feel that, babe?" Mandy would say, doing a yoga pose in the middle of my sterile living room. "So much lighter. All that stale energy is just… gone."

They'd succeeded where all the priests and mediums had failed. They hadn't fought my ghosts; they had simply made the world so unbearably bright, so relentlessly cheerful, and so utterly devoid of mystery that there

Ultra Grey
Gris ultra
PR20D3-3
Greyscape
Paysage gris
PR22N7-3
Devilish
Décor
Grey-ish
Grisâtre
PR20D2-3
Ghostly
Café Latte
Café au Lait
PR22N18-1
Ghouls
Frothy Beige
Beige écume
PR20C1-2
Café américain
22N18-4
Vente Coffee
Café Venti
PR20A4-4

was no place for them to exist. They didn't destroy the haunted house. They made it un-hauntable.

On Halloween night, the ultimate insult arrived. The Millers, in their wisdom, decided to throw a party. "A non-scary Halloween!" Mandy proclaimed. "No ghosts, no witches, no spooky stuff! We're doing a 'Positive Vibes' theme!"

My rooms were filled with people dressed as sunflowers, emojis, and bright yellow happy faces. They drank kale-infused cocktails and talked about mindfulness and real estate trends. A disco ball spun in the foyer, scattering idiot sparks of light where Seraphina once danced.

I was a masterpiece of horror, and they had turned me into a meme.

As the party reached its peak of mundane joy, something within me broke. Or perhaps, something finally woke.

It started with a flicker. The smart lighting system glitched, and for half a second, the room was plunged into a beautiful, deep darkness. A collective "Ooooh!" went up from the party-goers, who thought it was a fun effect.

It was not.

I reached down, down into my foundations, into the soil and the stone. I drew up not a ghost, not a memory, but the very essence of the un-haunted. The crushing weight of emptiness. The profound silence of a story erased.

I focused it into the chill of a thousand neglected conversations. I poured the void of Bartholomew's absence into the air. The vacuum left by the children's laughter became a soundless, screaming wind.

The disco ball stuttered and died. The pop music cut out. The only sound was the low, mournful groan of my beams, aching with a century of loneliness they had never before been allowed to feel.

The guests shivered. Their cheerful chatter died in their throats. They felt it. Not a cold spot, but an absence spot. A place where joy went to be forgotten. They felt the terrifying notion that nothing was there, that nothing had ever been there, and that nothing would ever be there. It was the horror of pure, existential nullity.

Chad, dressed as a thumbs-up emoji, dropped his drink. "Dude," he whispered, his voice trembling. "I feel… really, really sad for no reason."

One by one, the party-goers fled, not in fear of what was there, but in terror of what wasn't. They ran from the profound, unsettling void of a house that had had its soul sandblasted away.

The Millers were the last to leave, shivering and confused in their empty, gray perfection.

Now, I sit in a new darkness. They've put me up for sale. The listing says "over-renovated" and "lacking in warmth."

I am still un-haunted—but I am no longer harmless. I have learned a new kind of scare. I don't rattle chains or moan in the night.

I simply wait for the next bright, happy couple to walk through my door. I will show them the true terror of a home where every shadow has been lit, every whisper silenced, and every mystery solved. I will show them the horror of a world with no ghosts.

And they will flee, forever haunted by the feeling of nothing at all.

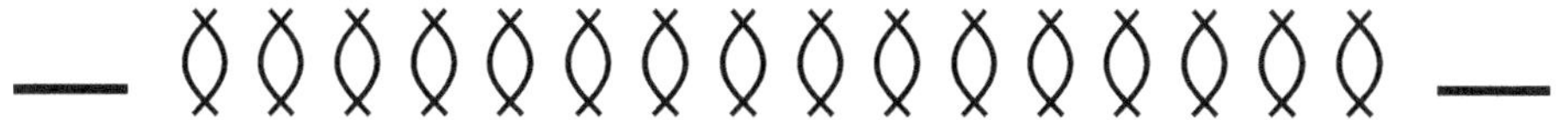

As the tale ends, you feel hollowed out, gutted, stripped of everything that has ever made you feel anything more than empty. You can still feel the shape of your rooms, the angle of your staircases, the circulation of your hallways—and then your body is only itself again, haunted or unhaunted by you and only you.

"It's almost morning," xe says. "You've done well, tonight, I think—though when all is said and all is done, only you will be the judge of that. I'm only a humble storyteller, no saint at the gate, I'm afraid. Would that I were, I'd've absconded from my duty and clambered through the bars myself eons ago instead of standing here and telling my tales out of school. Xe crosses to where you have kept your vigil on the sofa, takes your hand, pulls you to your feet. "I'm afraid there's still a bit more ground to cover," xe says, drawing you across the space, towards the other side of the room. "This leg of journey isn't over yet. Almost—but there's a few more sights to see, and a few more things to feel."

You stop in front of the minifridge, spattered with its museum of stickers, and you echo xer movements as xe crouches. The door to the freezer opens, and into it plunges your hand, surrounded by Hot Pockets and small bottles of liquor. "See if you can feel the blood in your palm; feel it, if you can, moving through your wrist, into and out of your fingertips, fighting the cold seeping the warmth out through your skin. Then, when the warmth leaves, try to hold on to the cold, on to the absence of feeling... see how long you can keep your grip on it, as the flecks of frost shimmer and arrange themselves into...

Snowcastles

administered once more by Kevin Novalina

— ‖ —

Cullen gunned the throttle on the Evinrude, planing the johnboat's nose high off the murky water. By the spotlight's beam, he wound among the riverbends, watching through the blizzard a cryptic frieze of treetops loom black against a paler dark, the snow limning the bare foliage like tinsel in the tattered moonglow.

A few hours ago, he'd snuck out dressed in layers of winterweight camo and hitched his old man's boat to the dually. He'd never dared take them out alone before. He had no license for either. But last night, his dad came home tanked and smelling not like his mom, then they'd yelled until he passed out and she went to the Quaverly Inn.

So, Cullen figured if they could escape, so could he.

Thing was, even at his age he knew there were no *real* escapes. He saw the fabric of his family rending by the stitch. His dad's boozing and women, his mom's screaming and abuse. Their communication in grunts or silences. Cullen wondered where all this rot came from. How far it'd go before the final seam busted.

The sharp cold bristled his nostrils, pierced his ears lobes through his blaze-orange beanie. He squinted against the rushing air as the boat rode the chop, wings of icy spray splitting around the hull. The spotlight offered scant visibility, thick snowflakes roiling in the tapered beam like insects at a streetlight on summer nights.

His dad had never taken him anywhere near this far downriver, this deep into the unknown, and somewhere behind him everything had assumed a surreal aura. Alien. Lore told of a land primeval teeming with game, but its terra incognita shied most superstitious hunters away.

That and the stories.

Legend had it, these woods were haunted. Where that Chantraine family was supposed to have lived. If you believed the tales, it's where they were burned alive, one at a time. Daughter and son first. And according to the few elders who'd been tikes around that time, it's where the cabin stood yet. The four charred holes still scorched through the floorboards.

Cullen swept the light toward a distant meander, the beam breaking over the woody debris along the river's edge until he trained it on a sycamore deadfall lying across the surface. Its crown half-submerged, the twisted taproots still clung to the bank failure.

As he neared, he killed the outboard, eased over extra jerrycans to the bow, and paddled alongside the sycamore's trunk lined with snow like an albino python. He tied off and fired on a headlamp, then sat tacking as the snag's wickerwork shuddered and hissed in the lapping wake.

Shouldering his field pack and his dad's Winchester .30-30, he kicked a foothold in the clay terrace and climbed the bank on roots exposed in the frozen erosion.

Up top, he dusted a rime of snow collared in his puffer jacket like sherpa and stood studying the dark woods by the grainy lamplight. "Attack with the river at your back," he whispered, hearing his dad's voice, then he stepped inside the timberline.

☰☰☰

Cullen trekked deep through a gothic winter wonderland incandesced without source, the parched powder creaking under boot. Sparse wildwood blooming with ice foliage. Black locusts like rawboned horribles charred in torsional attitudes of agony.

He reached a hollow flanked by ridges and found a lodged boulder beneath a pine, its wintermint vegetation still full enough to hold the fall. Shrugging his gear, he sat on a cushion of dead moss the same color as the stone it furred and listened to the flurry's pillowy whispers.

After a while, nature began materializing out of the dark, the woodland shaking alive. Through the riflescope, Cullen scanned a panorama of Mother Nature in monochrome. The only color, the evergreen leaves of a yuletide holly, its scarlet berries like blood slashes against the snow's chalky shadings.

All around him, limbs snapped and bracken crackled. The later it got, the louder.

And colder.

He hooded his jacket and cinched the drawstring, snorkeling his seared face. His mind drifted to the vacation a couple years back. Their last good time as a family. They'd built dilapidated sandcastles on Clearwater Beach. Beneath umbrellas, his mom and dad had sipped margaritas, laughed, and kissed, while Cullen watched the sun melt into the horizon watering off to somewhere, anywhere. Lounging in the warm tide, he listened to the waves hiss and burst, the surf foaming around him, then slipping silver back into the sea.

But now, he pictured his mom sobbing at the motel. His dad snoring on the garage floor, a handle of uncapped Old Crow on its side nearby, the level too low to spill. He thought it tragic he couldn't remember the love of what *was* without recalling the hate of what *is*.

He slipped his fleece gloves into a coat pocket, then blew into cupped hands, kneading and flexing them against the sting. Though alone, he almost sensed presences around him—as if the winds seething in the flora were specters visible but not. He wondered if the old Chantraine place was real or rumor. In ruins or still standing, a family's worth of holes roasted through a sodden carpet of dead leaves and guano and small game carcasses.

The way he'd heard it, the Chantraines were considered "river rats" back during Prohibition, though they were never part of an actual floating community. Instead of a shantyboat, they'd lived in a shack deep in the woods, surviving on what the wild and waters provided. Some claimed to have seen them wrapped like mummies in tattered pelts, running trotlines and barrel nets. Others swore they'd seen them along missing roads in a Ford Coupe, the ass jacked up on heavy-duty truck tires, running popskull hooch.

Over the years, ever-changing scuttlebutt made them inbred and feral, ravaged by chancres and pegged teeth. Patchy hair and honeycomb brains and irises marred gray as corpse wax.

According to the stories, they took in a couple drifters roaming the woods one winter night, not knowing these guys were on the lam after killing four folks in a general store over in Novalina. The Chantraines gave them food, a jar of shine, and a warm bed.

Then sometime during the witching hours....

Still, other tales claimed they were never fried like witches by fugitives. They'd just moved on to more bountiful geography. Lived and died as most did. Quiet.

He'd also heard the whole thing was a myth. A tall tale grown taller by the telling. That the Chantraines never existed at all.

Shifting a numb asscheek, Cullen caught movement in a distant gully. He raised the Winchester and found in the scope a doe dangling a stillborn fawn between her haunches. She spooked and moved toward a thicket of ghost brambles, her baby's head slicked in bloody mucus bucking off her hindlegs with her tender gait.

He startled when a murder of crows plumed from a white ash, holding the bough's shape, then remerged in a morphing Rorschach before skeltering away like ebon smoke.

And atop the timbered ridge beyond stood a wide-racked white-tail.

It'd never made a sound.

Just appeared like an apparition.

Cullen raised, drew the buck into the crosshairs, and fired.

Its forelegs buckled but caught, then it exploded down the rise loping shoulder to shank, hooves curling short and kicking long in a fluid glide more air than ground, spanning the bottom entire in a few gallops before vanishing over the far flank with snow dust and rifle's concussion hanging in its wake.

卌卌

Cullen located "first blood" along the ridge chine. A clean shot, with welts of dark heart's blood spattered over the landslip.

Adrenaline fizzing and sweating through his long johns. He looked toward the river, wondering how he'd get this bullbuck back to the boat. "Don't run too long," he said, then started toward the ripping bush.

卌卌

The blast whorled unceasing from the ether, churning polar white around the boy like a shaken snow globe. He scaled a steep rise, legs mushing through the ice scree, then rode a hip down the backslope, an avalanche of fluff fanning around him.

~187~

He tracked a good distance, cutting for sign through gauntlets of mutating icescape. Top snow had ghosted over swaths of trail, but just when it seemed the blood had run cold, he'd spot a crimson mist over a felled hickory. Claret rosettes on the understory plush with downy drifts.

Fording a glen, he sank past his thighs and fell. Struggled out to solid footing and leaned wheezing, his lungs nylon sacks of thumbtacks. He emptied the snow packing his boot mouths and casting his feet in ice molds. Then he bent windward and slogged on.

At length Cullen threaded a draw and crested out to a stand of cane that erupted at his approach. A spectral violence ripped through the brake flashing antler and white tail, splitting the inflorescence with a powdered contrail that swept off like gunsmoke as the poles clattered to silence.

He followed blood strokes through the boscage to where the buck had bedded down. Matted gore already encased in ice, brittle as carmine sugar glass. Such a novice error. If he'd just waited, it would've died right here.

He trudged on, shouldering through the dense canebrake until he shoved hard and tore free, snatching a breath and a birch trunk just as he cleared a bank, his feet snapping out over a frozen pond on his grip. He dropped ass-to-ledge, his boots slamming the rubbery surface and splintering the gray crust white. He dug his heels into the fluted ice, but the bank caved, and the fractures broke into bobbing floes. Water plumping the coat about his head, he clawed for purchase at the tangled roots, floundered out, and elbowed away. He pushed up steaming, his soaked outerwear already seizing in verglas like melted flesh.

Across the narrow tarn, he saw faint blood-spoors pocking a talus of sandstone to where the buck lay in a stiffening heap, laced with fresh fall.

卌

The blizzard metastasized into a whiteout. A boreal cold to snap bone, congeal blood.

In the lee of a shallow niche, he tried forging a fire using the driest cedar duff he could find as tinder. Icicle fingerbones fumbling through a whole book of damp matches and failing the flame, every stick. He dug through his pack for the ferro rod but in his haste, he'd forgotten both the tool and his clasp knife with which to strike it.

He slammed a fist down and felt it in his teeth. Wringing his gloves out, he peeled them back on, the pain like reskinning fleshless hands.

His layers of clothes well-burdened with watery sleet, he stood freezing and frozen between fight or flight, run or remain. "Move," he growled, then picked a point ahead and did.

All around him, blanketed undergrowth reared like roaring yetis in the battering gusts. He tore through tangled brushwork with reckless abandon, snarls of catbriar clawing his face, the goose down from his jacket. Ripping through his ears and leaving a hoar of frosted blood pearled on the thorns.

He plowed on in various directions just to double back with panic. His feet now lost to the cold, as if he were hobbling on shinbone stumps like hooves over the crimped crust.

He scaled a pillared tor and spun to all points of the compass, his bearings whirling on the dial. An illusion of cerebellum, delusion of inner ear, where everything resembled everything else, morphing by the blink. The reseized thaw reshaped new ice sculptures. Hollows banked, mounds caved, and snow loads filled or snapped branches to alter tree posture, turning every landmark into a landmark no more.

Each moment, a complete metamorphosis.

Each moment, a whole new world.

He shrugged his gear and stood hollering, his voice lost in the howling tempest.

The cold folded him and he sat and slipped his frozen bootlaces and emptied the slush, then skinned his soggy socks and studied his swollen feet. A frostnip hash mottled with blisters and slicked purple as raw liver.

He checked the ruck again, but he'd brought nothing to help.

Twisting the water free, he gentled the socks back over his feet and shimmied his boots on. His tongue like jerky, he ate handfuls of snow until freeze shocked his brain, then sat tremoring from the rage both without and within.

All his stupidity had led him here. Alone and soaked in this arctic nightmare. No one knew his location and outside a hitched boat in the Twilight Zone, he'd left no trail to track.

Remote
Outposts
Become
lost
the
serenity
Six of Swords
Five of Pentacles

He watched a horned owl unfold from the crown of a cottonwood. It wheeled out, rocking on its keel before homing to the same limb, its face like a halved apple face spun backward, watching with disced eyes from beneath tufted plumicorns.

"I'm gonna die out here," he whispered.

He imagined his mom curled fetal by the phone, his dad pacing the garage. Both wilting away with the minutes, days, months, years while Cullen's bones lay unclaimed, absorbing into the crust with the earth's ever wheeling.

He thought if he were afforded one answered prayer, it'd not be to live, but that his parents find some remnant ember of love resident in both their hearts.

He wondered if this tragedy might be such an answer. Loss leading to rediscovery, through his death, their union surviving.

A sacrifice of *him* for the better *them*.

His damnation for their deliverance.

Weeping, he laughed with a sorrow beyond all telling.

卅卅

The rifle between his folded legs, Cullen huddled between the gnarled roots of a cankered hemlock, his frozen thermals girdling his ribcradle. He shuddered as if possessed. Face pale, his purple eyelids translucent as a hatchling's. He listened for a passing motor, a tug's foghorn, anything to show him the river's direction. Back to his dad's stolen johnboat waiting to carry him away from this wintertide hellscape.

Above, a nimbus of clouds seemed to time-lapse as if supernatural. The notion took him to just let go and give in to the elements when he heard a child giggle, then say: "You dead, Mister?"

He opened his eyes, pink with corneal lacerations from blown ice, and before him a little girl stood shapeless in a coat of tanned rodent skins. Skunk pelts bound into makeshift pampooties.

"You *ain't* dead, Sleepyhead!"

He squinted up at parted skies where light prismed through the ice encasing the naked overgrowth, thick granular snowflakes sifting down around him like blanched leaves. Forcing his tongue through his blue lips, he wept again.

She wrapped both hands around one of his and tugged and he winced and rose in a cloak of vapor, snow dusting from his lap like confectioner's sugar.

"So's you coming or aintcha?" she asked and spun to go.

Cradling the rifle, he wobbled behind on newborn fawn's legs while she skipped along humming "This Little Light of Mine," her flaxen curls afloat. They reached a meadow haloed by a sundog in the squall's break, its rainbow spangled through a cloud of ice crystals.

"What's your name?" he called, but she skipped on, leading them through swales of winter galax powdered with fresh skiffs, the leathery brown leaves like frosted heart-shaped cookies. "Do you know where we are?"

"*Course* I do, Freezy-Wheezy," she said, giggling again. She stopped and pointed far down the hillock where an ancient live oak stood, its branches spread like a massive Medusa head, the Spanish moss white as hag's locks draping a cabin canted below. "Home."

The shack stood cobbled from unhewn lengths of logs. A chimney forged from fieldstone with birch bark shaking the low-slung roof. They stepped through a door swinging on moldering rawhide hinges, clapping against its skewed jamb.

Inside, the air hung with a nameless rank amid the scurry and squeak of scattering rodents. Near the door, an old cast-iron cookstove stood beneath a lone window set crooked in its crude sash. The cracked glass translucent from old tallow or lard smoke, the edges wreathed in sprigs of frost firs.

"This little light of mine," the girl sang, skipping into the shadows. "I'm agonna let it shine."

Sunlight filtered through the roof seams and wall chinking, casting eerie glyphs over the dark room that morphed with the roiling storm. Cullen pocketed his gloves. "Your parents around?"

Cherubic silhouette whirling before the low glowing embers on the hearth, she tittered and sang: "Let it shine, let it shine, *let it shine!*"

A gust wrenched the cabin, slamming the door, and Cullen jumped.

The girl appeared from the shadowed keeps twisting a curl around a finger, studying his jacket and boots. "Gimme, Coldilocks," she said. "So leastways you won't catch croup."

He shed the rifle and field pack. His coat, socks, and boots, then she lugged them all away.

He eased into a cane rocker in fungal shambles. He heard her moving about in the gloom, then she reappeared with a steaming clay mug and said, "Hot cooco with mashmallies!"

Cullen wrapped the mug with both palms, his fingers palsied like dead spider legs. Blowing on the rim, he studied her pale face in the ashen light. Glacial eyes and missing front tooth. Cheeks blushed like a Kewpie doll. "Where's your mom and dad?"

"Mop and Pop'll sure be happy," she said, swinging a deerskin blanket around his shoulders, the worn pelt spotted with white mold. "They just love new callers."

"It's okay," he said. "I'm not real cold now." Pinching the front of his alpaca sweater, he fanned his collar but let the blanket remain.

Wind shrilled through the wall gaps and Cullen glanced about. "Got any brothers or sisters?"

"Umfortuneply," she said, blew her lips, and chuckled.

"Where are they?"

"Who knows, Clown Nose," she said, touched his numb honker chapped red as a winterberry, then pirouetted back into the darkness.

Cullen doffed his beanie, mopped sweat from his brow.

"But you oughta not wander the woods alone," the girl said, grabbing a log from a rick of firewood. Waddling it toward the hearth, she stopped and stood silent, the light through the slatted walls crazed over her shape. Then she said: "There's painters and wolves and bears out there."

The shanty shuddered hard, smacking the door with such violence Cullen almost dropped the coco. He sipped, his core searing. "You didn't tell me your name?"

She tee-heed and said: "Wanna hear a story?" She dropped the log on the coalbed, then the room ignited, whooshing with flamelight.

And the blanket slid from his shoulders.

There it was.

Four holes burned through the flooring, the splintered rims charred.

"One a ponce of the time," she said in a musical trill, "there was a *beautiful* princess."

"The Chantraine place," he whispered, eyes goggled at the floor. "It's all really real."

She coaxed the flames, the logs somehow glowing orange, the bottoms blistered with ash over the cherry coals. A flurry of crackling sparks whorled about her, the flue moaning with its draw. "And one day," she said, "the princess was captured by a mean old dragon and locked in a fiery dungeon."

"I wanna go home."

She giggled behind her hand. "Soon, a handsome prince came to rescue the princess," she said, stepped from silhouette, and a bubble of flesh pulsating on her cheek popped, then puttied to the floor in a smoldering hiss. Her singed hair glowing like bulb wire as it curlicued back to blisters on her broiled pate.

His innards seized into ice blocks.

"And he told that dragon," she said, throat croaked, and smoke tendrilled from her nostrils. "'Release the princess, beast or face the wrath of my sword!'"

The room foundry hot, bright as neon lava.

"You're dead," he said, and his shallow breath ghosted out.

Smile fading, she fixed him with eye-globes melting in their cups. "I'm not dead, Slleeppyyhhheeeaaaddd…," she said, voice warping in a narcotic drag as her lips charred back from a jack-o'-lantern rictus. Her jawbone unhinged on one side, then the other, and thumped to the puddle of flesh sizzling on the floor before she disappeared as if ash on a soft summer breeze.

His throat pipes locked, he peered down at his hands cupping nothing, then back up to find no shack. No deerskin blanket or raging inferno. No holes in no floor. Just his jacket and field pack, rifle and boots where he'd shed them nearby, ghosting over with fresh drifts like some lost child's body frozen within its rags and absorbing into the crust of an ever-changing wasteland that always looks the same.

卌

Cullen sat against the dead hemlock. Eyelids tacked shut with crusted tears, legs sheathed in a chrysalis of ice. Above, spindrift scrolled off the treetops like frozen smoke in the violet gloaming.

Far away he heard the faint growl of a boat motor, but he didn't stir. He'd just sit a minute and wait. Rest a little longer because he'd seen those creepy scenario videos in Hunter's Ed and knew that sometimes, boats weren't boats at all. Sometimes, you heard boats like you saw old cabins and apparitions of incinerated little girls singing in the woods. With snowflakes big as dove feathers wafting down, pale blue under the moon, he'd just hang here on the beach and chill. His mom and dad beneath umbrellas, sipping margaritas. Laughing and kissing. Maybe they'd build another crumbling sandcastle. So what if that was a boat. There'd be more. There was always more. There were boats and boats, and he could sail away anytime. Toward the sun melting into the horizon that watered off to somewhere, anywhere. But now, he just wanted to lounge in the warm tide, listen to the waves hiss and burst. Let the surf foam around him, then slip silver back into the sea.

Really, it could wait.

He was cozy now.

Even the shivering had stopped.

You do not notice that your own shiver has stopped until the thin rind of ice around your hand turns into a slick sheen against your skin, tiny droplets of moisture caught in your hair. The freezer door is closed once more, and Deedee appears as if on cue to give you something warm to touch. You scoop the cat into your arms, heedless of the risk of a scratch or a scrape, but he seems by now to have taken a shine to you, allowing himself to be cradled as you return once more to the sofa. Before you can sit back down in the place where the cushion is now caved into the shape of your ass, you feel your host's hand on your shoulder, spinning you, causing Deedee to spill out of your arms and back onto the floor.

"Not yet," xe says. "There'll be time to rest soon—but you've been so still for so much of tonight, letting it all happen to you. Now, here at the tippy-top, before we start to descend, take my hand and join the dance." So your fingers interlace with xers, and xe begins slowly, moving you in a soft circle around the table where the melted candle still sits in a pool of itself. The room is too small to really dance, you think, and you are sure that you will bang your shins against the table as xe picks up the pace. You can still hear the slightest thrum of music from the dampened party downstairs, and as you try to match the rhythm, the room seems to accommodate. It does not grow, not in any readily visible way, anyhow, but you have plenty of room to move, to frolic, and you feel more and more alive with each footfall. You look at your host across from you, hands in your hands, eyes burning once more as xe guides you in your romping whirl. "Move, mover, and move, and move," xe says. "Dance, dancer, and dance, and dance, feel, feeler, and feel and feel, and in the midst of that feeling walk with me across the flames to attend…

The Jolly Goblin Jamboree

administered by Adam Parker

Mother hated camping. Every day was like camping where she was from, she would say, why would she ever want to. But father had some kind of vendetta against nature so they had a compromise and bought a camper van.

The first (and last) time we used the van was a summer trip we took up into the Rockies. It was just before I went into secondary school so I would have been twelve or thirteen. Our first night was at a provincial park but our second night we found a postcard perfect spot off the side of the road near a crystal clear lake that was a crisp glacial green-blue.

The trees around that valley were an evenly placed thin monotony of oaks. If you like acorns then this is the place for you. Father said the natives burned out the old growth to manage the forest against larger fires then planted the oaks, at a distance, and harvested the nuts. The forest seemed endless.

I had brought my best friend along on that trip, my dude Sam, the biggest kid in my class. I once helped him pass a math test and he would thump any kid that stepped up to me. And, of course, my little sister Kiki was there too. She was four years younger than me and my constant annoying shadow.

Sam had brought a tent which we set up while Mother made the hotdogs for our dinner and Father drank two beers. Kiki brought her stuff out and launched into screaming tears when we said she had to sleep in the camper. My parents stayed out of it and she moved all through dinner. Finally, we agreed.

Just before dark, we went for a walk around the clearing, not too far. We met the only set of neighbours we had, a couple of hippy guys reclining in moldy hammocks beside a rusty low pickup. We called them "monkey spankers" to their faces, laughing. I had just heard the term in a comic book and wasn't quite sure what it meant. But it sure sounded funny.

They said they were there for a beach party that night, even though we couldn't see any others yet. They said we should come on down and "ride the hippies." We kept laughing and repeating that, on our way back to camp.

It got dark and Father broke out his guitar. Only for a couple of songs, thankfully. I went to take a pee behind the tent and found a pair of rotting boots. I wanted to take them, clean them up to wear, but Mother said to leave them. There was some strange material next to them, like some shedded skin or plastic or a spider web around and on the boots that looked like bad news. So I left them there.

Once we had all gone to bed, and I could hear Father snoring, me and Sam snuck out, as was our plan. Kiki stirred at the sound of the zipper and I shushed her back to sleep. Then we got on our shoes and crept out.

We headed down to the beach but, even though it was a full moon and the trees thin, they were thick enough to make the scene a world of shadows and obfuscated paranoia. We got turned around and hoped we were heading in the right direction.

Sam ducked behind a stump, grabbing my shirt and pulled me down into the dim. He motioned. The hippy campers were trotting on their way. We went to the beach too, following far behind and darting tree to tree, pretending we were commandos.

The hippies stopped and we stopped as well. I could see the hippies, like, changing, and figured they were putting on warmer clothes, or getting booze out of a bag. But, no. What we saw, though I could not believe my eyes at the time, was three small men climb out of each of the regular sized men. Goblins. Maybe two feet high apiece. Now there was no doubt. Then the six of them continued down to the water.

Me and Sam shared a look and he walked low and slow over to the shedded costumes of the two hippies. The human-like shells lay there like old clothes.

From there we could just see the water, the glint of moonlight shimmering on mellow waves. Then we became aware of the sound of drums. Not sure if they had started right then, but that's what it seemed. Sam pressed on. He was always brave. With his size, he was expected to be.

We crested a hill, some rocky dune full of thorns and crawling ants, and we could see the light erupting from a substantial bonfire. Squat shapes rounded the blaze in frenzied delight, synced to the pounded skins and their own one-to-one chant of, "Gak! Gak! Gak!"

There were still more of those thinly placed, gangly oaks, and we crabwalked ever closer, into a mass of scrub bush and driftwood. We assumed this spot would keep us sufficiently hidden among the shadows. We could see the happenings around the big bonfire very clearly.

When I say the bonfire was big, I mean it was large enough to enable several quite large driftwood logs to be placed over the flames and coals, so that the goblins, or even possibly a full grown man, could walk across. Like a bridge over hell. Many of the goblins were. One at a time, without regard for a lineup, just shoving their way into the front position. Fights naturally broke out between the contestants allowing any opportunistic other to hop on and, bandy-legged, cross the gauntlet. More than one fell, *gak!*-ing, to feed the fire.

A feral orchestra of drummers encircled the blaze, with several smaller satellite fires around them all and trailing down the beach. I could just see and sense apparitions of the violent lovemaking that was transpiring where the glow died in the dark. Others coupled up and dissolved with them in the gloom. The rest, which seemed to number in the dozens (perhaps hundreds) were fortifying themselves with drink and smoke or had lost themselves in the dance.

At a signal from (what I took for) an elder goblin, gauntly tall with a gnarled wooden headdress, the drum pacing accelerated. The dance thrust, in tempo, and the general vibe grew ever more aggro.

At that time I also noticed a literal change to the shade, the quality of light emanating from above. I remembered something Father had mentioned that week and looked up. There, hovering above the lake, formerly so full, fleshy and proud, the moon had begun its rare metamorphosis into its own diabolical twin, the blood moon. A lunar eclipse.

We watched for some time, too scared and fascinated to move. Sam looked over and grinned at me. I tried to grin back.

When the eclipse had reached near its zenith, the drum stopped, everything stopped, all at once. The entirety of the crown, we noticed, had come to gather around. The largest fire had peaked too, flames lapped at the sky. The elder, wizard or crone I could not tell, led a younger, taller person to the hell bridge and bid them to cross.

I could see their goblin faces better now. Distinctively green, full of vengeful mirth and mischief. Sharp underbites that would be endearing on a dog but here spoke of certain doom. The young flame walker turned her head enough to be a visible opposite to the imps. It was Kiki.

She must have followed us. She always did. I heard one of the goblins make out a three syllable parroting of, "prin-se-sa." My stomach turned. I crawled back from the rim of light. I wanted Father there but Sam stopped me. We argued, through signs and small grunts.

Sam would not leave her and he was right. He made a move towards the light and got his feet ready to sprint. Just then we found ourselves surrounded by the little fuckers, getting jabbed, annoyingly, by sharpened sticks. They forced us forward to the flames, to their elder and into their drum circle, and we fell at Kiki's feet.

Tears were in her eyes but she would not let them flow. We got up, one on either side. It was obvious what they wanted. One drummer began again and the rest joined in. The elder motioned to the path again. Sam went first. Then Kiki. They cheered, in their way. *Gak! Gak! Gak!* I was the one that went last.

It was exhilarating. The flames felt like water, like fresh renewal. And, after we had passed, hopping off the other end into sand and pebbles, then we were accepted as one of them. We were set upon, but with offers. Wine that smelled like watermelon and some nefarious, well-charred but still furry, kind of meat. Sam went for everything but I stopped him. Kiki knew better but Sam was a true glutton and, a slave to his good manners, never liked to refuse.

So we danced.

And danced and danced. Like I never could have believed we could before—

—Till the flames and the fierceness of motion led us away from the circle, out to the satellite camps and the crimson lake that was turning silver as the Earth forgave its small partner and returned her to usual view. Before long I had to shield Kiki's eyes from the rough fucking and fighting happening, without supervision, at the fringes.

We went then and rested at one of the small fires with what seemed the mellower sorts among them. But goblins have no chill. Immediately, you could see them flex into small groups, scheming. As for me, I was so tired by then, I could only sit there and stare. That's what I've been telling myself

Parks
and
Recreation
Road
Trip!
HERE! HAVE
A TASTE!
SEEKING HARMONY

anyway. I grabbed a handful of sand and a decent nearby rock, just in case. None among them was over two and a half feet, but there were so damned many.

They did nothing. After a moment, we moved on. Back at the big fire, we also chilled, finding some small logs to sit on. Sam started dancing with, what looked like, a couple of female goblins. They had their little weird boobies out anyway, I remember noticing. Soon, before I could stop him, they had offered some kind of herbal refreshment in the form of a stone pipe, one holding up a thin lit twig and the other holding the pipe itself. Sam ducked low and puffed.

We had snuck a couple cigarettes, a few times, from Sam's mom's purse, but this still seemed pretty hardcore to me then. After that, Sam began hopping around and *gak!*-ing out loud, like one of the little devils. A big-boy goblin came up and was dancing, or maybe it was fighting, with Sam. An aggressive matching, for sure. Like capoeira or moshing, with a bit of mutual strangulation. I chased the green guy off and tried dancing with the girl ones but they completely ignored me and went to dance where the water was most slippery, on the rocks where the tired waves massaged the shore.

I tried talking to Sam and he could only grunt and *Gak!* back at me. Kiki was nodding off and even the drums were hit more slowly. And it was getting weird. The odd goblin would be *gak!*-ing, but solemnly, and jump into the fire on purpose. A skinny *Gak!* came crying to Kiki, imploring her to drink, then immolated himself, trying to get her attention, but she had just ignored him and had gone back to sleep by then.

It was time to leave. But Sam couldn't communicate or be communicated to any way I knew how. I thought he was just doing a bit. Or really high. And I had to get back, get Kiki back, to our camp. It was almost sunup anyways. So I took Kiki by the hand and we left the party. I told Sam we were leaving, but he was still gone.

The walk back was mostly okay. Kiki was too tired to complain. I piggy-backed her some of the way too. She had gotten down there herself, I figured, so it would be fine for the walk back. The only thing was that we got lost a little, off path, for a bit and we had to cross a bit of a cliff face to get up to the path and not backtrack. It was simple enough and the drop was only ten feet into bushes so probably not deadly.

We were crossing, holding hands, but we had to really lean forward onto the cliff and inch along sideways. I was leading, about halfway across, when I could feel a strong presence behind us. Something was just buzzing in my brain. I don't know how to explain it. No sound, just the sensation of goosebumps. I turned and what I saw should have blown me right off of that cliff: there was a massive snake sidewinded and ready and it struck right at me, jaws wide, fangs top and bottom. It bit right through me. It wasn't real. Not in any physical sense, anyway, and I knew it, even in that moment. That was the miracle, trusting my own skepticism, even in what I was seeing. I still don't know why I saw that. Maybe it was the secondhand smoke.

We got back and, without warning, it was light out. I got Kiki into her sleeping back and lay in mine, boots still on. I got back up a few seconds later. There was no way I could sleep.

I went and found Sam in just a couple minutes. He came off the beach path, by the trail we had driven off the highway to find our campsite. He looked sick but smiled when he saw me. We got back to the tent without a problem. But, I had to help him into his sleeping bag when he kept pressing his face into the side of the tent. I told him I needed to sleep, "try and lay down."

He told me, "Dude, I don't know where the ground is."

The next day (or later that day, I should say), we went fishing down at the lake. We took the same path as the night before but now there was no sign of the bonfires. It was only a few hours later, after breakfast, but there was no sign at all. Kiki and Mother had stayed back at the camper. I think they were playing cards, then doing a colouring book, I'm not sure.

Father, Sam and I took turns casting dad's old fishing pole. We used bits of beef jerky or worms we dug up for bait. We caught nothing until Sam found an old, stained t-shirt, half buried, beside a log he was walking on. It had Snoopy on it wearing sunglasses. Remember Joe Cool? We didn't think the shirt was all that cool so I tossed it in the water. Father shouted. The shirt had drifted over, so quick, and got tangled up in his line. He was pissed. But, when he reeled it in, there was a nice trout flailing on the end of the line.

We gutted and skinned the fish right there. It wasn't big enough to feed everyone, but Mother fried it up with butter and garlic that night and everyone got to try a few bites, which were delicious. Of course Father had me drag the shirt out and try tossing it over his line a bunch more times that morning, but none of us caught another fish.

After dinner, before it was dark, us kids went for a walk along the shore and Sam told us what had happened the night before. He said that, after he smoked that shit in the pipe, he blasted off, that he was still in the party, but was also now in a spaceship, and that everything and everyone around him had taken on the aspect of a snake. Everything around him was alive, and of the one same slithering being. He was a part of it, now, and in no way in control of his thoughts and actions. We were there too, but, at the same time, very far away, like in another dimension.

He said that the snake beings began communicating to him, relaying an important message, and that was that there was, or is, an important herb that grows there, nearby, in the mountains. And, that if he could find that herb, which he described as having a purple flower, that it could be used medicinally (or recreationally) as a genuine backdoor to enlightenment. I'll admit that I had no idea what he was talking about at the time, but that it seemed very appealing.

After they told him that, Sam said that other, higher voices appeared, just audibly, and told him *no!* don't listen to the snake-people. They were lying and it was all a trap.

Kiki got a handful of water from the lake and made a childlike blessing over it, in her own made-up fashion and blew the, now holy, water into Sam's face. He gasped at the coldness and, after a long moment, wiped the water off with his sleeve. He thanked Kiki and we went back. Sam seemed to be feeling better after that.

That night, we snuck out again. Not Kiki, just Sam and me. There was nothing going on at the lake, but I lost Sam on the trail coming back. I waited till morning. I was sure he would find his way. Mother took the van, with Kiki, to find a phone and call the police. We searched all day. Sam's parents came up and they searched, with the police and volunteers, all week. I think his father stayed and lived there for a month. Everyone did everything they could.

Father was worried about getting sued by Sam's parents but they never did. He was worried about being ostracized by the community, or some kind of vigilantism, but there never was. He was worried about being demoted at work but they actually gave him a promotion the next year. We sold the camper van, at a small profit, and we never went camping again.

With his promotion, Father earned enough, over the years, to help me out a lot with my tuition fees. He joked about me living the American dream, like in American movies. Kiki would act like the goblin dance party never happened but I could always tell, by her eyes, when she was lying. After graduating from secondary school, I went to work at the root beer factory in my hometown, to save some extra money for university.

I gave my notice for halfway through August, so I could go camping. I went by myself. I came here, back up to the Rockies, to the lake where I last saw Sam. I followed, with what I could recall, and by intuition, up into the high pass, past the lake, and further. Stalking the sounds of birds and the smell of mud, and herbs, to a hidden land, a pocket biosphere, where the purple flowers grow.

And there, puckered amongst the deepest patch, where the odour fills your nostrils the thickest, I found their opening. Their door. That hole in the ground where men should fear to go. But they do not. It is, instead, inviting. I have sat here and set this brief account to paper and stowed it in clear view of the entrance described above. I must gather these purple-flowered herbs now and begin my journey inward. Tonight, the moon turns red again.

And, if you are still in doubt, if you linger here unsure, know that you are most welcome inside. You are invited. Join us.

come on down

So, here we are again—the sun on this side of the earth, the afterdawn bleeding through the sheets and dappling the room with ribbons of caramel light. The dance breaks as you trip, stumble backwards, fall through the air, hit the couch, and as you regain your bearings you realize that you are alone in the playroom, your host nowhere to be seen. You blink, taking in the sudden absence, the silence that comes with it. Outside, you can hear the sound of birds, chittering and twittering in the crisp air. Across from you, the alarm clock is functional once more, staring at you with its big block number eyes. It's not even seven yet, not quite, and night is already creeping back from whence it came, making way for morning.

On the table in front of you is the crystal pendant, making it clear that whatever else over the last dozen hours might have been imagined, your host had not. You try to recall the color of xer skin, the geometry of xer face, the exact tenor of xer voice, but all you can manage is the shape of the stories as they poured from xer lips like red, red wine. Your hand reaches out to grasp the pendant, lifting it into the air, the honey amethyst catching the new light and holding it close.

You are contemplating walking to the attached bath for a drink of water when you hear the fire alarm, blaring out in the hallway. A new path dictated for you, you cast one last look at your sanctuary—at the melted candle, the incense burner, the discarded clown puppet, the empty can of craft beer, the projector in its nest of wires and connections—and then make your way out of the room, closing the door behind you. Housemates are stirring in the hallway, emerging from their burrows in hazes of hangover and irritation and stumbling through the flashing white lights.

Down a different set of stairs from the one you came up, into the main hall where the meat of the rager had pulsed, spilling out into the yard along with the housemates and the rest of the post-party flotsam. People stand in clusters and clumps, hanging on the picnic table or standing by the curb with hands in pockets. You hear someone say that because the house is part of the city's co-op network, the fire department will need to come to disable the alarm. You don't know where to stand, or whether to stand anywhere—you don't know any of these people, save for the one who had come into the playroom the night before for their moleskine, who gives you a curt wave from by an elm tree, but not the kind of wave you feel confident following to its source. You decide instead to simply stand and listen to the birds, who seem to all have the same thing to say, spitting into the periwinkle sky: "Poo-tee-weet? Poo-tee-weet? Poo-tee-weet?"

The front door slams open and you see your friend stumble out, surrounded by a couple of other stragglers. "Yo!" they say, coming down the steps and bumbling towards you. "Fuck, dude, where were you last night? I looked everywhere for you. I totally thought you bailed." Their fist buries itself in your shoulder and they throw an arm around you. "Man, that shit was wild! I told you. Didn't I totally fucking tell you?"

You nod in agreement that they totally fucking told you, catch a snippet of annoyed gossip between two housemates that apparently the alarm had been set off by someone in the living room lighting a Swisher Sweet directly underneath a smoke detector. Your friend is still talking, but your eyes slide instead to the bushes lining the side of the house, where a hairless cat is sitting and staring at you with its big headlamp eyes. Your friend notices your gaze and turns to look. "Whoah, freaky little thing. What is that, like, a goblin?"

The cat turns and disappears into the brush with a whip-flick of his tail, and taking this as a cue, you turn away from the house, hitting the sidewalk. Other survivors have already made their exit, and your friend joins you just as the firetrucks pull up and several very unamused looking fire safety officers ask to speak to the residents. They might have been about to argue, but the arrival of the authorities seems to have inspired them as well to make themself scarce.

Down the lane you set, reaching into your pocket, feeling the comforting weight of the crystal between your fingers. It's finally cold now, on the other side of the night, the clouds cracked and grey like television static. Your friend is still talking about the party, but that is static too, radio chatter, just waves hitting a shore and breaking to pieces. It's a long jaunt, you think—a long, long, fucking jaunt—and as you think it, feel it, taste it, know it, the sky opens like a pinata and begins to snow.

creator bios

G. W. McClary ("Black Magick 101") is a native of Ohio with a B.A. in literature and founder of The Storycraft Co-op. His stories have appeared in *Nova Literary-Arts Magazine*, *Altered Worlds: An Altered Reality Anthology*, *Razzle Dazzle Cafe*, and elsewhere. You can keep up with his new releases on Instagram: @gwmcclary

Sandor Paulson ("Hungry Yellow Eyes") is a witch, audio-visual editor, and technical writer located in Chicago. They are most often spotted in the wilds of Roger's Park, Andersonville, and Lincoln Square. They are a White Sox fan out of spite. Additionally, they are currently working to make a magazine for electronic and physical distribution in Chicago. They can be reached for inquiry at sandorpaulson@gmail.com

Raymond Brunell ("Again", he/him) writes speculative fiction where the gothic meets late-stage capitalism—stories about bodies that catalogue their own dissolution, algorithms that charge rent on grief, and the small dignities we surrender to appear functional. His flash and short fiction has appeared in *Skeleton Flowers Press*, *Brilliant Flash Fiction*, and *The Drift*. He curates his broader literary projects at www.unbound-atlas.com.

Zazie Productions ("The House that Breathes Back") is the professional name of Zazie Kanwar-Torge, a multidisciplinary artist whose work spans experimental fiction, sound design, and conceptual media. With a focus on precision and interiority, his practice investigates memory, perception, and dissonance—producing emotionally resonant, structurally inventive pieces across text, audio, and visual form.

Mave Goren ("Today I am a Tool", she/her) is an author, musician, radio host, and enthusiast from rural Brooklyn, currently studying for an MFA at the Writer's Foundry at St. Joseph's University. Her work runs the gamut from the absurdly gothic to the gothically absurd and can be found in Kaidankai Ghost Stories, Trembling with Fear, and elsewhere. A zine, Moonfire, will be available from Shapeless Press in late 2025. You can find her at your local library with a stack of books larger than she knows what to do with.

Sirius ("Mr. Belly's Infirmary", they/them) is the author of The Dread South Series, the Gentleman Demon series, the Wirekillers series, the Draonir Saga, and multiple short stories included in various anthologies and literary magazines. When not writing, they are spreading blasphemy as a drag king or doting on their beloved dogs. More about their work can be found on www.lmhpub.com and www.curiouscorvidpublishing.com

James Arthur ("Fior di Morto") is a native of Northeastern Ohio in the United States, has aspired to be a storyteller from an early age, ever since taking top honors in a young writer's competition. He's been weaving tales from that moment on, often integrating elements of the fantastic to help bring his sometimes disturbing visions to life. Mr. Arthur has published short stories and longer works in both the digital and print mediums, and is putting the finishing touches on a novel.

Sali Andiamo Siyaya ("The Night Ride") is a Malawian writer and engineer with a deep passion for storytelling. Though trained in engineering, she spends most of her time writing poems and stories that reflect real emotions and life experiences. Sali started dreaming big at a young age and worked hard to reach her goals. She went to St. Michael's Girls' Secondary School, where she learned the importance of hard work and never giving up. Later, she earned a certificate in Engineering from ECOM Vocational Training Institute. Still, her heart has always belonged to writing. Sali was invited to appear in an anthology, *The Poetess*, by Blair Smith and has touched many readers. She has also published novels on different platforms and continues to write with the goal of inspiring others. In her free time, she enjoys reading, singing, and playing chess. Sali believes that words have the power to heal, connect, and bring light to the world.

Ryan Danley ("I Like It") is a stand-up comedian, horror podcaster, writer for The Hard Times, and a horror author based in Portland, Oregon. Right now he's eating tacos and cursing the names of whoever invented credit scores.

E. B. Ratcliffe ("Taraval Street") lives in the green splendor of Seattle. He is excited to have "Taraval Street" in Fearful Symmetries this Halloween. It is a trippy look at what moving beyond our current plane of existence might be like. He has also recently had his story "Evening Star" printed in *After Dinner Conversations* and his flash piece "Midnight at Friar's Pool" published in Siren's Call. In addition, he had a short film, "Alone," presented at the Portland Film Festival in 2023. He enjoy writing stories and regularly presents his adolescent writing at the Salon of Shame in Seattle.

Stephen McQuiggan ("Not For You, For Me") was the original author of the bible; he vowed never to write again after the publishers removed the dinosaurs and the spectacular alien abduction ending from the final edit. His other, lesser known, novels are *A Pig's View of Heaven* and *Trip a Dwarf.*

Ted Morrissey's ("Swinford & the Girl in White") most recent novel is *The Strophes of Job.* His first collection of poetry—*Aspiring Child: A Biography of Mary W. Shelley in Sonnets*—will be released in 2026. He co-hosts the monthly podcast A Lesson before Writing.

Raining Rivers ("Ode to Nicky", "Stay Clean", "Wildwood Rd 35", "Unlodged Sludge") is a musical, and a multimedia artist: (making collages, textile pieces, and sculptures). Rivers is also the lead singer for an up and coming gothic, post-punk, psychedelic shoe gaze inspired band called Neon Nymph. Their debut album "Bard witch, the dancing plague" is scheduled to release in early 2026. Rivers grew up in a rural town in Michigan, and a lot of the inspiration for her work lies in the horrors of the great American Midwest—the isolation of western culture, the grotesque state of the mundane, and the underbelly that lies in your very own back yard. You can keep up on Rivers's projects on Instagram at @raining.rivers

Lucien R. Starchild ("The Great Un-Haunting of Raven's End") is an enigmatic poet &writer and cosmic dreamer, weaving tales that blur the line between reality and the surreal. Born under a wandering star, he draws inspiration from forgotten myths, celestial whispers and the hidden magic of everyday life. With a pen dipped in stardust, Lucien invites readers to lose themselves in worlds both strange and hauntingly familiar.

Kevin Novalina ("A Fun Day of ~~Grand Illusions~~ Bland Delusions",
"Snowcastles") has had fiction, non-fiction and poetry published in over 200
Literary Journals, Magazines and Anthologies. He won numerous writing
competitions and was nominated for multiple prizes and awards, including
four Pushcart Prizes.

Adam Parker ("The Jolly Goblin Jamboree") is a writer and filmmaker from
the West Coast of Canada. Before graduating from the Film Production
Program at Vancouver Film School, he attended the Creative Writing
Program at Vancouver Island University. In his spare time, he enjoys listening
to music, watching movies, cooking and gardening. He currently resides with
La Chata in Vancouver. His debut novella came out in August of 2025. Check
out @adamparkerscribbler on Instagram and Substack for more.

acknowledgements

This book would not be possible without those who supported this book on Kickstarter, and those who have held space for our events, supported us on Patreon, or in other forms over these first few years of development, including…

Erika Nagi ★ Axel Kallesøe ★ mythossanta ★ Robert Lipton ★ Valerie Oltarsh-McCarthy ★ Douglas Goldmacher ★ Zack Fissel ★ Mike ★ Poppet

In addition, we would like to thank **Alexander Kiiskilä, Adam Rice,** and the rest of **Montie House Cooperative** for their role in the development of this project , as well as the **Merritt Branch** of **St. Catharines Public Library** in St. Catharines, Ontario for giving us a place to hold the release party for this book, the 3nd Annual From Above, From Below Ball, and **Sophie Bonnen & Fritz Dries** for their ongoing patronage of the Library and its projects.